HUNGRY SPIRITS

This Large Print Book carries the
Seal of Approval of N.A.V.H.

HUNGRY SPIRITS

ALICE DUNCAN

KENNEBEC LARGE PRINT
A part of Gale, Cengage Learning

GALE
CENGAGE Learning

Detroit • New York • San Francisco • New Haven, Conn • Waterville, Maine • London

OS LT DUNCAN, ALICE

GALE
CENGAGE Learning™

LIBRARY OF CONGRESS CATALOGING-IN-PUBLICATION DATA

Duncan, Alice, 1945–
   Hungry spirits / by Alice Duncan.
      p. cm. — (Kennebec Large Print superior collection)
   ISBN-13: 978-1-4104-3369-5 (pbk.)
   ISBN-10: 1-4104-3369-2 (pbk.)
      1. Majesty, Daisy Gumm (Fictitious character)—Fiction. 2. Spiritualists—Fiction. 3. Pasadena (Calif.)—Fiction. 4. Large type books. I. Title.
   PS3554.U463394H86 2011
   813'.54—dc22   2010048696

Published in 2011 by arrangement with Tekno Books.

Printed in the United States of America
1 2 3 4 5   15 14 13 12 11
ED045

ACKNOWLEDGMENTS

Joan and Johnny Young have helped me out so often in the writing of my books, I can hardly thank them enough. I especially want to thank Johnny for his help with this book and another book called *Angel's Flight*. Not only did he tell me how to gauge when a 1920 Chevrolet needed to be refueled, but he assisted me in helping my heroine in *AF* escape from certain death through deft use of the gearshift in that automobile. I don't know what I'd do without either of you. Thanks for being my friends!

And then there are Mimi Riser and Dr. Alice Gaines. I've requested a couple of times now that Alice and Mimi and I do some kind of Vulcan mind-meld, but they keep refusing, dang it. But they've both helped me out of more plot problems than I can count — and this time Alice even did it in German!

Also, I'm still intensely grateful to my

cousin Jan Rotondo and my up-the-street friend, Virginia Majesty, for continued use of their last names.

I swear to heaven, I don't know what I'd do without my friends.

CHAPTER ONE

In a blissful bout of self-deception, I had imagined that when Anastasia "Stacy" Kincaid, daughter of my longtime best customer Mrs. Madeline Kincaid, got religion and joined the Salvation Army, many, if not most, of my problems would be over.

I should have known better.

Now, not only did I continue to get hysterical calls from Mrs. Kincaid herself, begging me to come to her mansion on Orange Grove Boulevard and read the tarot cards or conduct Ouija board sessions, I was now getting calls from Stacy herself. Wanting me to teach people to cook. *Me,* Daisy Gumm Majesty, who not only could, but did, burn water. Well, not the water itself, but I burned the pot so badly that it had to be thrown away.

But you probably don't know what I'm talking about. Please let me explain.

My name is Daisy Gumm Majesty. In late

1921, when the above transpired, I lived with my husband, my parents, and my wonderful aunt Viola in a neat little bungalow on South Marengo Avenue in the beautiful city of Pasadena, California. I pretended to commune with spirits for a living.

I guess further explanation is called for here. You see, in those days, shortly after the Great War and the dreadful influenza pandemic that, according to newspaper accounts, killed nearly a quarter of the world's population, you can't even imagine how many people had lost loved ones. Many of them, the ones with more money than sense, paid me good money to get in touch with said departed loved ones. I made it my duty to assure those left behind that their sons, daughters, husbands, wives, and/or cousins, aunts, uncles and friends were happy on the Other Side (whatever that is) and expected those remaining to be happy here on earth until they were called to the Great Beyond by God himself. Heaven forbid someone should contemplate suicide in order to be reunited with a deceased loved one.

That may sound weird and perhaps even slightly callous, but it's not really. Trust me. I helped many, many people in my own small way. Heck, I did it as much for myself as for them for I, too, had been horribly affected by the Great War and the influenza pandemic.

You see, my husband Billy Majesty, who lost both of his parents to the influenza and had been the love of my life since I could walk, had been set to enter the world of business as an automobile mechanic for the Hull Motor Works before the war. The wretched Kaiser and his accursed mustard gas had other ideas. Billy joined the US Army right after we were married in 1917 and went off to war, his regular handsome, jaunty self.

Slightly more than a year later, he came back a ruined man. According to all the doctors who worked on him in the US Army hospitals and at home, Billy probably would have recovered from the bullet and shrapnel wounds he'd suffered, although he'd have been in pain and limped a good deal, but the mustard gas had done him in. Not completely. Just enough to render him unable to walk, breathe or function properly for the rest of his life. His pitiful US Army pension wasn't enough to keep us fed, so I had to work. It was difficult for me to look at the Billy with whom I lived now and compare him to the Billy who went to war

9

all those years ago. He's the same, but . . .
well, he's not the same. He's a wreck of the
formerly jolly, happy-go-lucky Billy Majesty
I grew up with. Of course, his condition was
tougher on him than it was on me, but
still. . . .

At any rate, I have hated Germans ever
since, even though I know not all of them
are evil. In some ways, Billy was more
philosophical about the catastrophe his life
had become than I was.

"It was a war, Daisy. Lots of people suffered."

"Not everybody used that blasted mustard
gas."

"The Kaiser will get his reward eventually."

"I want him to get his reward *now*, Billy.
The same way he got you."

Billy would have sighed, but it was early
in the morning when this conversation took
place, and he couldn't take a deep-enough
breath.

See what I mean? Do you blame me for
hating the Kaiser? I guess his soldiers were
only doing what they'd been told to do, but
I still had no use for Germans. Irrational, I
know, but that's life.

Anyhow, ever since I was ten years old and
Mrs. Kincaid, the aforementioned best

customer, gave her cook and my aunt, Vi, an old Ouija board, I'd been fiddling with spiritualism. By this time, in November of 1921, I made a good deal of money at it. More money, certainly, than I'd have made doing anything else available to a young woman at the time. Sure, I could have worked at Nash's Dry Goods and Grocery Emporium as an elevator girl or a sales clerk, but I wouldn't have made a third as much money as I did summoning the dead.

Gee, it sounds awful when put that way. Still, it worked. And as I mentioned before, I did my level best to bring comfort and solace to the bereaved. When I was ten and began my career, I decided Daisy was too pedestrian a name for a spiritualist, so I began calling myself Desdemona, which sounded much more elegant. At the time, I didn't know that Desdemona was a world-famous murderee or I might have selected another cognomen but that, too, is life.

Billy didn't like my trade. He felt bad because he couldn't earn our living for us. I figured that when one was born into our station in life — that is to say, not rich — one did what one had to do in order to earn one's keep. And I earned a darned handsome keep doing what I was doing, by gum,

11

even though Billy claimed what I did was wicked.

In some ways I understood his qualms. I suppose it's not very nice to fool people. However, the people I worked for *wanted* to be fooled. If I'd refused to work for them, they'd have dug around until they found somebody else to do it for them, and at least I was an honest fake. I only worked for people who could afford me, and I never did anything underhanded like send trumpets flying through the air or manifest disgusting ectoplasm, or anything like that.

At any rate, that's how I earned a living for Billy and me, and my generous income also helped to support the rest of my family. Ma worked at the Hotel Marengo as the chief bookkeeper, which was a pretty darned important job for a female in those days. Naturally, she didn't get paid as much as a similarly employed man would have earned. I think that stinks, but it's the way the world works.

Pa hadn't been able to work for a few years because of heart problems. His first heart attack nearly killed him, and we wanted to keep him around for as long as possible. He's a good man — and they're almost as hard to find as honest spiritualists. When Pa had worked, he'd made a

12

good income as a chauffeur for rich people, a class abounding in the fair city of Pasadena.

As I mentioned before, Aunt Vi worked as Mrs. Kincaid's cook — and ours, too. Thank God for that, because neither Ma nor I could cook anything more elaborate than fried eggs. Even then, my yolks were always hard as rocks and the whites were burned on the edges.

I guess God gives each individual a different gift. That's another reason I don't consider my line of work wicked. If God had wanted me to be a ballerina, He would have blessed me with grace. He didn't. He blessed me with a gift for spiritualism.

So there, Billy Majesty.

But I digress.

To get back to my main point, Mrs. Kincaid had been my best customer for years, primarily because of her daughter Stacy, who was a pill. Stacy Kincaid had hated my guts for not quite as many years as her mother had employed me. She started detesting me when she became a "bright young thing" and I remained a sober and well-dressed Pasadena matron — well dressed because I sewed my own clothes. Not for me the devil-may-care, smoking, drinking, carousing life, believe me. I had

13

an image to protect and project, and I took my job seriously. I could waft better than anyone else I knew. Stacy had never held a job in her life and would never have to, either, so she felt free to fritter her life away in unsavory pursuits.

Frittering was exactly what she did, with utter abandon, until earlier that year when a series of unfortunate events transpired in a speakeasy and we both got arrested. I wasn't there to carouse, but to conduct a séance. Nevertheless, I got picked up anyway. The result of that disaster was that I helped the Pasadena Police Department capture a couple of vicious gangsters and an inside snitch. Inside the police department, I mean.

As I was going about this assistance — to be honest, I was forced into it by Billy's best friend and my *bête noire,* Sam Rotondo, a Pasadena police detective — Stacy was introduced to a friend of mine who was a captain in the Salvation Army. Said captain, Johnny Buckingham, ended up marrying Flossie Mosser, former gangster's moll, and Stacy ended up donning the uniform of a Salvation Army maiden. I'm not sure what her rank was. As far as I was concerned she was still rank.

The particular morning when all this

started, Billy and I had eaten the delicious breakfast Aunt Vi had made for us, and she and Ma had gone to work. Pa was walking Spike, the black-and-tan dachshund I'd got for Billy the year prior, as payment for a job of exorcism I'd performed for a client named Mrs. Bissell. I'm not a priest or anything, and the exorcism had been as much of a sham as anything else I ever did in the spiritualist line, but I'd helped Mrs. Bissell rid her home of its so-called "ghost," and acquired Spike for Billy, so it worked out all right. Mrs. Bissell, you see, breeds champion dachshunds. Her primary goal in life is to have one of her dogs entered in the Westminster Kennel Club Dog Show in New York City. Clearly, she didn't have to worry about earning a living, either.

Billy and I were in a philosophical mood that morning — well, there were two philosophical moods going on, but you understand I'm sure — and we had been discussing the events of the passing year. Nineteen twenty-one had started out a humdrum affair and then had grown into something rather more interesting, what with starving Russians dropping like flies; Sacco and Vanzetti being tried for their bomb-throwing escapade; Fatty Arbuckle being arrested; Rudolph Valentino making his smashing

15

debut in the moving pictures; the World Series being broadcast over the radio for the very first time ever (and Billy even got to hear it, because I'd bought him a radio-signal receiving set earlier in the year); race riots in Oklahoma of all places; and a cloudburst killing hundreds of people in Colorado; and Babe Ruth breaking tons of homerun records (in spite of him, the Giants beat the Yankees in the World Series). The Tomb of the Unknown Soldier was scheduled to be dedicated on Armistice Day, which was a few weeks away, and would take place in Washington, D.C. Naturally, I planned to push Billy's wheel-chair down Colorado Boulevard in Pasadena's parade as I'd done every year since the Armistice. There had also been a big gas explosion in Germany that had killed hundreds of people. Don't tell anybody, but I was glad about the last item. Billy told me I was being unnecessarily mean, and that the people who died were just working stiffs like we were, but I couldn't help it. It had been Germans who'd ruined my darling Billy, and I didn't care what happened to them, working stiffs or not.

Before we could get into a huge argument, the telephone rang so I got up to answer it, glad as I did so that I hadn't pressed the

German issue, since it would have ended badly. Billy didn't like the way he was any more than I did, and it wasn't fair of me to rub his nose in it. So to speak.

When I learned who was on the other end of the wire, I stared at Billy, who was drinking his coffee at the breakfast table in the kitchen. I know my eyes opened wide and my eyebrows must have soared, because Billy looked slightly alarmed. I shook my head to let him know it wasn't anything serious.

Ha. Silly me.

It took me a minute or two to shoo the worst of our party-line neighbors, Mrs. Barrow, off the wire. As I did so, I tried to think of something to say to Stacy Kincaid, who, to my utter astonishment and dismay, was the caller. No luck. "Um . . . Stacy, I'm not the one to whom you should be talking. I'm not a good cook. My aunt Vi is, as you know, but not I."

"Yes, yes, I know about your aunt, but she's busy all the time. I thought you might have more time."

Of all the nerve! As if I didn't work just as hard as Aunt Vi. My working schedule, moreover, wasn't restricted to the daylight hours, as was Vi's. Why, many's the time I'd had to work day *and* night, as spiritualism is often a nighttime pursuit. And I made more money than Vi. Still, Stacy was a fool if she didn't know I was a working woman with limited time in which to play games devised by her. I opened my mouth to tell her so, but she forestalled me.

"I know you work hard, too, Daisy, but this is important."

Nuts. I'd been going to throw my status as a hardworking, beleaguered breadwinner in her face, and now I couldn't do it. Still and all, I also couldn't cook, and that was that. "I truly can't help you, Stacy. I'm a lousy cook."

"Oh, but Daisy, this is for *such* a good cause."

If anyone had asked me as much as six months before if I thought Stacy Kincaid would ever be interested in assisting a worthy cause, I'd have said no after I stopped laughing. That day I only said, "Oh?" politely. Although I'd blown up at Stacy once and told her exactly what I thought of her and her selfishness, I'd tried since that one slip to be polite just in case any of my customers got wind of my behavior.

"Yes. Don't you see? People need your *help*."

I was already helping people, darn it, and

decided to say so. "I always try to help people, Stacy. And I do it using the one talent I have. You need to find someone who can cook. The notion of me teaching a cooking class is. . . ." I couldn't think of an appropriate word that wouldn't ruin my somber spiritualist image. "Um, it's just ludicrous. Trust me. You don't want me teaching your class."

"Yes I do."

Oh, brother. Making the face I wished I could make at Stacy, I looked at Billy. He only smiled back at me. Big help.

"No," I said more forcefully, "you don't."

"But, Daisy, I *do!*"

Somber spiritualist or no, I was beginning to lose my temper. "Stacy, there are undoubtedly hundreds of women in the City of Pasadena who would be better at teaching a cooking class than I would be. In fact, I'd wager that *most* of Pasadena's matrons are better cooks than I am. Why, I can't even fix toast without burning it."

I heard Billy snicker in the background, but I paid him no mind.

"Really?"

She sounded pleased to hear about this failure on my part, and I regretted my honesty. Still, nonsense was nonsense, and

Stacy was full of it. Among other things. "Yes."

After the slightest of hesitations, Stacy said, "Well, be that as it may, we still need you to do it."

This made no sense whatsoever. I felt like banging the receiver against the wall in an effort to make the words come out of it in another way. But I knew banging wouldn't have made any difference. It seemed that Stacy was still the bane of my existence, whether she was a Bright Young Thing *or* a Salvation Army maiden. Blast!

"But *why?*" The faintest hint of a whine had crept into my voice, and I told myself to stop doing that. I had long ago determined never to show Stacy the least hint of weakness. She was the type who'd pounce on a weakling and rip her to shreds with her well-manicured fingernails. Kind of like a lioness in the jungle who preys on the youngest, oldest or feeblest. She was that type. I didn't trust this religious transformation of hers one teensy bit.

"Because Captain Buckingham said you were the only one who would do."

My mouth fell open for a second. When my wits returned, I all but screamed, "*Johnny? Johnny* said that?"

"Yes. He did."

I couldn't believe that my friend Johnny Buckingham, bosom pal of my Billy for many long years, had sold me out to the enemy. Johnny, of all people! Why, I'd found a wife for him not very many months ago! And he'd turned on me in this unaccountable way! Well. We'd just see about this.

"Let me get back to you, Stacy. I really can't imagine teaching a cooking class."

"Captain Buckingham said you were the only one who could do it."

"So you said." The rat. I never in a million years would have thought Johnny Buckingham to be such a scoundrel.

"He did."

Sez you. "I'll call you back."

"Thank you, Daisy." The way she said it made me think she thought I'd agreed to her idiotic plan.

"I haven't said yes yet."

"You will," said Stacy. And she hung up the receiver, sounding as happy as the proverbial lark in springtime.

In his own quiet way, Billy was laughing when I slammed the receiver onto the hook and turned toward the kitchen table.

"I can't believe it," I told him as I went back to the table, sank into a chair, and picked up my coffee cup. After taking a big swallow — its contents were cold by then,

21

thanks to Stacy Kincaid; I swear, the girl wouldn't get out of my life, no matter what — I said grumpily, "It's not funny," since Billy still appeared amused.

"Sure it is," said my beloved.

I glared at him. "It is not. And I'm going to call Johnny Buckingham right this very minute and tell him so, too. I don't believe Stacy Kincaid for a second. She wouldn't know the truth if it bit her on the hind leg. Besides, Johnny couldn't have recommended me to teach a cooking class. Why, do you remember the time I tried to pack a picnic for us when we were kids?"

Billy laughed harder. It was kind of hard to tell, since he didn't dare laugh out loud or he'd fall into a coughing fit, but I had become an expert at deciphering his moods. His laughter didn't endear him to me that morning. Nor did his next words.

"The eggs turned out to be soft-boiled and the chicken was raw!"

He'd be rolling on the ground if he were still a healthy man.

Angry and hurt, I said, "It wasn't funny then, and it isn't funny now, Billy Majesty."

"Yes it was. And it still is."

"Bother."

"Face it, Daisy. You're a wonderful woman

in many ways, but cooking isn't one of them."

I huffed and got up, intending to telephone Johnny Buckingham instantly and clear this whole thing up.

But before I got to the telephone hanging on the kitchen wall, it rang again. With an aggrieved sigh, I yanked the receiver off the hook and almost barked into it. Recollecting myself, not to mention my livelihood, I sweetened my tone just in time to say, "Gumm-Majesty residence. Mrs. Majesty speaking."

"Hey, Daisy." Johnny Buckingham.

"You *beast!*" I hollered into the receiver. "How could you *do* this to me?"

His laughter in my right ear and Billy's in my left almost made me shriek.

"Calm down, Daisy. I know you don't want to teach the class."

"It's not so much that I don't *want* to do it as it is that I *can't* do it, blast it, Johnny! You know almost as well as Billy that I can't cook a bean, much less a meal."

"You can learn. In fact, I have a book here I got just for you."

I didn't understand this. Pleading for clarification, I said, "Why are you doing this to me, Johnny? There simply *have* to be people better qualified than I to teach other

23

people to cook."

"I'm sure there are."

Now this is when things got really stupid. I was hurt by his words. I. Who can't boil an egg. Was crushed because Johnny Buckingham, an old friend, had just told me the truth.

"But that's not the point," he went on to say.

"Oh? What, pray, is the point then?" I told myself it was no use getting mad at Johnny. He was another good man. And they, as has been pointed out before, are few and far between.

"We don't need a good cook, Daisy. What we need is someone who is kind, honest and good-hearted, and who can teach frightened women in a gentle and generous manner. We need you."

It was nice to hear those things spoken about my humble self, but still I said, "How do you figure that?"

"For Pete's sake, Daisy, you saved my Flossie's life. And you did it not because you're a reformer, but because you're a kind woman with a genuine open heart. You know good and well that if it weren't for you, Flossie would still be in the clutches of those dirty criminals. You're the one who gave her the self-respect to better herself.

You're the one who helped her see she could have a better life if she tried to find it. You know where she came from. Don't you realize that without your help, she'd still think of herself as dirt? You're the one who taught her to care for herself. You're the one who showed her there was a better way."

Good Lord. I had? This was news to me. Mind you, it is true that I'd helped Flossie tone down her manner of dress so she didn't stick out in a bunch of respectable people like a black beetle on a white sheet. And I guess I had kind of tried to bolster her self-confidence and tell her she was too good for the likes of Jinx Jenkins, the brute she used to live with and who used her as a punching bag. But I'd only done that because. . . .

Shoot, I'm not sure why I'd done it. Actually, I guess I'd helped her because she'd asked me to. She had shown up on our doorstep one miserable February morning, black and blue and with her eyes swollen almost shut, clad in a startling orange dress, and asked me to help her. So I had.

And now, because of that one good deed, Johnny was asking me to help others. Cook, of all things!

See? This is what happens when you allow

25

your good intentions to override your good sense.

Nevertheless, I knew when I was defeated. With a deep and heartfelt sigh, I surrendered.

"All right, Johnny." Wanting him to understand just how idiotic his idea was, I added, "But I'll hate every minute of it. And, what's more, it won't do any good. I'm a lousy cook, and you're only going to end up with a class full of lousy cooks if they take after me."

He laughed. How come all the men in my life were laughing at me that morning? "I know you are, Daisy, believe me. So consider this an opportunity for you to learn, too. I'll bring over that book I told you about in a few minutes."

Aw, crumb.

CHAPTER TWO

The book Johnny brought me was entitled *Sixty-Five Delicious Dishes,* by Marion Harris Neil. All the recipes were made with bread. It was published by the Fleischmann Yeast Company, so I guess that accounted for the bread angle.

I stared at the book glumly. A lovely young woman was pictured on the cover, and she held a plate upon which rested something that looked a lot like a tiny castle tower brimming over with green peas. I soon learned that the recipe pictured was called Eggs and Green Peas, which sounds kind of pedestrian given the castle image. The woman's hair was approximately the same color as mine, being a dark reddish hue, and we had the same basic facial features, but there the resemblance ended. The woman on the cover was smiling smugly. I, on the other hand, scowled. Naturally, my sour expression made Johnny and Billy, who had rolled his chair into the living room, laugh again. I frowned at both of them.

"It's only once a week, Daisy. On Saturday afternoons. You can do it. And the class will only last seven weeks, the last class being held between Thanksgiving and Christmas. Don't want to tie you up for the holidays, now, do we?"

"Huh." The comment was ungracious, but I was feeling about as gracious as a maddened rhinoceros by that time.

Pa, who had brought Spike back from their morning walk shortly after I'd hung up the phone the second time, took the book from my hands. He appeared puzzled. Sensible man, as well as a good one. "What's this all about?"

I was feeling too grouchy to explain, so Johnny did. As he did so, I saw Pa's eyebrows lift until they darned near got lost in his hairline. He knew about my cooking skills — I'm being sarcastic here — too. However, since he was a truly kindhearted man, he said mildly, "So you're going to teach this cooking class, Daisy?"

Shooting a black look at Johnny, I said, "That's what Johnny thinks. I doubt that I'll be able to do more than teach the students how to burn a chicken to a crisp." Or leave it raw in the middle.

"Hey," said my formerly wonderful husband. "I just read an article in *National Geographic* about Cajuns in Louisiana on the bayous there. They fix something called 'blackened' this and that. Maybe you can teach them Cajun cooking, Daisy. You can blacken a chicken for them."

He thought he was being funny, I guess. So did Pa and Johnny, because they all laughed some more. Even Spike wagged his tail. I should have taken a female dachshund, I guess, but Mrs. Bissell only offered me a male, mentioning something about breeding bitches or suchlike.

Ignoring them, I asked a question I should have thought about before. "Just who's going to be in this so-called cooking class, Johnny? Who are the poor dears I'll be inflicting my paucity of the culinary arts upon?" I love to read, and sometimes I get carried away with the poetry of the English language, especially when I'm feeling beleaguered.

Grinning broadly, Johnny said, "Flossie, for one. You did such a great job on her wardrobe and her sense of worth, I figured you could teach her to cook."

I'm sure my eyebrows soared like Pa's. "She can't cook?"

"Actually, she can, but she'll be in the

class too."

"Huh. Maybe she should teach it."

"That's the whole point, really. Or one of them. You see, she can cook, but she lacks the confidence to teach a class. I figured that since she loves and trusts you, she can learn how to teach from you."

"What if I can't teach either?"

His grin looked positively diabolical. "We all know better, don't we?"

Did we? Nuts.

Since I couldn't get out of teaching the stupid class that way, I asked another question that had been puzzling me. "How come you brought me *this* book?" I waved the soft-covered pamphlet — because it wasn't really much more than that — in Johnny's face.

He shrugged. "Bread's cheap. The women are poor." He gave me another grin. "The book was cheap, too. It was the cheapest one I could get at Grenville's Books. I had to get enough copies for the whole class."

Oh. Well, that pretty much stifled the rest of my sulky protestations. If there was one thing I knew about, it was poverty. Not that we Gumms were especially poor. In actual fact, we were better off than a whole lot of people, but that's only because we able-bodied family members all worked like slaves and, in spite of Billy's problems, had been remarkably lucky. Heck, if it hadn't been for Aunt Vi's Ouija board, I personally would have been in the soup. Or at least operating an elevator in Nash's. Other people weren't so lucky, and I knew it. There was still a bit of a depression going on even then, several years after the war ended. According to the newspapers, that was why people like Sacco and Vanzetti and other anarchists kept throwing bombs at people they believed were trouncing the poor working classes. Maybe they were right to resent the wealthy, but I still didn't approve of the bomb angle.

However, that's neither here nor there. On Saturday afternoon at two o'clock, I drove our lovely new self-starting Chevrolet (bought after receiving a most munificent gift from the mother of a woman I'd helped during the same episode that garnered us Spike) down to the Salvation Army on Walnut and Fair Oaks. There I went to their fellowship hall, or whatever they call it — we Methodists call it a fellowship hall — armed with the cookbook Johnny had given me and about six hours' worth of Aunt Vi's advice, ready to do this latest duty that had been thrust upon me. I felt like Frederic in *Pirates of Penzance:* a slave to duty.

I stopped dead at the door when I heard what sounded like Babel issuing from within the hall, and it was only then I remembered that Johnny had stopped telling me about students after he'd mentioned Flossie and the students' poverty. Evidently Johnny was close behind me, because someone took my arm and when I turned to see who it was, I saw Johnny.

My face must have shown my puzzlement, because Johnny said softly, "A few of your students will be foreign ladies who were brought here after the war. They're war refugees who have lost everything, you see, including their families and livelihoods and even their countries, some of them. The church is sponsoring them."

"Where are they from?"

"Different places. Belgium, mostly, I think, and I do believe there's an Italian lady."

Frowning, I listened some more. That language in there didn't sound French or Italian. Didn't Belgians speak French? I decided to clarify the matter and asked Johnny about it.

"Some of them speak Flemish."

"Flemish. Huh. It sounds like German to me."

He shrugged. "There might be a German

lady or one who speaks German in the mix."

You can understand how rattled I was when I burst out, "But I *hate* Germans!" I'm almost always more respectful than that.

He patted me on the back. "I know, Daisy. And I know why. And I don't blame you. But these women are as much victims as you and Billy." I didn't buy it, and I guess Johnny could tell, because he said, "Just go on in, Daisy. It'll be all right."

Like heck it would.

Shooting one last hateful glare at Johnny, I entered the hall. The chattering stopped, and Flossie came forward to greet me with a huge smile on her face. Flossie had turned out to be a very nice woman, and she looked quite pretty in a printed blue frock with long sleeves and a dropped waist. She'd let her hair grow out to its natural light brown — she used to be what they call a platinum blonde — and she had it twisted into a knot at the back of her neck. If I didn't know better, I'd think she was just another attractive young Pasadena housewife.

"Daisy! It's so good of you to do this!" She gave me a hug and a little peck on the cheek.

That's another thing. Until she met me and she and I started our mutual Flossie-redemption project, she'd sounded like an escapee from the slums of New York City's Five Points district, which is exactly what she was. Now, while she still had a slight New York twang, she used proper grammar. She'd been working awfully hard, in other words, and I felt a little guilty about my resistance to teaching this stupid class.

"Happy to help, Flossie," I lied nobly.

Good old Flossie. She didn't even realize I was being less than truthful. With an arm around my waist, she turned me to face the class. "Ladies, I'd like to introduce you to one of my very dearest friends, and the most good and talented person I've ever met, Mrs. Billy Majesty. Desdemona Majesty. We call her Daisy."

Good Lord. I felt myself blushing, mainly because I knew Flossie meant precisely what she'd said. Shoot. All I'd done was help her change her mode of dress a little bit. Well, and introduce her to Johnny. Nevertheless, I attempted to hide my embarrassment and smiled at the class. As I did so, I tried to pick out the German women among them, and was disappointed to find I couldn't. Gee, you'd think evil would stand out like a sore thumb, but it sure didn't then.

"Good afternoon, ladies," I said, striving for aplomb. After all, I knew I couldn't cook, and Johnny knew I couldn't cook, but

I didn't want these people to know it.

Nine women sat before me in a semicircle, all smiling, all eager. They'd each been provided a student desk. You know the kind I mean: a little wooden seat attached to a little wooden desk. Ink pots sat in the holes in the desks, and each woman held a pen poised in her hand over a lined note pad — to take down recipes, one presumes.

"Before you begin, Daisy, I'd like to introduce you to your students," Flossie continued.

Good. Now I'd know which of them to hate.

Hmm. When put like that, it doesn't sound awfully reasonable, does it? Well, never mind.

"I'll start at this end." Flossie pointed to the end of the semicircle on my left. "We have here Maria, Margaret, Hilda, Della, Gertrude, Mildred, Rosa, Merlinda and Wilma."

Since they all only smiled and nodded, I *still* didn't know which one was the German, if any of them even were. It was then I began to think that my irrational hatred of all Germans was stretching it a little bit. According to Johnny, some of these women were refugees who had lost everything, including their homelands. Clearly, none of these ladies had gassed my husband. Also clearly, they were all eager to learn how to cook in America. From me. Oh, boy.

"Good afternoon, ladies. I hope we'll all learn a good deal from this class." And *that* wasn't stretching the truth a bit.

The ladies all nodded eagerly.

Johnny had explained to me that I'd only be recommending simple recipes to the ladies, and showing them how to put the dishes together. He'd also explained that another reason he'd selected *Sixty-Five Delicious Dishes,* besides the price, was because it was the simplest, easiest-to-understand cookbook he could find in Grenville's bookstore. You'd think this would be an uncomplicated thing to do, but I was scared to death. I'd taken my many cooking failures to heart, and they embarrassed me.

Recalling Aunt Vi's instructions, the first thing I did was put on my apron — well, it was really one of Vi's, but I'd made it for her — and recommended that my students do likewise. They did. Obedient little rabbits, the poor dears.

Then I opened *Sixty-Five Delicious Dishes* and turned to page twenty-five. "Today we're going to make Bread and Macaroni Pudding, ladies." Another thing that was cheap in those days was macaroni, which

36

came in long tubes and which you had to break into small pieces. Aunt Vi had shown me approximately how big to break them, but sometimes the macaroni tubes didn't cooperate. Flossie, who had been warned in advance of my plans, handed out some macaroni tubes to the ladies.

I broke my macaroni. The ladies, after watching me intently, broke theirs. Maybe this wouldn't be so hard after all. We'd see.

"And now we need to boil our macaroni until it's soft," said I, only then remembering that I was supposed to have started heating the water before I broke the macaroni. Oh, well. The ladies didn't have to know that. Besides, the stove was in the back of the hall, so it almost made sense to do this part backwards. In any event, we all took our bowls of macaroni pieces and traipsed to the back of the hall. "Remember that you need to salt your macaroni water," said I, doing same, "and be sure to use plenty of water. The water needs to more than cover the macaroni, because the noodles will swell when they're cooking."

Aunt Vi had told me that; otherwise, I wouldn't have known. See what I mean about it being stupid for me to teach this class? Besides, didn't German ladies cook with noodles all the time? One of these women probably already knew the stuff I was telling the class. Actually, if one of them was Italian, she'd know all about noodles, too.

Never mind.

Eventually, we all got our noodles boiled until they were soft, and then drained them and went back to our original places, where we smashed our pieces of dry bread into crumbs, grated our cheese, melted our butter — I had to make another mad dash to the stove, because I should have done that while we were boiling our noodles — mixed everything together along with a little bit of mustard, larded our fireproof dishes, and layered everything into them, just as the recipe instructed. I was real proud of all of us when we stuck our dishes into the oven, which, thanks to Flossie, had been turned to a moderate heat. Truth to tell, I nearly fainted from relief, although my faint would have been ill-timed, since I still had to make sure our meals didn't burn to soot.

As our macaroni dishes cooked, I had planned to lecture the ladies on some of the uses for stale bread, which, according to the book, was so abundant in most households that the average housewife couldn't keep up with it all. Needless to say, I didn't know this fact from experience, although Vi confirmed the book's veracity in that regard. Astonishing what you can learn even when you don't want to, isn't it?

My plans suffered a check when, just as I was launching in to the economic value of frying bread in bacon fat in order to stretch the family budget in a tasty way, who should roll into the fellowship hall but my husband. Worse, he was followed by his best friend and my mortal enemy, Sam Rotondo, detective with the Pasadena Police Department. Sam and I had encountered each other before, almost always under unfortunate circumstances. Unfortunate for me, I mean.

I must have been standing there with my mouth open for quite some seconds, because it was Johnny — I don't know where he'd been lurking — who suddenly showed up and graciously introduced Billy to the ladies, all of whom muttered and fluttered. They appeared almost as embarrassed and disconcerted as I was.

"And this is Detective Sam Rotondo," continued Johnny, smiling happily. I guess he was glad Billy and Sam had joined the fray. That made one of us. "He's originally from New York City, but he moved here several years ago and is now working for the Pasadena Police Department."

More flutters and mutters.

"I didn't know you were going to come," I said, perhaps a trifle ungraciously. I wanted to ask if Billy had showed up in order to watch me fail, but that would have been unkind, not to mention self-defeating. After all, these women didn't know I was a failure as a cook. Yet.

"We just decided to drop by and offer encouragement," said Billy, smiling his winning smile.

Billy had always been a very handsome fellow. Even from his wheelchair, he exuded the charm that had won my heart when I was no more than a girl and used to follow him around, much to his annoyance. He got over it.

"Well . . . thank you." I tried to sound sincere.

"Please," said Sam, "carry on." He waved his hand in the air with a nonchalance I didn't believe for an instant. I squinted at him hard, but could not discern any deeper motive for his sudden arrival at this strange place. Strange for him, I mean. Well, and it was strange for me, too, but. . . . Oh, forget it.

Then I noticed the big clock hanging on the side wall and recalled our not-yet-burning noodles. Ignoring the men, I said, "Let's check our dishes, ladies."

So we once again trooped to the back of the hall. Praying hard, I opened the oven door and, wonder of wonders, all nine of our little dishes were bubbling away and looked wonderful! Pretending I knew what I was doing, I said with some satisfaction, "You see? The custard is almost set and the tops are getting brown. That's exactly what we want. We should give them another minute or two, though, to be sure of the custard."

The ladies nodded happily, and we discussed stale bread for another little while as we waited for our dishes to be perfectly done. One of them mentioned croquettes, and I started slightly. There were a couple of recipes in the little booklet for croquettes, little volcano-shaped things that looked far beyond my limited capabilities. I said something about maybe trying croquettes another time and then, thank God, it was time for me to open the oven door again.

"And there you go, ladies." I spoke with understandable triumph as the aroma of perfectly cooked cheese custard wafted into the room. "Do you all remember what your dishes look like? Let's take them out of the oven and sample our wares."

So we did.

Only there was one dish left in the oven.

Puzzled, I looked around at my class. Only eight women were left. "Where's . . . ?" But I couldn't remember their names. I mean, I could vaguely remember that somebody was named Margaret and somebody else was named Maria, but I didn't yet know which woman went with which name. "Has someone left?"

Then the ladies all glanced around. Evidently they didn't know each other, either, because one of them said uncertainly, "I think so."

"Hmm. Well, I'll take her dish out of the oven, and we can just leave it here. Perhaps she had to go to the powder room or something."

"I'll go check," said Flossie. She bustled off but came back empty-handed.

"Oh, well. I'm sure she'll return. In the meantime, let's see what we've made up and how it tastes."

So Billy, Sam and I bravely sampled my bread and macaroni pudding, as the other ladies sampled their own dishes, and Johnny, being the kindhearted gent he was, took a taste of everyone's dish. He paused longer at Flossie's desk than anyone else's. Flossie colored and fed him a spoonful of her macaroni, and it did my heart good to see the two of them so happy together. Darn it,

42

I could do *some* things right.

Appearing perfectly dumbfounded, Billy said, "Hey, Daisy, this is pretty good."

"Yeah," said Sam, loquacious as ever.

"Thank you." And I said no more. Occasionally I can keep my mouth shut, although not often.

I glanced back at the stove to see if the one wandering woman had returned to claim her prize.

But whoever the woman was, she never returned to the group that day.

Maybe she didn't think cheese and macaroni was worth her time? That made me feel pretty awful, to tell the truth.

CHAPTER THREE

We ate the leftover macaroni pudding at supper that night along with Aunt Vi's pork chops and brussels sprouts. My dish seemed a kind of paltry contribution to the meal, but the entire family raved. That's only because they, too, knew about all my previous cooking disasters and were being kind to me.

In order to divert everyone's attention, I said, "I wonder if that woman will ever come back to class again."

"If she does," Sam said, surprising me, "let me know, will you?" Aunt Vi had begged him to stay for supper. Everyone loved Sam. Except me.

I eyed him narrowly, mistrusting this fascination of his for my student defector. I could detect pretty well myself, and I detected more than casual interest in this police detective. "How come?"

He shrugged.

"There's something you're not telling us, Sam Rotondo. If there's a vicious criminal in my cooking class, I ought to know about it." I glared at him.

"There's no vicious criminal in there that I know about," he said, sounding slightly exasperated. "I just thought it was peculiar that as soon as a policeman showed up, she vanished."

"Darn you, Sam Rotondo," I said, all the frustration of my day at last finding a target. "What in the name of heaven do you want with a poor, innocent woman who's probably an impoverished refugee and who's taking a cooking class? She's a charity case, for heaven's sake."

Ma said, "Daisy," in a tone of voice I remembered of old.

Aunt Vi said, "Honestly, Daisy Majesty." She didn't approve of rudeness in any form, not even when it was directed at Sam Rotondo, who deserved it.

Billy snickered and said, "I thought I detected a German accent from one of the women. You ought to be glad the police are interested."

I glared at my beloved. "I thought so, too. Johnny said a couple of them were Belgian, but *I* think at least one of them's German."

"Ah." Billy scooped up more macaroni.

"I don't think a German lady would be taken in here, in the United States," said Pa thoughtfully. "We just fought a war with Germany."

"My thoughts exactly," I said, smiling at Pa.

"Not," Pa said, "that the poor women had anything to do with the war."

Bother. My family members were all so reasonable. "I suppose not," I grumbled.

"A very few Germans have managed to get into the United States illegally," said Sam.

"Illegally?" I'd never heard of such a thing. I'd always thought of deeds such as murder, kidnapping and theft as illegal. It never occurred to me that countries might have laws governing who could and who couldn't cross their borders. Which was silly of me, really, since I'd read about the Chinese Exclusion Act and stuff like that in school.

"Yeah. Only people with valid work permits, a sponsor and a job are supposed to enter the United States. The government is especially particular about Germans. We're taking in some of the Russian-Germans and a few Belgian-Germans, but they aren't allowing many German-Germans to enter."

I stared at him, undoubtedly rudely, for a

46

few seconds. "I didn't know there were such things as Russian-Germans and Belgian-Germans."

Billy enlightened me. "Oh, sure. Lots of folks, especially Jews, tried to get out of Germany before the war and during it. It's even worse there now, what with all the damage from the bombs. The war ruined crops and farmlands as well as cities, and thousands of people are attempting to start their lives over someplace else. Someplace that hasn't been ruined by the war, I mean."

"Well, surely Flanders and France were hurt worse than most places, weren't they?"

"That accounts for the Belgian immigrants," muttered Sam. "Although not too many have made it as far as the USA. I'm sure you've read about what a mess Russia is these days, what with that revolution they had over there right after the war and all."

"Are we not letting Russians in either?" I was beginning to think we Americans were rather snobbish. "Weren't the Russians our allies in the war?"

Again Sam shrugged. I wished I could heave a brussels sprout at him — speaking of things Belgian. "We're letting quite a few Russians in."

"Oh." I felt a little better about American kindness of heart. "But what's this about

Jews?" I knew Jews had been persecuted for centuries, if not millennia, because of their religion — Christians were mad at them because Jews killed Jesus, but I figured Jesus was a Jew, too, so I didn't buy that argument — but I'd never thought about such things in this modern day and age.

Sam waved his hand in a careless gesture. "We allow some Jews in. We really don't have much of an immigration problem here. Not in Southern California, anyway. Our immigration policies are so strict that most people can't get in. Those who can get in enter via Ellis Island in New York City."

"That's right," I said thoughtfully. "You must have met a lot of immigrants when you lived in New York."

He nodded, not looking especially happy about his experience with immigrants. He might have been thinking of the Bolsheviks or the Anarchists like Sacco and Vanzetti. That got me to thinking again, which can be a dangerous thing. "Are all immigrants radicals like those Italian guys who blew up the bank?"

Billy choked slightly. I realized he was laughing and knew I'd said something stupid. Again. "They didn't blow up a bank, Daisy. They shot a couple of payroll guards."

"Oh. Well, that's just as bad, isn't it?"

"Absolutely." I could tell my husband was trying not to laugh out loud at me. Nuts. I turned my attention back to Sam. "Well, are all immigrants Bolsheviks or Anarchists, Sam?"

"Of course they aren't." Again he sounded exasperated. "My father and mother were from Sicily, and they're not Bolsheviks or criminals." He eyed me coldly. "And neither am I."

Whoops. I'd forgotten for a minute that Sam was of Italian descent. "Sorry, Sam." Boy, I hated apologizing to that man.

He waved a hand as if to say, "Forget it."

"Daisy Majesty, I don't know what to do with you," Ma muttered.

Aunt Vi tutted.

"No," Sam continued. "Most immigrants are perfectly law abiding and are happy to be here and away from famine and the destruction of war. As I said, we don't allow many of them to enter. However, lots of them are going to South America, and some have sneaked across the border that way."

"Oh."

"What's supposed to happen," he said, repeating himself, "is that a fellow will have a job lined up and a work permit, and then he and his family can emigrate to one country or another — except this one,

49

where they're not generally welcome. If they want to come here, they have a better chance if they have a sponsor."

"Oh." That didn't sound right to me, although I couldn't put my finger on exactly why. "I thought people were supposed to send us their tired, weary and huddled masses yearning to be free." My sixth-grade teacher, Miss Ischy, whose grandparents had come here from Switzerland, had taught us that.

Billy laughed. It was more like a snort, actually. "That was then. So darned many of 'em came here that the government decided to crack down on immigration."

"I didn't realize that." Well, except for the Chinese, who, as I mentioned before, I had read about. My education regarding these matters seemed pitifully insufficient at the moment. I decided to visit the library and see what I could find out about the crackdown on immigration.

"But some of 'em manage to sneak in anyhow. Usually across our southern border with Mexico."

"Hmm." I took another bite of pork chop. Vi was *such* a good cook. No way in a million years could I ever even aspire to her degree of expertise of the cooking arts. I think you have to be born with the gift. Sort of like I was born with the spiritualism gift, if you know what I mean. "Mr. Kincaid tried to sneak out of the country the same way. Via Mexico, I mean." Mr. Kincaid, Mrs. Kincaid's ex-husband, was now languishing in prison, which was a good place for him. I'd always figured that Stacy got her unpleasant qualities from him rather than her mother, who was only flighty. Mr. Kincaid was mean and evil.

Sam frowned at me. He never did appreciate my involvement with the Kincaids. Which just goes to show how much *he* knew. If it weren't for Mrs. Kincaid, my family wouldn't be half so well off.

"Do you suppose these women have a sponsor?" I asked.

Sam shrugged. "My guess is that your friend Buckingham or his church are sponsoring the women in your class."

"Oh. That makes sense." And it sounded very much like something Johnny, who had a heart as big as the outdoors, would do. Flossie, too.

And thus the conversation died.

Ma and I washed up after supper, which we always did since Vi did all the cooking, and Billy, Sam and Pa set up the card table in the living room. They just loved playing gin rummy with each other. As Ma washed

51

and I dried, I couldn't help but think back to my first-ever attempt at teaching anything at all. "I can't believe I'm teaching a cooking class."

Ma laughed a little. "I can't, either. You're no better cook than I am."

"Well, at least you made a good raisin pie earlier in the year."

"It almost killed me, too." Ma laughed and I joined her.

"But I really do wonder what happened to that lady who disappeared."

Ma only shrugged.

The following morning we all walked up to the First Methodist-Episcopal Church, North, on Colorado Boulevard and Marengo Avenue, where I sang alto in the choir. Since Thanksgiving was fast approaching — for which meal I would *not* be cooking, thank God — the choir sang "For the Beauty of the Earth," a pretty song I've always loved, and I forgot all about cooking classes, German ladies, Russian immigrants, Sacco and Vanzetti and Johnny Buckingham.

On Monday, Mrs. Kincaid called in a tizzy. As usual. Actually, she'd been even more frazzled than usual lately, because she was planning for her wedding to a gentleman named Mr. Algernon Pinkerton. Mr. Pinkerton was a very nice, very wealthy fellow who had been a good friend to Mrs. Kincaid through all her travails with Mr. Kincaid, but Mrs. Kincaid didn't need much of an excuse to tizzy up, if you know what I mean.

"Please, Daisy, bring your cards. I simply *must* know if I'm doing the right thing in marrying Algie."

It would, thought I, be more to the point if it were *he* worrying about marrying *her.* Naturally, I didn't say so. "Of course," I purred. We spiritualists purr a lot. We also waft, but that would come into play later. "I'll be happy to do a reading for you." What the heck. She sure couldn't do worse than her first husband, and money was money. I could always use more of hers, and she sure seemed to like to give it to me.

Besides, I liked Mr. Pinkerton, although I wasn't sure I'd want to marry anyone whom folks called "Algie," which sounded like pond scum to me. However, Harold Kincaid, Mrs. Kincaid's son and my best friend, liked him. I knew from experience that Harold was a much better judge of people than I, so there you go.

After I hung up the receiver, I turned from the 'phone with a sigh to find Billy and Pa looking at me, both grinning. "Mrs. Kincaid," I said, although from their smirks, I presumed they already knew that.

Pa confirmed my presumption. "We heard."

"I don't understand why she keeps calling," said Billy. "I mean, once you read the cards, the message doesn't change, does it?"

"Not much," I confirmed as I started clearing the table.

"The cards don't say different things at different times?" Pa asked.

"Well," said I, "it all depends on what questions you ask." Then I stopped stock-still in the middle of the kitchen, marveling that I, who knew better, was actually talking as if there was really something to this spiritualism nonsense. I'm pretty sure I sighed again.

Changing the subject, I said, "I'm going to stop by the library before I go to the Kincaids' place. Does anyone want anything?"

"Yeah," said Billy. "Will you see if there are any new Zane Grey books there? I think he's published a new one."

"I'll check on it. I'm hoping Miss Petrie will have a new mystery or two for me."

"Nothing for me, thanks," said Pa. "I'm still trying to wade through *The Beautiful and the Damned."*

"I read that. Didn't like it." I wrinkled my nose. "I already know too many people who don't have anything to do with themselves but drink illegal booze and throw parties."

Pa chuckled. "You're just jealous."

"Am not. Any one member of our family is worth more than Gloria and Anthony and all their friends mushed together."

"Can't argue with you there," Pa acknowledged. "But I'm curious to know why everybody is raving about this book."

"I'm sure I couldn't tell you." In part, I blamed F. Scott Fitzgerald for Stacy Kincaid. Not now that she'd joined the Salvation Army, but before, when she hung out at speakeasies and smoked and drank like crazy.

Anyhow, a little after nine that bright autumn morning — to tell the truth, autumn in Southern California is a whole lot like the other three seasons — I drove our Chevrolet to the Pasadena Public Library on the corner of Fair Oaks Avenue and Walnut Street. I was meandering through the new novels, looking for Billy's Zane Grey book, when I bumped into the library page who was shelving books. I turned around to apologize and got as far as "Oh, I'm so —" when I realized I was looking into the frightened face of the woman who had run out of my cooking class on Saturday. "Oh. It's you." Stupid thing to say, but it's what came out.

"M-Mrs. Majesty," she stuttered, shocked. She had some kind of accent, but I couldn't pinpoint it.

I saw her swallow hard, and wondered why she was so darned nervous. So I smiled. "How nice to see you here."

"Thank you." It sounded more like "tank you," but I understood her. I did, however, wonder if this was the German lady. Not unlike a cuckoo in the nest, thought I unkindly. "Nice to see you, too."

And she fled with her cart. It rattled over the floors in a manner I'm sure Miss Petrie would not approve. I stared after her, bewildered. Then I decided to heck with it, and went back to perusing the new-book section, to see if I could find a Zane Grey book Billy hadn't read yet. And there, by gum, I found *The Men of the Forest* and *The Call of the Canyon.* I wasn't sure if Billy had read either of them, so I took them both.

After that, I went to the desk and asked Miss Petrie if she'd tucked away any new detective stories for me.

"I'm not sure if this is a mystery story," she said, "but it's by Mary Roberts Rinehart, and I know she's a favorite of yours."

I was thrilled. I thought I'd read all of Mrs. Rinehart's books, but when I looked at the one Miss Petrie hauled out from under her desk, I saw it was one I hadn't happened upon: *The Amazing Interlude.* "Oh, my, that looks great!"

"I haven't read it, but I hear it's a wonderful book."

Miss Petrie appeared to be happy that she'd made me happy. I thought that was sweet. So I checked out Billy's books, *The Amazing Interlude, The Great Portrait Mystery* by R. Austin Freeman (I really loved his Dr. Thorndyke stories), a couple of Oppenheim books I hadn't read, and *The Case of Jennie Brice,* which I'd already read, but had liked and decided to read again. I was happy when I left the library. As long as you always have books to read, you can never truly be unhappy.

That was my philosophy then, anyway.

At any rate, after I left the library, I drove to Mrs. Kincaid's house, where I was greeted at the front door by Featherstone, Mrs. Kincaid's butler. I thought Featherstone was swell. Except that he moved and spoke (when spoken to), he might as well have been a marble statue. I've never met anyone less effusive than Featherstone. I wished I was more like him, actually. My emotions are often perilously near the surface, which means I cry a lot, and I consider that a weakness.

"Good morning, Featherstone," I said brightly.

"Mrs. Majesty," he said soberly.

"Lead me to the lady of the manor, please."

Without batting an eye, Featherstone turned and said, "Mrs. Kincaid is in the drawing room. Please follow me."

I'd been in that house dozens, if not hundreds, of times. I knew good and well where the drawing room was. Far be it from me, however, to step on another person's livelihood. So I let Featherstone lead the way to the drawing room. When I entered the room, I was pleased to see Harold there. He hurried over to me.

"Daisy! Good to see you. What's this I hear about you teaching a cooking class?" He proceeded to laugh like your basic hyena.

Now I love Harold Kincaid. He's a great friend, and we liked to chat and go places together. That morning I have to admit I'd as soon have chucked him upside the head with my pretty beaded handbag. "It's not funny, Harold." I frowned at him. "Besides,

58

how'd you even find out I was teaching the stupid class?"

He waved airily. "Word gets around, my dear. Stacy told me."

I should have figured as much, except that Harold and Stacy don't speak much on a regular basis, Harold sharing my opinion of his sister.

He went on, "Say, Daisy, we need to get together one of these days and have lunch or something."

Although I was still smarting slightly from his laughter, I said, "Sure, Harold. I'd love that."

"Del had to go to Louisiana for a family thing — I think one of his aunts died or something — and I've been awfully lonely." He sighed heavily.

Former Lieutenant Delroy Crowe Farrington, Harold's . . . um . . . well . . . friend. . . . Oh, heck, they were lovers. That had shocked me when I'd first learned about it, but it didn't any longer. Both Harold and Del were wonderful people, and I don't think Del had ever said an unkind word about anyone or had ever done anything underhanded in his entire life. In actual fact, he was probably nicer than Harold, but I was closer to Harold than I was to Del — perhaps for that very reason.

I find perfection difficult to deal with. Not only that, but Del was probably the most handsome man in the entire universe. Harold was more of a normal-type person. More like the rest of us, if you know what I mean.

"Well, I'll try to perk you up, Harold. You must be missing Del."

Harold took my hand. "You're a gem, Daisy."

"Oh, Daisy!"

I turned to find Mrs. Kincaid rushing up to me. She was a pleasant-looking lady of early middle age, and she dressed beautifully. A trifle plump, her skin always looked freshly powdered, which it probably was. Near as I could tell, Mrs. Kincaid had never had to do anything more difficult than paint her nails in her entire life. Come to think of it, she probably hadn't had to do that, either, since she had a lady's maid to do her hair, paint her nails and even draw her bath, for Pete's sake. I wouldn't mind being rich, but I don't think I'd care for anyone doing all that stuff for me. I like my privacy. In the case of Mrs. Kincaid, however, I was glad she used a maid, because one of my old school friends, Edie Applewood, had just been promoted to the position of lady's maid. Edie and her husband both worked for Mrs. Kincaid, in fact.

Moderating my friendly tone to a more spiritualistic one, I held out both of my hands to Mrs. Kincaid. That two-handed reach thing is effective when you need to calm someone down, I'd learned over the years. Makes people think you're only interested in their welfare and are there to help them or something.

"Oh, Daisy! I *need* you to do a reading for me!"

"Of course, Mrs. Kincaid."

Harold tipped me a wink over his mother's shoulder. I didn't even crack a smile. See? Told you I was good at my job.

"I'll be off now, Mother," Harold said, kissing Mrs. Kincaid on her softly powdered cheek. "I'll give you a call, Daisy."

"Thank you, Harold."

So Harold, who was a costumer for some studio in Los Angeles but still took time to visit his mother and do other stuff like that, took off, and I once again read the tarot cards for Mrs. Kincaid. The cards told her exactly what they'd told her before: that she and Algernon Pinkerton were destined to be very happy together. The cards always said that because *I* always said that. I'm not big on predictions as a rule, since you never really know what predicament life is going to fling at you or how you'll get yourself out of them, but I figured that particular prediction was relatively safe. After all, Mrs. Kincaid and Mr. Pinkerton had known each other for a million years and they still liked each other. What could go wrong?

Of course, as soon as I thought the latter to myself, I remembered all the things that *could* go wrong and that *had* gone wrong and that *might* go wrong, and began to doubt my prediction, but I didn't take it back. Shoot, the two of them were rich, and as much as I hate to admit it, money really does help heal a multitude of woes.

Which is just one more reason Billy should be proud of me, darn it.

CHAPTER FOUR

The Amazing Interlude wasn't a mystery. In actual fact, I was almost sorry I'd checked it out of the library. The book told the story of a young American woman who wanted to help with the war effort in Europe. So she went to France and started a little soup-kitchen-type place, fell in love with a French soldier, and lots of things happened. Not only that, but at the end, you couldn't tell if the two lovers would be together forever, or if the soldier would be killed or gassed, or a bomb would take the roof off the soup kitchen and the heroine, Sara Lee, with it. The story left me up in the air and feeling kind of blue. I'd faced enough real problems from that stupid war. I didn't want to read about fictional ones.

In other words, the book made me cry. I think I already mentioned that I do enough crying on my own and don't really need books to help me along. I finished reading it, but decided I wouldn't be rereading it anytime soon.

Thus it was that I was almost glad when Saturday rolled around again and I had to teach another class in cooking. I read *ever* so much better than I cook, but *The Amazing Interlude* had truly ruffled my feathers, and I wanted to forget it. That Saturday, moreover, I was going to spread my wings and fly. Or try to. Aunt Vi had spent two solid days — well, two solid evenings, anyhow — teaching me how to make chicken croquettes, and I was going to do my best to impart this newfound knowledge to my students. As for my family, I doubt that any of us will ask Vi to fix chicken croquettes for supper again for a long, long time.

Be that as it may, I felt minimally confident as I parked our Chevrolet at the Salvation Army, climbed out and headed to the room where my classes took place. Flossie greeted me warmly, and I was pleased to see that none of my students frowned at me. I guess their bread and macaroni pudding of the preceding Saturday had met with their approval — or at least hadn't made anyone sick. Although I was too nervous about the impending lesson to take note of the women's faces or count their number, I decided it might be a good idea for the students to wear name tags so I could try to learn their names. Oh, well. I guess I should have thought of name tags before the class began.

Holding up my copy of *Sixty-Five Delicious Dishes,* I said, "Please turn to page nine, ladies. Today we're fixing chicken croquettes." I smiled winningly, or tried to, my courage waning slightly.

Then I reminded myself that these women didn't know I couldn't cook. Didn't help. And it didn't matter, either, since I was here and so were the ladies of the class, and there was no escape.

Because I'd already telephoned Johnny and given him a list of ingredients our class would need, everything was prepared ahead of time and in the Salvation Army's kitchen facility at the back of the hall. Still smiling, I read the very short, very simple — so far — recipe and then told the ladies, "Let's all go to the icebox and fetch our ingredients."

Fortunately for me, Flossie had already chopped a whole mess of chicken, so I didn't have to deal with that part of this ordeal. It would have been bad for my class's morale if I'd chopped a finger off.

I felt rather like a mother hen with several chicks as I led the way to the kitchen, and we divvied up our chopped chicken, eggs, and stale bread. Now came the hard part.

"First of all, we need to crush our bread," said I, as if I knew what I was talking about. "The easiest way to do that is to put the stale bread between two pieces of paper and crush it with a rolling pin." Aunt Vi had taught me as much.

"But first," I said, remembering perhaps the most important part of the entire operation, "I need to light the oven. A moderate oven will be best for these croquettes." Not that I knew this from personal experience. Vi had told me so. I was *so* glad I'd remembered to light the oven, I nearly giggled, but restrained myself.

Since we were all still in the kitchen, we took turns placing our chunks and slices of hard bread on pieces of paper on the wooden cutting board, covering them with another piece of paper and smashing them into crumbs. This was the first time it occurred to me that cooking might well be a good way to relieve the strains of life. There's something about pounding something into submission that's vaguely satisfying.

After all the crumbs were crumbed, I said, "And now we need to measure our cold chicken. We'll each need approximately three cups' worth."

I was so glad Flossie had chopped the stupid chicken! The first time Vi had shown me her chopping technique, she worked so quickly I couldn't even see the butcher knife or what she was doing with it. So she slowed down, and I managed to get a handle on the technique. Not a good handle, mind you, but a handle. Still, I was intensely glad that I didn't have to try to chop anything that day.

Thanks to Flossie, in no time at all, I had the required three cups of chopped chicken prepared and in my mixing bowl.

Lest you think the hard part of this recipe was over, let me tell you that the *really* difficult part was yet to come: when we mixed our chopped chicken, bread crumbs, eggs, salt and pepper together and tried to fashion the mixture into little volcanoes. Vi told me that if the mixture didn't stick together at first, just add a little water, but I didn't want to do that since it smacked, to my mind, of incompetence; and I didn't want my students to grasp my own personal ineptitude. I mean, how would you like it if you learned your algebra teacher had failed a class in basic mathematics? Would such information inspire confidence in his or her ability as an instructor? I think not.

As my students chopped and stirred, I noticed that the student who had run out on the class last Saturday had come back, although she seemed to be trying to hide. I couldn't remember her name, drat it, and decided to ask Flossie to make name tags or little paper tents for the students' desks for our next session.

After everyone had their chicken and crumbs in their mixing bowls, I carried a carton containing eighteen eggs and my own mixing bowl back to the head of the class. It then occurred to me that I could learn everyone's name when I passed out the required two eggs each to my students. Thus it was then I discovered my frightened student, who had placed herself in the back of the class behind the largest woman, was named Gertrude, not a name I personally favor, but certainly not awful enough to induce a person to hide from the world. Odd.

However, there was no time to worry about another person's idiosyncrasies at that point in time. I had to demonstrate — I, Daisy Gumm Majesty, who was the least talented cook in the entire universe — how to shape chicken croquettes into neat little conical shapes.

"Now, ladies, what we need to do is beat

our eggs very well."

"How well?" a student asked. She would.

But I had an answer for her. Aunt Vi had given it to me, bless her heart. "Beat them until they're light and frothy," I said with authority. As if I knew a light-and-frothy egg from a penguin.

Beating-egg noises ensued.

After a minute or two, I asked, "Is everyone ready?"

Nods.

"Very well. What we need to do now is mix our eggs with our chicken and bread crumbs. Be sure to season the mixture with salt and pepper." Vi always said "salt and pepper to taste," but I wasn't sure what that meant, so I didn't add that part. "If you like, you can add a little powdered mustard, although I prefer to save the mustard for ham croquettes. Chicken is a milder meat, so the mustard might be overpowering." And if you think I made that up on my own, you haven't grasped the extent of my ineptitude yet. A few muttered comments from the ladies seemed to agree with Vi's opinion on the mustard issue, which pleased me.

They followed my instructions. If I'd had more confidence in my ability to teach the stupid class, this blind obedience might have given me a sense of power, but it didn't. I was still too shaky to don the mantle of power. Heck, even competence was an elusive trait at that moment in time.

"And now, ladies, we need to shape our croquettes into little cones and place them flat side down on our buttered baking tin." I picked up a glob of the mixture and began shaping, praying like mad that the stupid stuff wouldn't crumble to bits as soon as I put it on my buttered baking pan. As I prodded and shaped my chicken, I said, "When you make these at home, you may decide to fry them in hot fat rather than bake them. That's perfectly all right. Since there are so many of us and only one stove, we're going to bake ours today."

Murmurs from the class told me they thought my reasoning was sound. Only it wasn't my reasoning. It was, as ever, Vi's.

My first croquette didn't fall apart. Gathering courage from this auspicious beginning, I began shaping another one as I chatted to the class. "Croquettes are a great way to use dried bread, and you don't even need to add meat to them. Plain croquettes made only with bread and eggs make a tasty side dish. Or they can be served for breakfast as a cheap-and-easy dish." I'd learned this little tidbit from the cook booklet. "You can also make ham croquettes, if you like.

Croquettes, aside, if your bread is too old to be eaten fresh with butter, you can crush it into crumbs and create bread dumplings for stews or soups." Another clue from the booklet. The Fleischmann Company gave all sorts of nifty tips in their tiny recipe collection.

A second perfectly sound croquette appeared! Firm and solid and looking amazingly like a dunce cap — which I decided not to take personally — it joined its fellow on my buttered baking tin, and I began to truly relax for the first time since class began.

Some of the students finished shaping their croquettes before I did, but that didn't discourage me. After all, they only had to shape their glop into volcanoes; I had to talk whilst doing same.

"And now, ladies, let's take our tins to the oven. Then we can all wash our hands."

They laughed, as well they might. I don't know how Vi does it. Personally, I don't enjoy having chicken-and-bread goo on my hands. It feels sticky, dirty and awful.

The rest of the class went well. As our croquettes baked — mercifully, they didn't take long — the class and I discussed uses for dry bread once more, and I made the mistake of asking if anyone had a special recipe from the booklet she'd like us to attempt in an upcoming class.

One of the ladies raised her hand. I think it was Merlinda, but I'm not sure. Smiling, even though I'd already recognized my error, I said, "Yes?"

"The recipe on the front cover looks good. How about teaching us how to make that one?"

Ah. The pea castle. The one recipe in the entire booklet that scared me more than any other. Even croquettes didn't seem as daunting as that stupid little bread castle brimming over with green peas. "Perhaps we will in another week or so." I smiled winningly again and hoped the class would forget I ever said that. Then, in order to divert the class's attention from my last, idiotic question, I asked, "Can anyone think of other uses for stale bread that we haven't covered here?"

Thank God they knew more about cooking than I did! We discussed French toast, Welsh rarebit, and toasted sandwiches using older bread, and one of the ladies even mentioned croutons. Croutons? I didn't even know what a crouton was until one of my students — I think she was Belgian, or maybe French — enlightened me. Oh, boy. And I was the teacher. It was almost enough to make one melancholy.

Fortunately, our croquettes were done about that time, so I didn't have to endure any more blows to my confidence. We all traipsed back to the kitchen, removed our croquettes from the oven, carried them back to our desks, and took small bites. They were actually quite tasty. Astonishing.

The class dispersed, taking paper bags full of their baked croquettes with them, and I finally let out a sigh of relief. Not only had I got through another class, but nobody in the person of Sam Rotondo or my husband interrupted us that day.

Flopping down on my desk chair, I gazed at my croquettes with befuddlement. I'd actually created those little volcano-shaped things with my own two hands. And they were edible. It nearly boggled my mind. Flossie found me there, musing about the mysteries of life, after she'd seen the students off to their various domiciles. Which reminded me of something I'd been meaning to ask her.

After enduring several minutes of Flossie's gushing gratitude — she couldn't be made to understand that I was a total fake — I said, "Say, Flossie, do you know that woman, Gertrude?"

"Gertrude Minneke? Of course. She

moved out here after coming to grief in New Jersey. I guess her family fell on hard times. Her folks died in the influenza, she kind of hit the skids, and she and her brother decided to move West hoping they could turn their lives around. The Salvation Army in some city in New Jersey helped them out. Why?"

"I only wondered why she seems so scared all the time. She actually ran out on the class last week."

Flossie's pretty eyes opened wide. "Scared? Do you think she's frightened?"

"She sure looks like it. Today she was hiding behind that large woman — what's her name? Maria? — and she tried to hide from me when we went to the kitchen."

"Hmm. I didn't notice. Perhaps she felt embarrassed because she bowed out of the class so suddenly last week."

"I'm surprised she came back again, if she's so frightened."

"Oh, I don't think she's really scared. Only embarrassed. You see, she told me later, the next day, that she'd begun feeling ill, so she left."

"Ill? I hope it wasn't anything we cooked."

Flossie thought I was joking, but I wasn't. It would be just my luck to sicken an entire class of eager ladies who were trying their

74

very best to create new lives for themselves. After she got over her fit of amusement, Flossie said, "Oh, Daisy, you're such a character."

I was, was I? Well, we'd see.

She then said, "No, it wasn't the delicious macaroni dish. She said she just thought she'd better leave, but she didn't want to disrupt the class, so she didn't tell anyone what was going on with her."

"Ah. I see." Flossie's explanation made sense, I guess.

"These croquettes are wonderful, Daisy," Flossie went on. "You're so good to do this for us. I'm hoping I'll learn enough about teaching from you that I'll be able to teach another class if we decide to do this again."

"I'm sure you'll do a *much* better job than I'm doing, Flossie. I honestly don't know how to cook. If it weren't for my Aunt Vi, I'd never have been able to do it."

"Nonsense. You're a wonderful cook, Daisy."

Oh, brother. But I'd never yet been able to convince Flossie of any of my many failings. For some reason, the woman insisted on thinking the best of me in spite of myself. I decided to drop that subject in favor of something else that interested me. "Say, Flossie, exactly what does this sponsorship by the Salvation Army entail? I mean, what do the people who partake of it have to do?"

"Oh my, it's a wonderful program, Daisy. Johnny is so pleased with it. It was all his idea."

It pleased me to see how happy Flossie was with Johnny. And vice versa, too. They made a lovely couple. I liked to think that Billy and I would have been so happy had the blasted Kaiser not butted in and ruined everything.

"What happens is this," Flossie said. "We get applications from various parts of the country. You know, from other churches. We take as many individuals as we can, but our church can really only support ten at a time."

"Ten? But there are only nine students."

"Yes, but we're also sponsoring Gertrude's brother, Eugene."

"Ah. Yes, I remember you told me she's here with her brother. I see. I wonder why she seems so nervous all the time."

"I don't know. Maybe she's just worried that she won't be able to learn what we're teaching."

I could appreciate that, since my feelings were approximately the same. "If she's so nervous about it, I wonder why she came back today then."

"Oh, she has to. You either have to partici-pate in all the benefits of the program, or you have to drop out of it. Since both she and her brother are involved, she probably doesn't dare *not* come back, even if she's as nervous as you say. I don't see it myself, but you're standing in front of the class so you'd have a better view. You see, the Salvation Army finds housing for all the participants. Most of the women stay here, actually. We have a building where we can house people. The apartments are small, but they're serviceable. The Salvation Army also finds them jobs and offers them classes in the skills necessary to build a life. Eugene, for instance, works as a busboy at two local restaurants. He's also learning how to be an automobile mechanic, which pays much better than restaurant work."

Just like my Billy. I'd have sighed again, but I didn't want Flossie to think I was unhappy or brooding or anything.

"I saw Miss Minneke in the library earlier today."

"Yes. We found her a position as a library page."

"Ah."

"The truth is that most of the women we sponsor, especially the war refugees like Hilda Schwartz and Maria Colbert, are almost embarrassingly grateful to us for our assistance."

"I can imagine. Where are Hilda and Maria from? And do you think you could make little paper name tents to put on their desks, so next week I'll know who's who?"

"Wonderful idea!" Flossie beamed at me. It was nice to know at least one person in the world thought I was swell. "Hilda's from Switzerland originally. She came to the USA from Belgium, where her family was killed during the war. She was totally destitute, and she's grabbed onto this program of the Salvation Army's like a lifeline."

I grimaced. "How horrid. What a terrible war." Darned Germans.

"Yes. It sure was. Well, you know that better than anyone." Flossie gave me such a sympathetic smile that it almost made me cry. "Anyhow, Maria was originally from Italy, but she was living in France when the war started, because her husband was French. She came over here after the war ended because France was such a mess and her husband was dead. Killed in the war."

"Oh, my. So many people lost so much." At least Billy hadn't been killed, although I know he sometimes — perhaps often — wished he had been.

"So true. I guess in many ways, we here

in America are lucky. At least the war wasn't fought on our soil. We lost too many men, but we didn't suffer through bombing raids, and the famines and starvation that followed the conflict."

"You're absolutely right, Flossie. Sometimes I get to feeling blue about Billy and what happened to him, but you're right that we have much to be thankful for. At least our homes are intact and we have food and clothing."

"You know, Daisy, Johnny and I pray for you and Billy every day," Flossie said. "Johnny's told me more than once how brave you are and how terribly your Billy suffers. I remember when he was so sick earlier in the year. Johnny said he feared for his life, and I'm sure you did, too."

This time, I *did* cry. Stupid emotions. But Flossie was a true pal, although we'd come to know each other in a somewhat odd manner, and I appreciated her for her goodness. Johnny, too, even though he had got me involved in this wretched cooking class.

My curiosity about Gertrude hadn't abated, however, and I determined to find out more about all of my students during next Saturday's class.

CHAPTER FIVE

Mrs. Bissell, the lady who'd given us Spike as a reward for cleansing her house of a ghost, called that evening just as I finished setting the table and Aunt Vi was about to call us all to dinner. Mrs. B. wanted me to conduct a séance at her big mansion on the corner of Foothill Boulevard and Maiden Lane in Altadena two weeks from that day. I enjoy conducting séances because it's fun to put on my Rolly voice and pretend to commune with spirits.

"Mrs. Roger Baskerville passed on recently, you see. Mrs. Baskerville was a champion dachshund breeder with whom I've been in communication for decades."

Goodness gracious. Hounds of the Baskervilles, by gum! Only these hounds had little short legs and long bodies and would never even think about attacking and mauling anyone — unless it were a person bearing food. I said, "I see," in my most spiritualistic voice.

"I'm hoping that if you can get in touch with her, she'll be able to advise me on what I need to do in order to get my dogs to Westminster."

Oh? Curious, I asked, "Since you were in communication for so long, didn't you ask her that before she crossed over the vale?" Naturally, I cloaked my question gently, in a soothing purr.

"Oh, my, yes," she said. "But I figure she knows more about life's mysteries now, don't you think? After all, she's Over There now."

Right. And I could truly commune with spirits. I only said, "I'll be more than happy to do that for you, Mrs. Bissell." And before the day came, I'd check a book out of the library on how to breed and show dogs. They probably had one. The library had everything, bless it.

"Wonderful, dear. You can see my latest litter while you're here."

"I'd love to do that, too."

The litter she was talking about, naturally, wasn't technically hers, but that of one of her dogs. Dachshund puppies are probably more adorable than any other thing on earth, barring kittens. But kittens grow up to be cats and are, therefore, not as commendable as dogs, at least if you're me. I know some people love cats. I don't dislike them. I just don't want one, if you know what I mean. Besides, Spike absolutely adored chasing the neighbor's cat, and I wouldn't want to risk having one in the house, lest he actually catch it. Anyhow, I was telling the truth when I said I'd love to see the new litter.

Dinner, as usual, was delicious, even though we had to use my leftover croquettes as a side dish. Everyone ate them and commented politely upon their tastiness, but I'm pretty sure the rest of the family was as sick of chicken croquettes as I by that time.

The following day, the telephone rang just as we were getting ready to leave for church. Since the 'phone was usually for me because of my profession, I answered it.

"Gumm-Majesty residence. Mrs. Majesty speaking." Naturally, I used my most soothing voice.

After a short hesitation, a low, silky voice on the other end of the wire said, "Desdemona Majesty?"

I believe I've explained about that Desdemona already. "Yes."

"Mrs. Majesty, this is Miss Emmaline Castleton."

Wow! Mr. Henry Castleton's daughter! I

knew all about her. Well, I knew all about *him.* He was one of those railroad robber barons who made zillions of dollars building railroads across the country. He'd settled in Pasadena some years back and built a positively fabulous hotel on South Oak Knoll Avenue, which, naturally, he called the Hotel Castleton. I liked to go down there sometimes just to walk around. For the sake of my livelihood, I hid my excitement. I did, however, make sure my spiritualistic voice was in full throb.

"Yes, Miss Castleton? What can I do for you?"

When you're in a business like mine, you have to be careful. I definitely didn't want Miss Emmaline Castleton, undoubtedly one of the richest people in the universe, to know what a thrill it was to have her call me. But the truth was that people I didn't know never called me except when they wanted me to work for them. I regret to say that dollar signs began to dance in my head.

"I understand you're going to conduct a séance at Mrs. Bissell's home in two weeks."

It wasn't exactly a question, but I answered it anyway. "Yes, I am."

Another pause ensued. Evidently, this woman was either timid or didn't know what she wanted. At last she said, "I hope to meet you there, then."

Oh? Well, hmm. Deflated, I said, "That would be very nice, Miss Castleton."

I glanced over my shoulder to see Ma standing there. I think she'd begun to hover impatiently, but when she heard the name Castleton, her mouth dropped open and she only stared at me.

"Well," Miss Castleton said, "I don't merely want to meet you. I'm hoping that perhaps you can help me. In your capacity as a spiritualist, I mean."

Whew! Feeling more confident, I slathered the spiritualistic charm into my next words. "I'd be more than happy to help you if I'm able to, Miss Castleton."

I heard a soft sigh rustle through the telephone wire. "Thank you. Madeline Kincaid has told me so much about you. So has Mrs. Bissell."

That was nice. I said, "Ah."

"Then we'll meet in two weeks," said she in her soft, low voice. She sounded sad, actually.

"Yes," I said, getting confused again.

She replaced the receiver on her end so softly, I didn't even hear a click. I waited on the line just to see if any of our party-line neighbors had been listening, but I didn't hear any other clicks, either. Nuts. I

84

wouldn't have minded if the nosy Mrs. Barlow had heard me speaking to Miss Emmaline Castleton.

As I pushed Billy's wheelchair up the street to the First Methodist-Episcopal Church on the corner of Marengo and Colorado, as usual, and after I'd answered Ma's eager questions about my call from an honest-to-God Castleton, I pondered that telephone call.

Everyone in Pasadena knew who the Castletons were, and most of us knew more than that about the family. For instance, I knew that Miss Emmaline Castleton, she of the recent telephone call, had been engaged to marry a young man who'd been killed in the war. I expected that was why she wanted me to work for her. I'd actually met her intended once, at a party I'd worked for Mrs. Bissell. Occasionally, you see, if the cause was good enough, I would read palms and so forth for charity events, and that event was one of those events, if you know what I mean. I think the cause had been to make money for crippled soldiers' families, a cause I more than fully supported.

Interesting. Now I could hardly wait for Mrs. Bissell's séance! I resolved, on my next trip to the library, to look up articles about the Castletons and Miss Castleton's late fiancé, as well as books on dog breeding and showing. But by that time, we'd reached the church, so I had to stop thinking.

Billy always sat in the congregation with my parents and Aunt Vi while I donned my choir robe and took my place in the alto section. I was in the choir room donning said robe when the choir director, Mr. Floy Hostetter, broke into my musings, which weren't very interesting anyway.

"Mrs. Majesty?"

I looked up. "Yes, Mr. Hostetter?"

Mr. Hostetter referred to a notebook in his hands. "Would you and Lucille Spinks like to sing a duet next week?"

Would I? Why not? I liked performing. If I didn't, I wouldn't be a spiritualist. "Sure. What song do you have in mind?"

"Since Thanksgiving is approaching, I'd like for the two of you to sing 'This Is My Father's World.' "

"Oh, I like that one. Have you asked Miss Spinks yet?"

"I'm going to do that right this minute." Mr. Hostetter bustled off, presumably to find Lucy. I didn't doubt that she'd agree to the plan. Lucy and I sang duets quite often and our voices blended well together. Plus, we liked each other, a definite asset when we had to sing together. She was the soprano and always got the melody, but I didn't mind since I never had too much trouble learning my part. Next life, I want to come back as a soprano, however. Sopranos have much less work to do than the rest of us, who have to learn parts and sing them in spite of what the melody is doing.

I'd just buttoned my robe when, sure enough, Lucy bustled up to me, smiling. She's a performer, too. "Daisy, Mr. Hostetter told me he'd already asked you about singing a duet next week."

"He did. 'This Is My Father's World.' That's a nice one to begin the Thanksgiving season."

"I love the tune to it. We can practice on Thursday." Thursdays were choir-practice days. "But we probably should plan another get-together or two before next Sunday."

After mulling the matter over for approximately ten seconds, I said, "Why don't you come over tonight after supper? We can practice then."

"Good idea. But won't we need a piano?"

"I can play our piano at home," said I, feeling slightly superior even though I was an alto. "I'm sure Mr. Hostetter will let me take the music home."

"Oh, that's right! I forgot you could play the piano. I'm so jealous. My mother made me take piano lessons when I was little, but I hated practicing. Now I wish I'd kept it up."

"I always enjoyed practicing, which probably means I'm strange, but it's true."

We laughed about that for a minute. Then I said, "And you can come over next Saturday evening, too. That way we'll be fresh and ready on Sunday."

"That sounds wonderful."

I had a brilliant idea — at least it seemed like one at the time. "I know! Why don't you come to dinner on Saturday? Aunt Vi is a marvelous cook, and we can practice after dinner. I can take you home afterwards." Lucy lived with her parents on Los Robles Avenue not too far away from our house — not that distance mattered, since I had our lovely new Chevrolet.

"Thank you! I'd love to do that."

We entered the choir loft that Sunday as happy as two tuneful clams.

The rest of that day was peaceful if not happy, and Billy and I took Spike for a walk after dinner, which we ate at noon on Sundays. I think everyone does, although I'm not sure why. Aunt Vi fixed fried chicken, carrots, mashed potatoes and gravy, and she'd baked an apple pie for dessert. We all ate too much. Therefore, it felt good to get out into the fresh air and walk off some of our overindulgence.

I was eager to chat with someone about Miss Emmaline Castleton and what she might hire me to do, but Billy held negative views about my work, so I held my tongue during our walk. While I pushed Billy in his wheelchair, he held Spike's leash. Since his illness earlier in the year, he'd nearly stopped trying to walk. That worried me because I didn't want him to give up on life completely. Yet I didn't want to nag him, either. Billy didn't take kindly to nagging. Still, I decided to hazard a question, believing that to try to do something and fail must be better than not to try to do anything at all.

"Would you like to practice walking a little bit, Billy?" Then I held my breath and prayed he wouldn't get mad at me.

He didn't. "I don't see the point, but if it would make you happy, I'll give it a try."

It wasn't a particularly gracious response on his part, but I didn't react. "Why don't I take Spike's leash, and you can hold on to your chair?"

"Why not?" The words came out on a weary sigh, and my heart gave a spasm.

So I took Spike's leash and Billy struggled out of his chair, which I held steady so it wouldn't roll away from him. I was developing the world's strongest arm muscles, thanks to my husband's delicate health. Every now and then I'd look at my shoulders in the mirror and hope they wouldn't get any bulkier. Muscles are fine on football players, but I had an image to protect. A delicate, wafting mien, along with a pale and mysterious look, is my stock in trade, for the love of goodness. It was a mien difficult for me to maintain at the best of times, as I was naturally a robust and healthy person.

Nevertheless, I'd do anything for Billy. He'd sacrificed his health — indeed, his life — for his country. The least I could do for him was bear up through the aftermath. "Are you steady?" I asked once he stood beside the wheelchair.

"I think so."

"Do you want to put your arm around my shoulder or hold on to the chair?"

"I'll try using the chair."

In the crisp November sunshine, Billy's face looked pale and pasty, and it worried me. I'd talked to Dr. Benjamin dozens of times about the state of Billy's health, or lack of it, and the doctor and I both knew the poor man was probably not long for this world. I wanted to cry whenever I thought about losing my darling Billy — even though he'd stopped being darling in approximately 1918. He was still my Billy, and I still loved him, so I put up with his uneven temper and tried my best not to react when he lost it. Today, he only looked weak and sick, and I wished I could take his burdens onto myself.

Such was not to be, however, so I attempted to maintain a cheery aspect for all three of us. Spike, of course, didn't have any trouble being cheerful. In fact, I do believe the dog would have been happy if it were he, and not Billy, whose health was so precarious. I suppose a person can learn a lot from a dog, if he — or in this case, she — wanted to. Dogs suffer the slings and arrows of outrageous fortune just as humans do, but you don't see a *dog* dwelling on its problems or getting crabby and brooding, do you? No, you don't. Dogs seem very accepting of their fate.

Unfortunately, Billy and I were humans, and we didn't have Spike's ability to look on the bright side of life.

It occurred to me that perhaps Miss Emmaline Castleton might understand the burdens I had to bear, but then I told myself not to be absurd. Miss Castleton was rich as Croesus. I was only a poor middle-class fraud. For some reason, that thought made me sad, and I wondered if Miss Castleton had anyone to confide in about her secret woes. I hoped she had a dog to keep her company, at least.

Then, my mental wanderings came to an abrupt halt.

"I can't do this any longer," Billy said after we'd walked no more than half a block.

Instantly I held the chair still. "Are you sure?"

"Dammit, of course I'm sure." His voice held a bitter combination of frustration and anger.

I swallowed the retort dancing on my tongue, since it wouldn't have done any good. Besides, Billy hated his problems even more than I did. "All right. I'll hold the chair while you settle yourself."

Growling like a sulky bear, Billy did as I recommended. "Why don't we go back home." It didn't sound like a question.

I swallowed hard. "You don't want to walk any farther?"

"Oh, I *want* to walk," he said. "I *can't* walk, is the problem. There's no point in both of us ruining our health."

"Walking is good for us, Billy," I said, keeping my voice gentle. "Walking won't ruin anyone's health. Besides, Spike needs his exercise. Vi's been feeding him too many treats." This wasn't technically true, but I'd noticed before that changing the topic of conversation from Billy's unhappy condition to Spike sometimes settled the tension that seemed to build up around Billy and me every time we were alone together, a fact that made my heart ache. My heart always ached in those days. Stupid heart.

At that moment, a car pulled to a stop at the curb beside Billy, Spike and me. Spike began his usual happy-greeting dance, punctuating it with gleeful barks, and I looked over to see none other than Sam Rotondo climbing from the machine. It was one of the few times since I'd met him that I'd been happy to see Sam. Billy never acted grouchy around Sam, although I don't know why that was. Maybe he didn't think being grouchy was manly or something.

"Good afternoon, you two."

"Hey, Sam," said Billy, cheering up slightly.

"What are you doing here?" I asked. I hadn't meant the question to be impolite, but it certainly was.

"I was just out for a Sunday drive and thought I'd stop by and see if you'd like to join me," said Sam, ignoring the tone, if not the intent, of my question.

"A drive?" Billy said.

"A drive where?" I asked.

Sam shrugged. "I don't know. We can drive up into the foothills, if you want to. I'm sure Spike would like to chase some chipmunks."

I was sure he would, too. I glanced inquiringly at Billy, who seemed to be pondering Sam's offer. It was a very nice offer. Sam knew how Billy hated being the way he was, and to give him credit, he did his best to assist in making Billy's life more bearable. Heck, he and Billy and my father played gin rummy together all the time, and I'm pretty sure it wasn't because Sam loved the game, but because it was something both Billy and my father, who had bad heart problems, could do. Maybe he wasn't quite as bad as I liked to think him.

Naw.

"A drive sounds like a good idea," Billy said after thinking about it for a minute or two. He didn't sound awfully enthusiastic, but he never did about anything at all anymore.

"It does," I agreed, kind of surprised to discover I wasn't fibbing. "Are you sure you want Spike and me to go along, too?"

"Sure. Why not?" said Sam with another shrug.

"We'd better tell my folks we're taking a drive so they don't fret." I'd caused my parents enough worries this past year. I'd been on my best behavior ever since February, even though the incident then hadn't been my fault. Well, not much of it had been, anyhow.

So Billy, Spike and I rolled on home, and Sam followed in his car, a nice, roomy Hudson. Then Sam and I got Billy into the front seat of his machine, and Spike and I piled into the back. Thanks to my huge dinner, I fell asleep to the desultory conversation between Billy and Sam, which centered mostly around sports. Billy used to love to play baseball, and evidently Sam had played football during his youth in New York. I awoke when the Hudson turned off the paved road and onto a bumpy dirt track.

"Where are we?" I asked groggily.

"I thought we might drive to Millard Canyon," said Sam.

"It's pretty up there," added Billy.

"Spike will love it," I said through a yawn. Patting my mouth, I said, "Sorry."

Billy grinned, which was a distinct improvement over his mood prior to Sam's sudden intrusion into our Sunday.

It was a rocky climb in the big car, but eventually we made it to the canyon, which truly is a pretty place, with a nice stream running through it and lots of trees and bushes and cabins. People with money used the canyon to get away from the trials of city living every now and then. I understand they aren't allowed to buy those cabins, but have to lease them for something like a hundred years. Sounded strange to me, but I wasn't rich and wouldn't ever be able to rent, lease or buy a getaway cabin anywhere at all.

Sam had thought of everything that day. When the Hudson came to a stop, he went to the auto's rear end and untied a folding metal chair he'd stowed away. I hadn't even noticed the chair before, which goes to show how observant I am.

"I thought you could sit on this while Spike chases squirrels, Billy," he said.

It was a brilliant idea, but I didn't say so, my relationship with Sam being what it was. I did, however, smile at him. "Thanks, Sam."

"Yeah," said Billy. "That's a great idea." He smiled, too. I think that was the first genuine smile I'd seen on my poor husband's face all day long. I spread a blanket over his shoulders, and he huddled in the chair, looking almost happy for quite a while as we watched his dog romp.

The air was chilly in the foothills, but Spike didn't mind. He chased around like a dog possessed, barking at squirrels and birds, leaping in the air after falling leaves, and at one point jumping into the stream.

"Hey!" I hollered. "It's too cold for that!"

But Spike didn't think so. He had a rip-roaring good time. So did Billy, who said, "What the heck, Daisy. He's wearing a fur coat."

Actually, I was enjoying myself, too, until Sam said, "Say, did that woman come back to your class yesterday? The one who disappeared during the first class?"

There went my good mood. I glared at Sam. "Yes, she did. What I want to know is why *you're* so interested in *her,* Sam Rotondo."

This time he gave me a half answer, which was about twice as much as he'd given me before. "I'm not really interested in her at all. I just think it's curious that as soon as the law showed up, she vanished. That type of behavior makes my detectival instincts stand up and salute."

"Hmm. That's the only reason?"

"That's it."

"You're not thinking she's a criminal or anything? There's not a wanted poster for her up at the police station?"

He growled, "Cripes. No, there's no wanted poster up at the police station. If there were, I'd have arrested her by now. I don't know *what* she is. I only thought it was odd that she ran away as soon as I arrived."

I didn't believe him, and it took a good ten minutes for my happy mood to return. Thank God for Billy's dog or it never would have.

The rest of our outing passed peacefully enough, and Sam drove us home in time for cold chicken, green salad and potato patties that Vi'd made from the leftover mashed potatoes from dinner. This, after I'd absolutely *stuffed* myself at noon. I'll never have the "slim, boyish" figure the fashion magazines tell us we women are supposed to have, I guess.

Sam, Billy and Pa played gin rummy after supper as usual, and Aunt Vi and Ma read. I practiced playing "This Is My Father's World" on our piano in order to be as competent with the music as possible when Lucy showed up.

She did that very thing during my third run-through of the music.

"Hey, Lucy," said I, opening the door for her. I waved to her father, who had drawn his automobile up at the curb in front of our house, to let him know all was well.

"It's cold tonight," Lucy said, shivering to prove it, as she came in. I took her woolen coat and hung it on the coat tree beside the front door. She wore the same outfit she'd worn to church that morning, a pretty tweed suit in muted browns with a loose belt tied just below her waist. Lucy was long and lean, like the magazines kept telling us we should be, so the style worked on her very well. You wouldn't know she had a curve on her, if you know what I mean.

"Let me introduce you to everyone." Then, deciding that was a stupid thing to have said, I amended the statement. "Well, I guess you know everyone in my family." Leading her toward the piano and pausing beside the card table, I said, "Lucille Spinks, you know my family, but this is Sam Rotondo. Sam's a detective for the Pasadena Police Department."

To my utter astonishment, Lucy blushed! When I introduced her to Sam! Good heavens, what did this mean?

Sam and Pa had risen politely when Lucy entered the room. Billy smiled at her from his chair. "Hey, Lucy," said he.

"Good evening, Billy."

Sam, bowing slightly, said, "Pleased to meet you, Miss Spinks." I'd never known him to be so polite.

"Happy to meet *you,* Detective," Lucy said back at him, her cheeks positively glowing.

Well, for heaven's sake. I didn't know what was going on with Lucy, but I decided I didn't like it. After a round of "hellos" from my family, but before she and Sam had stopped grinning at each other, I yanked Lucy toward the piano.

Our rehearsal went really well, except that Lucy kept sneaking peeks at Sam as we sang. In an attempt to discern what fascinated her so, I looked at him once or twice as well. Sam wasn't a bad-looking man. He had an olive complexion that went well with his last name, black hair and brown eyes. He was tall and not skinny, as Billy was, but not fat either. I expect he weighed a little more than he'd like to if I'd asked, which I never would, of course. I still couldn't understand Lucy's fascination, however, and I couldn't figure out why said fascination rankled with me. *I* sure didn't have designs on Sam Rotondo! Shoot, I'd resented him for a couple of years by the time that night rolled around, mainly because he kept suspecting me of doing illegal or immoral things.

I decided that my irritation stemmed from

the fact that, if Lucy's attraction was recip-rocated, Sam might desert my family and, therefore Billy, for Lucy instead. Billy'd lost too much in his life already; he couldn't afford to lose a good friend like Sam, too.

That explanation didn't sit comfortably with me, but it was the only one I could come up with that would account for the unusual reaction I had to Lucy's obvious curiosity about Sam Rotondo. The sole comfort I could garner from the situation was that Sam seemed oblivious to Lucy's fascination with him. I decided not to think about it. We got a good deal of practicing done that night, and Lucy's father picked her up, so I didn't have to drive her home. Not that I'd have minded.

Lucy and I practiced our duet again on Thursday night at choir rehearsal, to the applause of the rest of the choir and Mr. Hostetter. Their approval made me feel a trifle better about life in general.

This happy attitude lasted until Saturday night, when Lucy came to dinner at our house. I'd conducted myself quite well at the cooking class that day, amazingly enough. Flossie had made name tents, so I got to fix names to faces. Gertrude still appeared more frightened that I deemed appropriate, although I didn't know why and nobody told me.

We fixed crumbed potatoes, the recipe for which appeared on page eighteen of *Sixty-Five Delicious Dishes*. It was the simplest recipe I could find in the stupid book, because I already had enough to do that day. I'd aimed to conduct a subtle and clever interrogation of my students, paying particular attention to Gertrude Minneke, but I didn't get the chance to do so, because she ran off the instant the class was over, clutching her crumbed potatoes as if she expected them to save her life. Nuts.

I took the leftovers home for dinner. Dinner was, of course, wonderful, because Aunt Vi cooked it. My paltry potatoes went pretty well with the beef loaf she fixed. Thank goodness none of my family members mentioned my cooking class, because the fact that I taught the class at all still embarrassed me. This, in spite of three weeks of moderate successes. It was evidently going to take me a good deal more than three weeks without a disaster to overcome a lifetime's worth of cooking failures.

At any rate, Lucille Spinks came to our house for dinner, which was tasty, and we aimed to practice our duet afterwards. Ma offered to wash and dry the dishes for us since we needed to practice, but we helped her. We already knew the song, after all, and were only getting together for one last rehearsal. Besides, Ma worked very hard during the day. She shouldn't have to work at night, too.

When the dishes were done and my family was ensconced in the living room reading, I trotted to the piano and played the music through once. And then Lucy and I began singing. We sounded pretty good together, but she positively *grilled* me for information about Sam Rotondo in between verses.

"Is he a married man?" she asked. I think she was attempting to act as if she were merely slightly curious, but she did a mighty poor job of it.

"He's a widower," I told her, trying hard not to snap.

"Oh, the poor man!"

Right. "I think he's over it now."

Lucy gave me a puzzled look. "How can you get over the death of someone you loved enough to marry?"

Good question and one I couldn't answer. Yet. "Well, I didn't mean it that way. But I think he's over the worst of his grief."

"How did his wife die?"

Boy, she just wouldn't let the subject drop, would she? Holding in my temper, whilst wondering why I was in a temper in the first place, I answered. "She had tuberculosis."

"Oh, that's so sad." To my absolute amazement, Lucy snatched a hankie from her pocket and dabbed at a leaky eye.

"Yes," I said. I think I meant it, but I was so confused by that time, I'm not sure.

"He's not from around here, is he?"

Fighting my aggravation at Lucy's probing, I said, aiming for sweetness, "He's originally from New York City. I believe he and his wife moved to California for her health, but by the time they got here, it was too late."

Lucy tsked. "Does he have any children?"

Sam Rotondo? A father? I thought not. I couldn't even imagine such a thing. "Um . . . no."

Lucy gave a mournful sigh.

To forestall more Sam questions, I inquired brightly, "Do you think we have the song down well enough, or should we go through it one more time?"

Thank God she responded to my question instead of asking me for more information about Sam Rotondo, the bane of my existence. We sang the song again. Then she thanked Aunt Vi for a lovely dinner, said good-bye to my parents and Billy, and we left.

When I drove her home, however, she started in on the Sam issue once more. I considered driving the Chevrolet into a tree but restrained myself.

"Do you know how old Detective Rotondo is?" asked Lucy.

"No." Sensing that was too short an answer, I elaborated even though I didn't want to. "I mean, I've never asked him. I think he's a little older than Billy. Late twenties or early thirties maybe?"

"Perfect," Lucy said in something akin to a purr.

"Perfect for what?" I asked, hoping my peevishness didn't come across in the question.

"Well, I mean . . . I mean . . . I. . . ." Lucy's words stuttered to a stop.

"Are you interested in him in . . . in a romantic way?" I asked at last, even though her interest had been obvious from the moment of their meeting.

I'm sure she blushed again, but it was too dark in the machine to see. "Well, I think he's an awfully attractive man. And he's a detective and all. I think that's very . . . interesting."

"Hmm. Maybe."

Lucy tossed her head. "*I* think being a detective must be interesting work. And at

105

least he's alive and employed. So many young men aren't these days."

"That's the truth." Not only had thousands of our young men died, thanks to the evil Kaiser, but the country had been in a financial slump ever since the war ended.

"And, yes. I guess I am interested in him," Lucy said at last. "I don't know about the romance part." She giggled.

Nuts.

CHAPTER SIX

In spite of Lucy's inexplicable interest in Sam Rotondo and my irritation resulting therefrom, she and I sang our duet beautifully in church the next day. As we sang, I was surprised to see Sam sitting in the congregation next to my family. Even though he'd visited our church before this, I was pretty sure Sam wasn't a Methodist. Weren't all Italians Roman Catholic? It then occurred to me that he might have come on account of Lucy. For some reason, that made my spirits sink. What was the *matter* with me, anyhow?

My surprise at seeing Sam, however, paled in comparison to the astonishment I felt when I espied my student escapee, Gertrude Minneke, sitting in the very back row of the church. What in the world was *she* doing there? Not that I begrudged her attendance at my church, but I should have thought she'd attend services at the Salvation Army, if she went to church anywhere. It occurred to me that nothing in my life was going the way it was supposed to be going, even down to people attending the wrong churches, and that was making me grumpy; and *then* it occurred to me that I should probably just give up trying to figure things out. Life was complicated, sometimes more often than not, and there wasn't a blessed thing I could do about it.

Shoot, perhaps Sam had come to church to keep tabs on Gertrude, although I couldn't think how he'd have known she'd be there. Maybe he'd set spies on her. Since he wouldn't tell me why he was interested in her comings and goings — or goings and hidings — there was no way for me to know. My brain was beginning to hurt, so I decided it would be better to concentrate on singing the song and forget about other people's actions.

In spite of my fuddled musings, everyone seemed to enjoy our duet. The minister even complimented Lucy and me on our "lovely voices." I suppose he'd have said something nice even if we'd stunk, but we didn't. We were good.

After the service I'd rid myself of my choir robe and joined my family in the fellowship hall, where the congregation always gathered after church for cookies and tea and coffee. I spied Gertrude at the back of the hall, all alone, looking like she wanted to run away. Then I spied Lucille Spinks, her hand on Sam's arm, gushing at him, while he looked down upon her, a bemused expression on his face.

I turned my back on the two of them and aimed myself at Gertrude.

She slid around a corner just as I approached, but when I, too, turned the corner, she was waiting for me in the hallway. I smiled benevolently at her, or tried to. "It's so nice to see you here, Miss Minneke."

"Thank you, Mrs. Majesty." She looked nervously up and down the hallway. She gave a big gulp and blurted out, "Mrs. Majesty, may I speak to you for a moment?"

"Of course you may." Oh, boy! Maybe I'd finally learn why she was as skittish as a spooked bunny rabbit! "Is something the matter, Miss Minneke? You seem a little . . . worried about something."

"Oh, no!" cried she. I didn't believe her. "There's nothing wrong. I . . . I just wanted to come to this church today. Your duet was beautiful." She added the last comment perfunctorily, as if she thought she needed to say something nice about me.

"Thank you."

"I wanted to see you and where you went to church."

How very odd. Rather than saying that, I said, "How did you know I went to this church?"

"Captain Buckingham told me."

"Ah. I see." But I didn't. Why had she asked Johnny where I attended church? I probably should have asked her, but I didn't want to appear too awfully nosy.

We stood there, staring at each other, for several seconds. Then Gertrude said, "Well, I probably ought to be getting home now."

"Won't you stay for a while after we chat and have some cookies and coffee?"

"Oh, no. I really don't. . . ."

"Ah. There you are."

Startled by this new voice, I turned to see Sam Rotondo standing in the doorway. "Were you looking for me?" I don't think I hid my incredulity very well.

"Billy was asking where you went," he said.

"I'll be right there." When I turned around again to ask Gertrude if she'd like to meet my family, she'd vanished.

What in the world was going *on* with that woman? I turned back to Sam and prepared to return to my husband.

But Sam was staring down the empty hallway. "Was that who I think it was?"

Sighing, I said, "If you thought it was Gertrude Minneke from my cooking class, the one who keeps running away, then yes, it was."

"She ran away again."

"I guess you're just a frightening fellow, Sam."

He frowned at me. "There's something odd about that woman."

"I suppose there's something odd about all of us," I said, shrugging and wishing everybody would revert to behaving as I expected them to. I was really annoyed that Sam had butted in just when I might have been able to get to the bottom of the Gertrude puzzle. "What made you come to this church today, for instance? That seems odd to me."

He shrugged. He did that a lot. I decided I was going to hit him if he refused to answer *that* question. I might have hit him if he said he came to church to see Lucy, too.

"I just thought your song was pretty and decided to hear it in the venue for which it was created. The two of you sounded very good together."

Oh. Well, that took the wind out of my sails. I said, "Thank you," humbly.

Billy and my folks were seated at a long table in fellowship hall, and Lucy and her family sat with them. I plunked myself down next to Billy's wheelchair.

"Where'd you run off to?" Billy asked.

"I thought I saw one of my students."

"One of your students?" This, from Lucy. "What are you teaching, Daisy? I thought you read palms for people. I didn't know you taught school, too."

Billy snickered, blast him.

Ignoring him, I said, "I'm only teaching a seven-week course at the Salvation Army."

"Oh?" Lucy sounded positively fascinated, curse her. "What's the subject you're teaching?"

Have I mentioned that Lucille Spinks was tall and skinny and had rather rabbity teeth? Well, she did. Not that she was ugly or anything.

I took a deep breath and tried to recollect if Lucy knew about my many cooking failures of the past. I wasn't sure, but you never knew about these things. Bravely daring, I said, "Cooking."

Lucy didn't burst out laughing, so I guess she was ignorant of my past misdeeds in the kitchen. "Oh, my. How fascinating. Why are you teaching the class at the Salvation Army?"

"Captain Buckingham is a friend of ours. He's the one who asked me to teach the class."

"Oh! I think I remember him from school. Johnny Buckingham, isn't it?"

"He's the one, all right." I wished she'd drop the subject.

Not Lucille Spinks. She seemed determined to drag the issue on forever — or until someone ratted me out. "Who are the students taking the class?"

Another deep breath calmed me enough not to holler at her. "They're nine ladies whom the Salvation Army is sponsoring. They all need help for various reasons. Some of them are war refugees and others are people who were down on their luck. The Salvation Army is helping them out. They're good at that sort of thing. They never turn anyone away." I'd learned this bit of information from Johnny, who'd hit the skids after he got back from the war. He'd begun drinking heavily and credited the Salvation Army for saving his life. I have no cause to doubt his reasoning on the subject.

"Oh," said Lucy. "How nice of them."

Was it my imagination, or was Lucy making cow's eyes at Sam? I couldn't tell. "Yes. They're a very helpful organization. Very inclusive. As I said, they never turn anyone away."

Then Lucy proceeded to grill me about the Salvation Army much as she'd grilled me about Sam the prior evening. By the time we finally left the church for home, I was more than ready to escape. Sam, naturally, was invited to partake of our noon dinner. It occurred to me he might have gone to our church that day just so he could come to dinner at our house, but even I, who didn't give Sam much credit for anything, gave him more credit than that.

Harold Kincaid called me on Tuesday of that week and asked if I'd like to partake of luncheon with him. As I mentioned earlier, Harold didn't live in Pasadena and he worked as a costumier at a moving-picture studio in Los Angeles. But he'd gone to visit his mother that day, and we generally got together when he was in town.

"I have to be fitted for a tuxedo," said he, not sounding particularly happy about it.

"I'm surprised you don't have tuxedoes at the studio."

"We do." Harold sighed deeply. "But Mother wants me to get a brand-new one for the wedding. She's in a dither about it."

"Yes," I said. "She's been dithering a lot

114

recently. I thought she'd calm down after your sister got religion, but she hasn't."

"Lord, no. She'd probably approve if Stacy had been saved by an Episcopalian, but Mother disapproves of the Salvation Army because they allow poor people to join their ranks. She equates poverty with evil."

I laughed at that. "Shoot, that's one of the reasons I like the Salvation Army. Because they don't care if you're rich or poor, and they don't turn you away if you've slipped up in life."

"You and me both. But you know my mother."

"I certainly do. She's a lovely woman and my best customer, but she is . . . um . . . a little scattered."

Harold almost howled with laughter.

When he stopped laughing, I said, "Anyhow, I'd love to join you for luncheon. Do you want to meet somewhere, or do you want to pick me up?"

"I'll pick you up. Say twelve-thirty?"

"Sounds good to me."

I hung up the 'phone, happy to have something to look forward to for once.

Billy, who'd overheard the conversation, didn't seem at all pleased.

"Harold," I told him.

115

"I heard. I don't know why you like that fellow so much, Daisy."

Borrowing a gesture from Sam Rotondo, my mortal enemy, I shrugged. "He's nice. And he's funny, too."

"He's a faggot, for Pete's sake."

"He's a nice man," I insisted. "In spite of what you think, I don't think he had any control over . . . that aspect of his personality."

"That *aspect of his personality?* Nuts."

So there we went again. It seemed to me that anytime I managed to look forward to doing something, Billy would object to it. Kind of took the joy out of life, if you know what I mean. Be that as it may, I said, "Would you like to join us?"

"No! Cripes, Daisy, I don't like hanging around with people like that."

"People like what, Billy Majesty?" My temper began to erode. Billy's reason for disliking Harold really irked me. It's one thing to dislike someone because he does bad things or is mean-tempered or malicious or does something horrid to you. It's something else entirely to dislike someone just because he's different from you. "Like kind? Sweet-natured? Generous and funny? Are those the types of people you don't like to hang around with?"

116

"Dammit, Daisy, you know what I mean. I don't like homosexuals, for Pete's sake!"

"Why not? Are you afraid Harold will try to seduce you or something?"

"That's disgusting, Daisy," Billy said solemnly.

"I just wish you could see past Harold's one . . . quirk —"

"You call men loving men a *quirk?*"

"Yes I do! He can't help what he is, Billy, any more than you can help what you are."

And if that wasn't the wrong thing to say, I don't know what was. I swear, my mouth gets me into *so* much trouble. I should have learned by that time not to argue with Billy, but it annoyed me that he had such a skewed opinion of a gentle and lovely man. Harold had helped me out more than once when I'd desperately needed someone to rely on. Of course, it didn't help that he'd been with me when the police raided the speakeasy where I was conducting a séance, but that wasn't really Harold's fault. He had intended to be helping me on that occasion, too.

In any case, my ill-chosen words precipitated one of the heated arguments in which both Billy and I ended up hating ourselves. Or maybe we both just hated me. It didn't matter; I knew it was wrong to argue with my husband. Poor Billy. He really deserved a better wife than I.

By the time Harold drove up to the curb in front of our house in his lovely, jazzy red Stutz Bearcat, I was in a dismally blue mood.

"I'm sorry, Daisy," Harold said with true sympathy when I explained why I appeared so downcast. "Your poor husband has a lot on his plate."

"I know it. But so do I, Harold! And it makes me mad that he judges people the way he does."

"We all do it, sweetie. Believe me, your Billy is no different from ninety-nine percent of the people in the world. Men like Del and me are considered worse than murderers and rapists and other criminous people."

I brushed a tear from my cheek. "That's not fair, Harold."

"Too true, but there's not much I can do about it. Or you, either. Besides, you've told me more than once that you hate Germans, and I defy you to name one genuine German you know and tell me why you hate that person."

Grumpy now, I said, "You fight dirty."

"But it's the same thing, Daisy. Your hatred of Germans is as irrational as your husband's hatred of men like Del and me."

"That's not true. Germans started that war and almost killed Billy. Neither you nor Del has ever done anything awful to Billy. Or anyone else, for that matter. At least not that I know about."

"True. But that doesn't matter. People fear what they don't understand." He frowned as he steered his car. "Anyhow, let's talk about something else. This subject is too depressing."

"All right." After sniffling once or twice and blowing my nose, I asked, "How'd the fitting go?"

"Like a dream. If Mother survives until the wedding, it should be a grand affair."

"I hope Stacy isn't going to wear her Salvation Army uniform."

"Lord, no! Mother would have a connniption fit if she did. No, Mother's having a dress made for Stacy, too."

"And Stacy isn't arguing about it?"

"Oddly enough, she isn't. She's really taken to this Salvation Army stuff. She's actually trying to modify her behavior."

"Good Lord. It doesn't seem possible."

"She's so self-righteous about her religious turn, she's harder for me to take than she was when she was drinking and smoking and getting arrested." Harold chuckled.

I'd have joined him, but I was feeling sorry

for myself. Instead, I sighed again. "If she keeps behaving rationally, I might have to change my opinion of her, and I'd hate to do that."

Harold grimaced. "Don't do anything so rash yet. This Salvation Army kick is still young."

"I suppose you're right. She'll probably have a relapse once the novelty wears off." I regret to admit that I hoped she would.

"Oh, I'm sure she will."

Harold took me to a lovely and wildly expensive Japanese restaurant called the Fujiyama, where the food was delicious and the decor was quite exotic. I'd never eaten Japanese cuisine before, and this restaurant was one of two of the ilk in Pasadena, the other being a place called the Manako. I was terribly impressed with something called tempura, which was basically vegetables coated in a light batter and fried, then dipped into some kind of yummy sauce. Thanks to Harold and lots of good food, I felt slightly more cheery when we left the place and walked to the parking lot at the rear of the building.

And darned if I didn't practically stumble over Gertrude Minneke! She stood in the alleyway leading to the street where the car was, talking to a man in a waiter's uniform whom I'd seen carrying dishes inside the restaurant. They were deep in conversation, and both of them appeared worried. Good heavens, now what?

"Miss Minneke!" I said in a bright voice.

Both Gertrude and her gentleman friend jumped about a foot and a half. When she landed, Gertrude swirled around, her hand pressed to her bosom, her eyes nearly bugging out of their sockets. "Mrs. Majesty!"

"I didn't mean to startle you," I told her, feeling a trifle guilty, although I don't know why.

"Oh, that's all right." She kind of panted the words. "Um . . . please meet my brother, Mrs. Majesty. This is Eugene." She took the hand of the waiter, as if showing him to me. "Eugene Minneke."

"Pleased to meet you," said Eugene. His back-East accent was stronger than Gertrude's. I could swear he also didn't mean what he'd just said.

"Likewise," I said, holding my hand out for him to shake. "And this is my very good friend Harold Kincaid."

Both Minnekes gave Harold tense smiles, and Eugene and Harold shook hands.

"It's nice to see you, Mrs. Majesty," Gertrude said in an uncertain voice.

"Yes, indeed," I agreed. We were both lying; I could tell.

Taking Harold's arm, I said, "Well, we need to run," and hurried us along, sensing that Gertrude and Eugene wanted to be alone to continue their conversation.

"What the devil's wrong with those two?" Harold asked as he opened the door for me to enter his auto.

"I don't have a clue. Gertrude is in my cooking class at the Salvation Army, and she keeps disappearing every time I spot her anywhere."

Harold got in the car on the driver's side. "They both looked as nervous as cats."

"I agree. Gertrude even went to my church last Sunday. She said she wanted to talk to me about something, and then she ran away again."

We both agreed that this was strange behavior on Gertrude's part, but I was no closer to learning the reason for it. I decided that I was going to have a long chat with Gertrude after our class next Saturday.

When Harold dropped me off at home, I got into the Chevrolet and drove to the library. There I found every book I could find about dog breeding and showing. Oddly enough, there were quite a few of them.

And then I toddled down to the periodical section and looked up all the articles I could find in old newspapers about the Castletons.

Sure enough, I found a long article about Miss Castleton's late fiancé. His name had been Stephen Allison, and he'd died in Flanders not long after the United States had entered the war. The most complete article I discovered was from the *Pasadena Evening Post,* a newspaper we didn't subscribe to. The article mentioned that Mr. Allison and Miss Castleton had planned to marry, but had decided to postpone the wedding until after Mr. Allison returned from the war. Unfortunately, by the time he returned, he was in no condition to marry anyone. He'd been buried at the Mountain View Cemetery in Altadena, the same place where Billy's mother and father were laid to rest.

I closed the newspaper, feeling tears sting my eyes. Darn it, why was life so hard? True, Miss Castleton had tons of money, but she didn't have Stephen Allison any longer and, although I hadn't met her yet, I'd have wagered a good deal that she'd rather have him than her father's money.

The article had said she resided at her father's mansion in a part of town called San Marino. In later years, Mr. Castleton would donate his gigantic house, grounds and collected art works, both paintings and sculptures, to the City of Pasadena as a museum. At that time, the place was a grand home. I wondered if Miss Castleton wandered the grounds, missing Stephen and wishing her life could be different.

By that time in my life, I'd known for decades — well, slightly more than two decades, at any rate — that rich people and the rest of us aren't the same. Rich people didn't have to worry about dying from want and starvation, for instance. Still, people were people, and I had a strong feeling that Emmaline Castleton and I had a lot in common, even if we came from opposite ends of the social ladder. In short, I felt sorry for her.

Bother.

CHAPTER SEVEN

Saturday arrived at last. That was the date set for Mrs. Bissell's séance, and my introduction to Miss Emmaline Castleton. I really wanted to meet her and find out why she'd called me. I sensed another good client in the offing, but I tried not to build myself up too much. After all, you never knew about these things. Perhaps she only wanted to hire me for a charity party or something.

But the séance would be held at night. Before I could commence communicating with the dead, I had to survive dealing with the living at another cooking class, a task far more difficult than raising the dead, at least for me. As you can probably tell, my confidence level hadn't risen perceptibly by that point in time as regards to the art of cookery. This is probably because I'd tried to make breakfast for Billy and me that morning, and my efforts were not universally successful. At least I didn't burn the toast. The eggs suffered a far more severe fate. Billy only laughed, so that part was all right.

At any rate, I'd selected a very simple recipe for my class to make that day, not for their sake, but for mine. The recipe, for scalloped cheese bread, resided on page nineteen of *Sixty-Five Delicious Dishes,* a book against which I had begun to harbor quite a grudge.

The only thing I looked forward to as far as that class went was finally discovering why Gertrude Minneke behaved like a frightened deer every time a representative of the police department showed up in her vicinity. By that time I'd decided that, as much as I didn't want to agree with Sam Rotondo about anything at all, I did agree it was the presence of law enforcement that so frightened Gertrude.

To facilitate my chat with Gertrude and to soften her up, if such a thing was possible, I decided to gently ask the ladies in my class to tell the rest of us a little about themselves as our scalloped cheese breads baked. Flossie, bless her heart, brought the name tents again, so I could call the women by their proper names.

"Let's all turn to page nineteen, ladies," I

said, smiling as if I were happy to be there.

Pages rustled.

"We're going to make scalloped cheese bread today. As I'm sure you know, both cheese and bread are cheap commodities these days, and they can be combined to make many tasty dishes." Aunt Vi had told me so; therefore, I knew the statement to be true.

We went through the recipe step by step — there weren't many of them, thank God — and then we carted our filled baking dishes to the oven in the back of the hall. As our cheese breads baked, I put my crafty plan into action.

"Until our dishes are cooked through, I think it would be nice to learn a little bit about each other." Noticing uneasy glances pass among my students, I smiled and said, "I'll begin with me." They all laughed. If they only knew how little there was in my life to laugh at.

Nevertheless, I gave them a short summary of my life up to that date, leaving out the more unpleasant parts of it, most of which involved my husband and his ruination at the hands of the Germans.

"And now, who'd like to introduce herself first?"

A resounding silence filled the hall. I

sighed inwardly, but remained undaunted. Darn it, I wanted to know who these women were! Especially Gertrude and the woman whom I suspected of being German. I squinted at the name tent on her desk. "Hilda Schwartz? Would you like to begin? Tell us a little about yourself."

She started slightly, an indication to my mind that she wouldn't at all like to begin. She swallowed her nervousness, however, and told us the following tale in a heavy and, I believed, Germanic accent: "My name is Hilda Schwartz, and I'm from Switzerland."

"Switzerland! Oh, my, I'd love to visit Switzerland someday," I said, aiming for a rapturous tone. In truth, it had never crossed my mind to visit Switzerland, although I'd read *Heidi* when I was a kid.

My enthusiasm seemed to calm Hilda somewhat, because she smiled and went on with more confidence. "My country is beautiful, with big mountains and grassy meadows."

"What language did you speak there, Hilda?" Was I crafty, or was I not crafty?

"Oh, we Swiss speak many languages. Some of us speak Italian, some of us speak French, and some of us speak German. In my part of Switzerland, we mostly speak

German."

Hmm. She might be telling the truth, I guessed. Just because a person spoke German didn't necessarily mean she was from Germany, evidently. I'd have to ask Billy, since he knew considerably more about the world than I did, thanks to his subscription to *National Geographic.*

"I see," I said. "And why did you come to our country?"

Was it my imagination, or did Hilda stiffen a little? It was probably my imagination.

"Oh, it was the war," she said with an air of gravity that seemed unfeigned. "My brother" — she pronounced it *brudder* — "fought in the war, and he died in France."

"Oh? I thought Switzerland remained neutral during the conflict." I smiled sweetly, or tried to.

She swallowed. "Switzerland was, but we were living in France at the time the war started, and he . . . he joined the French army."

"Really? Why were you in France?" I maintained my smile and tried not to feel guilty about my nosy questions.

"I was working as a nanny. My brother Hans was a . . . a chef."

"Oh, my! A chef! I'm surprised he didn't teach you how to cook."

I could tell she was grinding her teeth. Evidently, that chef comment had been a mistake. I got the strong impression she was making up her history as she spoke.

"We never were home at the same time," she said, solving that particular problem with one deft blow. "Hans was my last relation in the world. Our parents were dead, and I didn't know what to do after the war ended. But the nice Salvation Army people agreed to sponsor me."

Did that answer all my devious questions? I wasn't sure. But it looked to me as though Hilda was through talking. She clamped her mouth shut, smiled at me and folded her hands on her desktop as if challenging me to question her further. I decided not to, although I longed to ask her if her connection with the Salvation Army had occurred all the way from Switzerland, or if she'd managed to get herself onto this continent before her sponsorship began. I reminded myself that I could probably ask Flossie or Johnny.

Unfortunately, our scalloped cheese bread didn't take long to cook, and we hadn't got as far as Gertrude before we had to retrieve our dishes from the oven. But that was all right. She wanted to talk to me and I could detain her after the class. I might still be able to discover answers to her strange behavior.

By gum, the scalloped cheese bread was pretty tasty, thereby making this my fourth success in a row. And there were only three more Saturdays of this nonsense left. The cheese bread and the knowledge that more than half my torture was behind me was almost enough to rebuild my confidence from the morning's breakfast catastrophe. As my students, holding their dishes wrapped in towels to absorb the heat, filed out of the room, I wanted to clasp Gertrude by the arm in order to prevent her escaping again, but Flossie forestalled me by coming over and thanking me for the hundredth (or perhaps thousandth) time for teaching the class. Bother! There went Gertrude, sliding out of the room. Would I *never* learn the woman's story?

"You're welcome, Flossie. I'm happy to do my part." And if that wasn't a bold-faced lie, I didn't know what was.

Flossie stayed and chatted with me until I was sure Gertrude was gone for good, at least for that day. I was impatient at first, but Flossie was so good-hearted and well-meaning that I eventually relaxed. After all, except for nosiness, what did I care how many evils possessed Gertrude Minneke and her brother? Well, except that I didn't want anyone to suffer unnecessarily, of course. Still, Gertrude's woes were none of my business unless she wanted me to know about them. Drat it.

But I was wrong! As I gathered my notes, my recipe booklet and my now-lukewarm baking dish and prepared to depart for home, lo and behold, who should show up but Gertrude Minneke! I'm sure I looked as pleased as I felt, because her steps faltered a bit as she approached me.

"Um . . . Mrs. Majesty?"

"Yes, Miss Minneke? I hope you'll confide in me. I'll try to help you if I can."

"Oh, thank you!"

"Would you like to sit down?"

"Yes. Thank you."

So we sat ourselves in two of the student desks, and Gertrude began her tale of woe.

"Mrs. Majesty, thank you so much for agreeing to talk to me today. I hope you'll be able to advise me on what to do."

"I'll do my best." I refrained from telling the poor dear that my judgment had been faulty a whole lot in recent years.

"You see, Eugene and I are from back East."

"Mrs. Buckingham told me you're originally from New Jersey."

Gertrude's expression sharpened. "You've talked about me?"

Oh, dear. There went my mouth again. "We didn't *talk* about you," I lied. "Mrs. Buckingham has given me a little background information on all of my students, to aid me as I teach the class. She's from the eastern United States, too. New York City, in fact."

"I see." She hesitated for a moment, then said, "I guess that makes sense."

"I'll be happy to help you if I can," I told her once more, wishing she'd get to the good stuff.

She sucked in a deep breath and then blurted it out. "Eugene was falsely accused of a terrible crime back in our home state. But he didn't do it, Mrs. Majesty! I know Eugene, and he couldn't have done it."

I was shocked. I'd expected to be told about financial worries or family problems, but not crime! No wonder the woman was afraid of the coppers. In actual fact, I didn't quite know what to say.

"He didn't do it," Gertrude insisted again. "He *couldn't* have done it. He was with me at the time, so I know he didn't do it."

"Um . . . exactly what didn't he do, Miss Minneke?"

She gulped and hesitated and then landed

133

the blow. "He was accused of killing a man."

Murder! Good heavens!

Here I need to take a slight detour to explain something. I've always thought of myself as a fairly rational person and even generally unbiased, if you discount my problem with Germans, and you might even say that particular prejudice was almost justified. But I haven't admitted to something else here. Every time I was introduced to a young, healthy man in those days, I wanted to ask him if he'd volunteered to fight for the freedom of Europe, as my Billy had. I suspected Eugene hadn't, although he looked old enough to have done so when I'd met him. Perhaps this suspicious attitude on my part was unjustified, but I still had it, and it had faintly tarnished my initial impression of Eugene Minneke.

Very well, my confession is out of the way. Now I'll take you back to the rest of that Saturday afternoon's conversation.

Gertrude must have taken note of my shocked expression. She clutched my arm. "Oh, but he didn't do it, Mrs. Majesty. He couldn't have done it. He was with me! And," she continued stoutly, "we're going to prove it."

"I . . . see." I peered closely at her, trying to decipher if she was sincere or merely

134

shamming sincerity. Naturally, I couldn't tell one way or the other. I read novels all the time where people see anger or grief or falsity or truth in other people's eyes or expressions, but I've never been able to do likewise. Maybe it's a device novelists use to help their plots along. Maybe other people are more discerning than I. Phooey. "Um . . . do you think it was wise of you two to flee the state? I mean, wouldn't you be more apt to find proof of his innocence in New Jersey?"

She shook her head so hard, her bun nearly collapsed. I'd had my hair cut and shingled the year before, but none of my students were up-to-date in that way. They probably couldn't afford a visit to a barber.

"No! That's the point! The police refused to believe him. They *wanted* him to be guilty! Oh, don't you see?" She snatched a handkerchief from a pocket and sniffled into it. "If the situation hadn't been so dire, we'd have stayed there and fought the accusation, but the corruption in the police department back East is foul. It's hard for people who live out here to understand how bad it can be back there."

Hmm. Sam had talked a little bit about corruption in the big back-East cities. He didn't like it at all, which was another one of the reasons he'd moved to the glorious West. Still unsure what to say, I murmured, "I'm so sorry."

She stopped sobbing after a moment or two, swallowed hard, and continued her narrative. "It's partly Eugene's fault. He'd fallen in with some low company."

Aha. Now we were getting to the nub of the issue. "That happens sometimes," I muttered, wondering if it were true, or if likes were attracted to likes. Had Eugene fallen into low company because he'd started out low himself? Or had he allowed himself to be seduced by low company because he possessed a weak character?

It beat me.

"But he didn't do anything wrong, Mrs. Majesty. I *know* he didn't."

She'd already told me that. Several times, in fact. "I see."

"You probably wondered why I ran away during our first class."

Boy, did I ever! "I was curious," I said sweetly.

"It was because I thought that policeman had come for me."

"Why would he come for you? I thought it was your brother who was in trouble."

"If they connected me with Eugene, they'd try to get at him through me." There was more than a trace of bitterness in her voice, as if she had experience related to what she'd just said.

"Ah. I see." I tried to recall my brief meeting with Eugene. He didn't especially look like a crook, but I suppose the same can be said for a lot of crooks. Heck, if criminals all *looked* evil, they'd be easier for the coppers to spot and catch, wouldn't they?

"I . . . I just wanted you to know why I'm nervous, I guess," Gertrude said lamely. "I don't suppose there's anything you can do to help us."

I didn't suppose so, either, although I decided that saying so would come across as unnecessarily cruel. "Well, if you think of anything, please let me know. I'd be happy to help." Thinking I'd better, I added, "If I can." I don't think that was a lie; I mean, if Eugene truly *was* innocent of wrongdoing, I'd be happy to help prove it. It still seemed to me that he was in the wrong part of the country for such an attempt to be made, but what did I know about crime and punishment? Not a blessed thing is what, although Sam had talked to my family a little bit about some of his more intriguing cases.

"Please don't tell anyone we had this chat today, Mrs. Majesty. I'm afraid that if anyone knew, they'd get in touch with the authorities in New Jersey, and that would mean Eugene's capture. We can't allow them to know where we are until we can secure evidence of his innocence."

There she went again. "How are you attempting to find this evidence?" I asked in genuine curiosity.

"I'm in constant touch by mail with friends in New Jersey who are trying to help us."

Hmm. Odd way to go about it, if you ask me. But you didn't, and neither did Gertrude.

"And you think you can do this at such a distance?"

She nodded vigorously. "Oh, yes! Our friends are doing everything they can to find proof of Eugene's innocence."

"How kind of them." I probably sounded rather dry, because what they were doing sounded nuts to me. Then again, I'd never been falsely accused of a crime. Well, except by Sam Rotondo once or twice — but the crimes he accused me of were a whole lot less vile than murder. Perhaps the Minnekes were taking the proper course of action.

"They're being very kind and . . . and helpful," said Gertrude firmly.

"Very well," I said. "I won't tell anyone."

Why should I? There wasn't a single reason to do so that I could think of at the moment.

"Thank you, Mrs. Majesty."

"You're welcome."

And with sniffles and a drooping demeanor, Gertrude left the hall. I sighed, recollected my personal effects, and did likewise, only without the sniffles and droop.

Lucky me, Sam Rotondo was playing gin rummy with Billy and my father when I got home.

"Hey, Daisy," said Billy, sounding more cheerful than usual. "Sam's staying for dinner."

What a surprise. I walked over and kissed my husband's cheek, smiled at my father, and even gave Sam a halfhearted facsimile of a smile. "Hello, all."

"What's that you've got, Daisy?" Pa asked.

"What? Oh, this." I uncovered my baking dish. "This is scalloped cheese bread. It actually tastes pretty good." I'm sure they could all hear the astonishment in my voice.

Billy grinned. "Maybe you should make that for breakfast, then."

I gave him a playful swat on his shoulder. "Maybe I should."

Pa laughed softly.

Sam said, "Gin!"

He would.

I didn't really mind Sam's presence too much, especially when I smelled the delicious roast-pork aromas issuing from the kitchen. After I greeted the men and gave Spike the pats he craved — holding my scalloped cheese bread far out of his way as I did so. Spike didn't care if I was a lousy cook. He'd eat anything — I carried my pitiful contribution to the meal to my aunt, who was paring potatoes to roast. Oh, boy. This was one of my very favorite meals in the world.

Mother, Aunt Vi and I chatted as I set the table for dinner. Ma worked half days on Saturdays as the chief accountant for the Hotel Marengo. It was a good job for a woman in those days. Actually, it was a good job for anyone, but my mother had it!

Dinner was superb, as usual, and it got me to musing about things. I didn't understand why only one person in my family had been blessed with the ability to cook well. Wouldn't you suppose such a talent to permeate the whole family? Heck, you expect the children of musicians to possess a sense of rhythm and so forth, don't you? And don't artists spawn artists? So how come I couldn't cook? Perhaps I'm mistaken about the qualities of families. Heck, I must be. Ma couldn't cook any better than I could.

It occurred to me then that the wretched cooking class I was teaching might cure me of my incompetence. That happy outcome didn't seem likely, but stranger things had happened, I reckoned.

At the table, I considered telling Sam about Gertrude's confession, but I didn't, figuring it wouldn't do any good. Also, if Gertrude was correct and Eugene hadn't done anything wrong, I'd be doing both Minnekes a disservice by blabbing. Besides, I'd promised. I didn't feel comfortable keeping the secret, though. I didn't know Eugene *or* Gertrude Minneke. Maybe they were both guilty as sin. Maybe I should ask Johnny Buckingham about the two of them. Johnny would probably think I was crazy for my interest. Phooey.

"Did that student show up today?" asked Sam.

His question firmed my resolve not to relate Gertrude's tale to him. Darn him, if he wanted my help, he could at least tell me what dire deeds he suspected Gertrude of committing! "Yes, she did."

"Did you ask her why she runs away every time I show up?"

I said a short, "No." Then, in an effort to

divert the discussion from Gertrude, I said, "Have you been in touch with Lucille Spinks, Sam?"

He gave me a puzzled look from across the table. "Who?"

Good Lord. I said, "Lucille Spinks. I thought you and she were forming a fast friendship."

I guess my words held an edge, because my mother looked at me sharply. I smiled at her to show her that my intentions were honorable, even if they weren't.

"I can't place her," Sam admitted after mulling over my question for several seconds.

"Gee whiz, Sam! She's the one I sang the duet with at church."

"Ah, is that her name?"

"Sam Rotondo, the woman practically fawned all over you at church last week!"

By gum, Sam blushed! I never thought I'd see the day. "I believe you're mistaken about that," he said stiffly.

"Honestly! I can't believe you didn't notice."

Billy chuckled.

"Well, I didn't," said the stolid Sam — stolidly, of course.

I rolled my eyes but decided to give up on that topic, which was just as well. I didn't like to think about Lucy taking Sam away from Billy — which sounds stupid, but I'm sure understandable.

Anyhow, after I'd helped Ma wash and dry the dishes, it was time for me to prepare for Mrs. Bissell's séance. Autumn had arrived and the night air was nippy, so I selected a sober black evening dress I'd made with some fine woolen material I'd got on sale at Maxime's. I liked the costume a lot. It had a straight, tubular, hip-length top — that is to say, it was supposed to be straight. I had some unfortunate curves I couldn't get rid of even when I bound my breasts, but I did my best. What with my black handbag and stockings and shoes, and my subdued black woolen coat, I probably looked like a funeral director, although my purpose was opposite to that of an undertaker, whose job it was to plant dead people. Mine was to revive them long enough to communicate with the séance's participants. It actually felt good to know I was about to tackle a job for which I was fitted and leave the perils of cooking behind for a while.

When I looked in the mirror to judge the effect of all that black, I was satisfied. For my job, I cultivated a pale, ghostly appearance. As nature and heredity made me, I wasn't pale and ghostly, but rather vigorous and healthy. Powder helped to disguise that unfortunate fact, even if it couldn't cover all my freckles. Freckles and spiritualism just don't go together. Nevertheless, freckles were a part of me, and I did my best to lessen their impact. Not that I wanted to appear ghoulish, but sobriety, somberness and an air of otherworldliness were mandatory. My efforts to achieve same pleased me that night.

"You look beautiful, Daisy," Pa said when I walked into the living room. I wish Billy would say stuff like that.

"Yeah, Daisy, you look great," Billy concurred. I doubt he'd have said it if Pa hadn't commented on my appearance first, but it was nice to hear him compliment me anyway.

Naturally, Sam remained mum.

"Thank you both."

"Do you know what time you'll be home?" asked Billy.

"I'm not sure." It was then eight o'clock. "I expect I'll be back by midnight. Generally Mrs. Bissell serves refreshments after these shindigs, and I like to stay for a while, because sometimes séance attendees will hire me for their own séances and so forth. I'm looking forward to meeting Miss Castleton in person. I'm hoping she'll hire me for something."

Billy shook his head. "I don't understand how people can believe in that stuff."

"I don't either," said I with an effort toward lightness. I *really* didn't want to fight with my husband any more about my work. I thought he was unfair about it, and he thought I was wicked to trick people, and there didn't seem to be any middle ground for us to navigate.

Pa shrugged. "It's a living."

Bless him. His practical attitude was exactly my own. See what I mean about family characteristics? I'd inherited my father's penchant for practicality. So why hadn't I inherited my aunt's skill in the kitchen? It's one of those mysteries of life, I reckon.

"Take care, Daisy," said Ma. She came over and gave me a hug. "You do look lovely, dear."

"Thanks, Ma." I was touched. When my siblings, Daphne and Walter, and I were growing up, Ma had impressed upon us the insignificance of outward appearance. I suspect she'd done so in order to imprint upon us the importance of honesty, chastity, piety and so forth over our outer shells, and she'd done a good job of it. I don't think any of us are vain. Still, it was pleasant to

hear nice things about my looks every now
and then.

After I gave Billy another kiss on the cheek
and petted Spike, who always wanted to go
with any of us when we went anywhere, and
fending Spike off at the door — he'd have
run out and jumped into the Chevrolet if
I'd let him — I drove to Mrs. Bissell's huge
mansion on Foothill Boulevard and Maiden
Lane. I parked the Chevrolet in the circular
driveway in back of the house and strode to
the back door, which led out onto a sun-
porch. Once I got inside, I'd have to stop
striding and do a lot of wafting, but I wasn't
on duty yet. I heard excited yapping issuing
from the kennels. In older times, the kennels had been the stables, but all the rich
folks in town drove automobiles now.

My surprise was absolutely genuine when
none other than Hilda Schwartz answered
the door after I twisted the ringer. Good
Lord, my students were popping up all over
the place.

Her eyes opened wide. "Mrs. Majesty!
How nice to see you." She stepped back and
held the door for me to enter. "Oh, my, you
look so pretty tonight."

"Thank you. I'm here to conduct a séance
for Mrs. Bissell and some of her friends."

"Ach," said she. "I heard about that, but I

didn't know you was the one." Her w's sounded like v's. "I never . . . uh . . . my English not so good. I don't understand spirits and things like that."

"I think your English is very good," I told her politely. And it was. I decided not to comment on the spirits question, since I not only didn't understand them; I didn't even believe in them.

Hilda's face colored a little. She had lovely coloring: all blonde and blue-eyed and clear-skinned. No freckles marred her complexion, and she looked charming in her black maid's dress and white apron. "Thank you," she said.

"You're welcome. I didn't know you worked for Mrs. Bissell."

"Ach, yes. The Salvation Army got this job for me. Mrs. Bissell is a . . . what do you say? A kind woman."

"She is indeed. And I love her dogs. She gave me a puppy last year."

"Lovely dogs. In my homeland, many people have dachshunds."

They did, did they? I'd always thought dachshunds were a German invention. I didn't hold Spike's origins against him, since he'd been born in Altadena, California, and was therefore as American as I was. But I'd always thought Swiss folks had Saint

Bernards and big dogs like that. I should think a dachshund would sink into the snow and smother during the rougher parts of the year. "Ah. I didn't know that."

Hilda nodded enthusiastically. "Yes. Many, many dachshunds."

"Interesting."

As Hilda led me to the huge living room where a group of people had gathered and were chatting and laughing together, I contemplated Sam's words about German Jews and how the USA sometimes allowed Jewish immigrants to enter the country. I was certainly no expert, but Hilda didn't look Jewish to me. And would the Salvation Army have extended its well-known generosity in order to assist a Jewish lady to come to America? Actually, it probably would have. Great organization, the Salvation Army.

But I didn't have time to worry about Hilda. It was time to begin wafting and acting mysterious. Mrs. Bissell bustled over to me when she saw me, hauling another woman — not Miss Emmaline Castleton, because this woman was too old to be she — with her. Mrs. Bissell was a very pleasant woman, a little on the heavy side, but hale and hearty and quite generous. She'd paid me a fortune for a job I'd done for her last year, and that was on top of giving us Spike. I'd have taken Spike alone in payment because I'd wanted to provide Billy with a companion, but she'd insisted I take money, too. Some people are so darned nice.

"Mrs. Majesty!" cried she. "I'm so glad you could do this for us. My friend Margaret Spencer is simply *dying* to get in touch with her aunt."

Interesting phraseology, I thought. "I'd be happy to do that, but I thought you wanted me to get in touch with the late Mrs. Baskerville."

"Oh, I do! But can't you do both?"

Putting on my most arcane smile, I murmured, "I'm sure Rolly will be delighted to assist both of you."

"Oh, thank you!" Mrs. Bissell went on, "Mrs. Majesty, please meet a very good friend of mine, Margaret — Mrs. Wilbur — Spencer."

Oh, boy. I'd heard about Wilbur Spencer. He was an important lawyer in town and was reputed to be wildly wealthy.

I held out a white, well-manicured hand to Mrs. Spencer. "How do you do, Mrs. Spencer? I'm very sorry about your aunt's passing." I maintained my spiritualist voice, which was another skill of my trade, being soft and low and crooning.

149

"Thank you, Mrs. Majesty. Mrs. Bissell has told me what a great service you performed for her last year. My aunt's passing wasn't unexpected, but it was a blow. She reared me, you see."

"Ah. That makes your loss even more difficult to endure."

We chatted some more before we went into the séance room — in this case the breakfast room — and sat in the chairs arranged there. Mrs. Bissell also had a dining room, but the table in that room was too large to accommodate a séance comfortably. I always asked my séance clients to limit the number of participants to no more than eight. Mrs. Bissell's dining room could seat twenty people! Have I mentioned she was rich? Well, she was. Heck, my family wouldn't know what to do with two rooms designed solely for meals.

I still hadn't met Miss Castleton, although I spotted her among the séance attendees. She looked almost as funereal as I did. She had gorgeous blonde hair that was cut in a most becoming bob, and that night she wore a black dress, shoes, etc., just as I did. Her face was naturally ethereal, I guess, and it didn't look to me as though she had to powder away any pesky freckles. I envied her looks, actually, because she appeared naturally ghostly. At least I assumed she did. She looked pretty ghostly, anyhow. But I couldn't dwell on Miss Castleton yet. I had a séance to conduct.

Mrs. Bissell had prepared, or more likely had one of her servants prepare, the breakfast room with a single cranberry-colored lamp in the center of the table. The lamp held a candle, and it was the only source of illumination I allowed during séances. Hilda Schwartz was the one who turned off the electrical lights when Mrs. Bissell asked her to do so.

The séance went smoothly. I went into my "trance" after about five minutes of mumbo-jumbo. Then the fun began. My spirit control, Rolly, told Mrs. Spencer that her aunt was happy on the Other Side, and that she wanted Mrs. Spencer to carry on with courage and never to forget the great love she — the aunt — bore her — the niece. By that time, this stuff came to me as easily as falling off a log.

After we'd run the aunt thing into the ground, I had Rolly get in touch with Mrs. Baskerville. This "contact" was more fun, because it had to do with dachshunds. My library research came in handy here. Mrs. Baskerville told Mrs. Bissell that she should continue as she'd begun and that, sooner or

151

later, if she kept her breeding stock pure and did her best in the show ring, she'd have a dog in Westminster. Perhaps even more than one. I could tell Mrs. Bissell was pleased with old Rolly, even though my — I mean his — advice was no more than common sense.

When Mrs. Baskerville had been dealt with, a few other people asked questions of departed loved ones, and Rolly obliged them all. I believe I've already mentioned that I'd made Rolly up when I was ten years old. There were occasions when I wished I'd named him something more dignified, but it was too late to change his name now. Anyhow, most of my clients spelled his name Raleigh, and that was dignified, wasn't it? Rolly had a lovely Scottish accent. I'd learned how to fake a Scottish accent very early in my life, because I'd gone to school with a girl who came from Scotland. Glasgow, to be precise.

I'd been hoping that Miss Castleton would ask Rolly a question, but she didn't. It occurred to me that I was, in a way, auditioning for a job. Well, we'd see what came of all this nonsense, I reckoned.

And then I came out of my trance and it was time to see the puppies. Mrs. Bissell led all of us out to her kennels, where the man whose job it was to tend to the dogs turned on the lights and showed us the latest litter. Dachshund puppies are probably the most adorable creatures on earth (I think I've already mentioned that), and Mrs. Bissell bred some beauties. Most of these guys were black and tan, like Spike, but there were a few reddish-brown ones, too. I wanted to take them all home with me, but Spike would probably have objected. Well, and the rest of my family, too, of course. Not to mention Mrs. Bissell.

After the puppies came refreshments in the big living room. Mrs. Bissell served little sandwiches with their crusts cut off, pastries, tea and stuff like that. After the huge meal I'd consumed at home, I didn't really crave food, so it was easy to maintain my above-it-all spiritualist pose in the face of food. Several of the séance participants wanted to talk to me, however, so I stayed and chatted for a while. It had been a busy day, though, and I was tired, so I left shortly after eleven. Not, however, before I'd booked two more séances. I always told Billy I was good at my job, and I really was, even if he didn't want to admit it. Unfortunately, Miss Castleton wasn't among the folks who chatted with me and/or hired me. I began to wonder if she'd changed her mind about meeting me. Oh, well.

Hilda was the one who opened the door for me to leave, and I decided to see if I could learn more about her. I still believed she was German, and I hoped I could confirm my suspicion with some cleverly worded questions, provided I could think of any, cleverness not being one of my major skills.

"It's so nice to see you here, Miss Schwartz. Isn't Mrs. Bissell a lovely lady? I'm glad you got a job with her."

"Ach, yes. Mrs. Bissell is so kind."

"Say, Hilda, I've always been interested in Switzerland. Tell me about it, will you?"

Did she appear to be slightly dismayed? We were standing on the patio outside the back door, and it was dark out there, so I wasn't sure.

"Ach," she said, "I don't know much to tell. Switzerland is a pretty country."

"Lots of mountains," I suggested.

She seemed to brighten. "Lots of mountains. Green valleys. Nice people."

"And cuckoo clocks," I said, feeding her another clue.

"Ach, yes! Cuckoo clocks. Yes."

"And dachshunds," I added cleverly.

"Dachshunds." She nodded. "Lots of dachshunds."

I didn't believe her. I could believe a Saint Bernard or a — Darn. What was that dog Billy had told me about? Oh, yes — Swiss mountain dogs. But dachshunds? I didn't think so. Speaking of mountains . . . "Can you yodel?"

"Yodel?" She swallowed. "Ach, no. No yodel."

I got the impression she didn't know what *yodel* meant. Hmm. Very interesting.

"Where in Switzerland were you born, Miss Schwartz?"

This time I could tell she was unhappy with my question. "Uh . . . I was born in the country," she said.

I didn't believe her. "I see. Was there a city of any size near you?"

"A city? Ach . . . ach, yes!" She sounded relieved that she'd managed to think of a Swiss city. "Geneva. We was near Geneva."

Where Frankenstein came from, by gum! "How interesting. As I said before, I'd love to visit Switzerland one day."

"Yes. Pretty country," Hilda confirmed, and she scuttled back inside the house before I could ask her about Swiss chocolate. Or was it the Belgians who made the best chocolate? I couldn't remember.

But Hilda didn't seem to know a whole heck of a lot about what she claimed was her native land, either. I reminded myself that I didn't know much about America's own Southern states. Or New Hampshire or Maine, for that matter. Or even Illinois or Nebraska.

On the other hand, Switzerland was a whole lot smaller than the United States. One would expect a native to know about yodeling and cuckoo clocks and the kinds of dogs endemic to the country of one's birth.

She peeked out the door once more, before I'd taken more than a couple of steps toward the Chevrolet. Oh, boy! Maybe she was going to tell me something more.

"Mrs. Majesty?"

"Yes?"

"Thank you for the class, Mrs. Majesty. You helping us a lot."

Since I was tired and wanted to go home and get to bed, I decided not to resurrect the subject of Switzerland. "Thank you for coming to it, Mrs. Schwartz."

"Miss Schwartz," she corrected. "I not have a husband."

"I see. Well, husbands aren't necessarily all they're cracked up to be." I knew, as soon as the words left my lips, that I shouldn't have said that. My darned mouth!

But Hilda didn't seem to understand what

I was talking about. A bit dreamily she said, "I like to marry someday."

"I'm sure you will," I said, trying to redeem myself in my own eyes, if not hers.

"Yah. I hope so."

And that was that. I went to the Chevrolet — and I didn't have to crank the thing because it had a lovely newfangled self-starter — but before I could depart, another figure wafted toward me from the patio.

By gum, it was Miss Emmaline Castleton! Oh, good! Maybe I'd get another job.

She appeared to hesitate when I spotted her. Thinking she probably wouldn't be able to see me in the dark, I nevertheless pasted a friendly smile on my face, and said, "Miss Castleton?"

As if having come to a decision, she walked firmly toward me. "Mrs. Majesty? May I speak to you for a minute?"

"By all means," I said. "Would you like to go back inside?"

"No." She shook her blonde head. She had the prettiest hair. "I don't want anyone else to know I'm talking to you."

Mysterious. "Very well." I bowed my head in a gracious gesture of capitulation.

She came up to me, stopped, and seemed again to be uncertain what to do next. Since I didn't know what her problem was, I couldn't offer her any clues.

Eventually, she said, "Mrs. Bissell and Mrs. Kincaid have both told me a little bit about your background, Mrs. Majesty."

Good Lord. Did she mean that Mrs. Bissell and Mrs. Kincaid told her I used to sell raspberries door-to-door when I was a kid? Did they tell her that Mrs. Kincaid gave my aunt my first Ouija board, and that's why I started messing around with spiritualism?

"I mean," she explained, "about your husband's problems." She bowed her head.

It took me a minute because I had to swallow the lump that instantly formed in my throat when she said those words. She spoke so very softly and sympathetically, I darned near started crying. Then I remembered she had problems of her own. "Yes," I said in my softest, most soothing voice. "I understand you also suffered grievously from that war."

She nodded. "I did. I . . . Stephen Allison and I had planned to marry, but he . . . he died."

"Yes. I remember reading about his passing. That war caused more grief than anyone should have to endure."

"I agree." She stopped talking again.

Darn it, I wished she'd get on with it! To speed her up, I asked, "Are you interested in getting in touch with Mr. Allison?"

Her head snapped up. "Stephen? Good Lord, no!"

Oh. Well, that took the wind out of my sails. I didn't know what to say.

Fortunately, Miss Castleton continued. "What I'm interested in is getting some information about the Salvation Army's program for sponsoring immigrants."

Boy, I wouldn't have figured that to be her problem in a billion years! "The Salvation Army's program?" said I, stuttering slightly. "But. . . ."

She shook her head. "I know, it sounds absurd, but I have a reason for asking. I need to know if . . . if a person I know can get help there."

This woman had access to most of the money in the world, and she wanted the Salvation Army to help her? I still didn't understand. Instead of saying that, I said, "How did you know about my dealings with the Salvation Army?"

"Harold Kincaid told me you were teaching a cooking class there. He also told me a little bit about the program you're helping with."

Hmm. It made sense that Harold and Emmaline Castleton knew each other, both being in the very wealthy segment of Pasadena society. However, I still didn't know why she was interested in the Salvation Army. "Um . . . are you interested in volunteering at the Salvation Army?"

"Yes." Then she shook her head again. "No." She lifted her hands and let them fall in a classical gesture of frustration. "Oh, it's all so complicated!"

Because I was tired, and because I felt her pain, and because I was nosy, I said, "Perhaps we should get together somewhere else at another time. Somewhere we can talk in private, I mean, and not have to worry about being interrupted."

She leaped at that suggestion. "Yes! Oh, yes, Mrs. Majesty. Thank you so much. Won't you come to my house for luncheon? Um . . . the day after tomorrow? Or Tuesday? Tuesday would be better, although I'm terribly anxious about this whole thing."

"Tuesday would be fine with me," I said in a low, caressing tone. "When you say your house, do you mean . . . ?"

"I mean my father's palace." She sounded sarcastic. Then she brushed her hand over her eyes, and said, "I didn't mean that the way it sounded. Father is a wonderful man. He just doesn't . . . understand some things. I desperately need advice, Mrs. Majesty. Please come on Tuesday."

"I'll be happy to, Miss Castleton." And that was no fib. I'd been fascinated by that gigantic estate on South Allen Avenue and Oxford Road for years. I'd love to be able to see it in person.

"Thank you, Mrs. Majesty. I'll tell Stickley to admit you at the gate."

From that, I assumed Stickley was the gatekeeper, as Jackson was Mrs. Kincaid's gatekeeper. "I'll see you then."

We shook hands on it, and I drove home, mulling over my conversations with Miss Castleton and Hilda. I didn't know enough about Miss Castleton to mull much of anything at that point, so I figured our conversation was over.

After our little chat, I was pretty sure Hilda came from Germany and not Switzerland. Should I do anything about that? It was altogether possible that she was in the country legally, after all. I suppose I could ask Johnny Buckingham to dig a little deeper into her background. Or I could talk to Sam about her. If anyone discovered she was here illegally, the authorities would deport her.

I expected my heart to leap at that thought, but it didn't, surprising me. It then dawned upon me that I liked Hilda. Even though she was probably a German. I liked

her a good deal more than I liked Gertrude
Minneke, in fact, and I was willing to keep
Gertrude's secret.

Oh, bother. I hated having secrets. Shoot,
I generally didn't have any secrets at all,
and now I had *two* of the darned things to
bedevil me!

CHAPTER EIGHT

The next day was horrible. We all went to church in the morning, and that part was all right. So was lunch, which was pork ribs and liberty cabbage. Oh, very well, it was sauerkraut, but that was German, and I still called it liberty cabbage, even though the war had been over for several years. Anyhow, pork ribs, which Aunt Vi cooked in the oven with liberty cabbage, apples, and potatoes was one of my favorite meals.

But after lunch, when I was planning which spiritualistic outfit to wear the following day when I visited clients, I discovered by accident that Billy had managed to secrete several bottles of morphine syrup in the back of our closet. If I hadn't been searching for a shoe I needed, I never would have found his stash.

Ma and Pa had settled in the living room and were reading the Sunday edition of the *Pasadena Star News,* and Aunt Vi had gone upstairs to her quarters to take a well-deserved afternoon nap. Billy and Spike had gone out in the backyard, where we'd planted two orange trees: a Valencia and a navel. Having both trees was great, because it meant we had lovely fresh oranges all year long, or just about. Besides, the blossoms smelled heavenly when they were blooming. Sometimes I'd go out back just to breathe in their scent.

That afternoon, I stared into the box containing the morphine syrup, confounded. I was well aware of Billy's morphine use, but I generally picked up his supply from Dr. Benjamin. At least I thought I did. Where had he come by all this stuff? More importantly, why had he come by it? He didn't need to stash morphine syrup away, for Pete's sake. I didn't mind visiting the doctor for him. An awful thought came to me then, and my knees almost gave out. I managed to get myself to the bed, and I stayed there for several more minutes, brooding and feeling a great, sick weight on my heart.

Then, because I couldn't think of anything else to do, I went out back to talk to Billy. He sat in his chair under the navel-orange tree, flipping through the latest edition of *National Geographic,* one of his favorite magazines. I think he liked it because before we were married, we talked about traveling the world someday. He didn't look up when I shut the back door. Pa had built a ramp both in the front and back so Billy could maneuver his wheelchair, which was one of those modern ones with the big wheels that enabled the person in it to move about by himself. Or herself, if that was the case. Spike had rolled himself up in a little doggy ball and resided lazily on the grass beside the wheelchair. He was so relaxed, he only wagged his tail when I showed up. I've never, ever regretted getting Spike for Billy. They were constant companions, and Billy never treated Spike rudely, as he did me.

"Billy?"

He lifted his head, but he didn't smile. "Hey, Daisy."

I walked over and crouched down next to his chair. "Billy, I found all that morphine syrup you had stored in the closet."

His lips pinched, and his eyebrows lowered. Then he said, "Dammit, Daisy, what were you doing snooping around in my things? Can't I have *any* privacy? Isn't it bad enough that I'm a damned cripple? Do I have to give up all my freedom, too?"

I told myself to hold on to my temper. "I wasn't snooping. I was looking for a shoe. I found the box by accident. What I want to know is why, Billy. Why do you have so much morphine syrup?"

"That's my business."

"Where did you get all that stuff, Billy?"

He gave a harsh laugh. "I'm not going to tell you that."

"But —"

"And I'll tell you right now that if you get rid of those bottles, I know where to get more."

I was flummoxed. "But I can get plenty of morphine from Dr. Benjamin."

He stuck his nose in his magazine again. "Not plenty enough." His voice had turned into a surly growl.

My voice cracked a little. "What do you mean, Billy? I know you're in a lot of pain, but —"

He slammed his magazine down onto his lap. "Dammit, Daisy, don't you understand? I hate this life of mine! I hate the body I can't use any longer. I hate that I can't do anything. I hate that I can't walk, can't work, can't breathe half the time, and I . . . I just hate it. I hate that I can't be a proper husband to you. Can't you understand that?"

I felt my chin tremble and tried not to break down. "I do understand that, Billy, but I don't want anything to happen to you. You can take too much of that stuff, you know, and it'd kill me if that happened. I know you're in pain, and I —"

He interrupted me again. "I love you, too, Daisy, but you need a whole man. You don't need a wreck like me. For God's sake, do you think I *like* being this way?"

My voice broke, and I had to speak through tears. "I don't *want* anybody else! I know you hate being the way you are now, Billy, but I'd die if anything happened to you."

"For God's sake, Daisy, something *has* already happened to me."

"I know it, and it's horrible. But I've loved you my whole life, Billy. I don't care if you're confined to a wheelchair."

He slammed his hand over his chest. "*I* care, dammit! And I hate it. This life is more painful than I can stand, and one of these days, when it gets too bad, I want to know that I have an option. One of these days, when I can't stand it any longer, I'm going to use that syrup, and nobody's going to stop me."

I stared at him, horrified, for several seconds. "You'd . . . you'd really kill yourself? On purpose?"

He hesitated for a second, his lips a thin,

flat white line. Then he said simply, "Yes."

"Oh, Billy!" And I buried my head in his lap and cried, right on top of the *National Geographic.*

To give him credit, he didn't want to hurt me. He stroked my head and murmured, "I've loved you for almost as long as you've loved me, Daisy. But my life is hardly a life at all anymore. I'm not a husband to you. I'm a burden to your whole family. Do you think I enjoy knowing that?"

"You're not a burden, Billy. And I know you think you are and don't enjoy it," I burbled. "But I try to make your life better, Billy. Truly I do."

He sighed shallowly, the only way he could sigh. "I know you do, sweetheart. And I know I'm rough on you a lot of the time. I don't like the way you support me. I don't like that you *have* to support me. God, I hate being helpless."

Sniffling pathetically, I said, "Spike would be awfully lonely if you left us, Billy. And I'd be devastated."

He said, "Ha," bitterly.

"Oh, Billy."

We sat there for several more minutes, until my tears dried. Then I sat on the grass beside the chair and drew Spike into my lap, feeling hopeless and helpless and wishing I could wave a magic wand or something and cure my husband's many ills. Damned Germans and their damned mustard gas.

Then I thought about Hilda Schwartz and gave a huge sigh. Darn it. I couldn't even hate the entire German race any longer. Was nothing sacred? Recalling that box full of morphine syrup, I bleakly acknowledged that, no. Nothing was sacred. Not even life, for my darling Billy.

The next day, when breakfast was over and Billy and Spike were cozy in the living room with Pa, I canceled the appointment I'd had with Mrs. Kincaid. I didn't want Billy to overhear.

"Are you sure you can't come, dear?" She sounded shaky, but that was nothing unusual.

"I'm very sorry, Mrs. Kincaid. I need to visit the doctor. It's . . . it's important." I didn't want to confess that my visit was about my husband. Mrs. Kincaid knew about Billy's problems, but not the extent of them, or of the despair those problems caused him. Not to mention me. "Perhaps we can reschedule our appointment."

She hesitated a second or two, then said slowly, "Yes. I suppose we can do that. Are you unwell, Mrs. Majesty? I certainly hope you aren't."

"Oh, no. It's not about me." Drat. I hadn't even wanted her to know that much. She wouldn't have minded, of course, but Billy didn't like his problems broadcast to the world, and I felt honor-bound to keep his confidence. Besides, I aimed to keep this particular doctor visit a secret even from Billy.

"Is it about your poor husband?" Mrs. Kincaid's voice fairly throbbed with sympathy.

I sighed, then said, "Yes. It is."

"That poor, poor man."

He was that, all right. I didn't say anything.

"Very well, dear. Do take care, and ring me when you're able to come over."

"I will, Mrs. Kincaid. Thank you. Perhaps. . . ." I was going to mention the morrow, but recalled my appointment with Miss Castleton just in time. "Perhaps I can come on Wednesday. Would that be all right with you?"

"Wednesday would be fine, dear. Is ten o'clock all right with you?"

"Yes. Ten o'clock on Wednesday. See you then." I hesitated for a second, then blurted out, "Thank you for your understanding, Mrs. Kincaid."

"Of course, dear."

So I went to see Dr. Benjamin. I'd talked to him many, many times about my poor beleaguered husband, but Billy had never threatened to commit suicide before. I'd always just sort of assumed he'd keep on trying to survive until pneumonia or bronchitis or some other vicious disease attacked his ruined lungs and took him away from me.

The worst part for me was that I could see his point. I wouldn't want to live the way my Billy lived, either.

Dr. Benjamin kept morning office hours, and he visited patients in the afternoon. He regularly called on Billy, but this wasn't his day for doing so. His wife acted as his nurse and receptionist. I was fortunate to be the first one in the office that morning, so I didn't have to wait. Mrs. Benjamin ushered me right into the doctor's office.

"Good morning, Daisy," he said, smiling. He was a genial man and one who took a genuine interest in his patients and their families.

"Good morning, Dr. Benjamin." That was as far as I got before I began leaking tears again. Darn my sentimental nature! I'd hoped to get through this appointment without bawling, although God knew I'd cried in front of Doc Benjamin plenty of times before this.

"Oh, my dear child." He came around his desk and patted my shoulder. "Is something the matter with Billy, Daisy?"

I nodded miserably.

He sighed. "Would you like a glass of water, my dear?"

Shaking my head, I said, "No. That's all right. I'm sorry to be so pitiful."

"You're not pitiful, Daisy. You're a very brave young woman who's suffered grievously. You and your Billy are strong people who have endured unnecessary pain and hardship on account of other people's mistakes."

I swallowed hard and got right to the point after wiping my eyes with my hankie. "Billy's managed to get hold of an extra supply of morphine syrup from somewhere, and he says he's going to use it when he can't stand his life any longer." I looked at the doctor, and I'm sure that all the pain I felt was there on my face. "Dr. Benjamin, he says he's going to *kill* himself."

Dr. Benjamin didn't say anything until he'd rounded his desk and sat in his chair once more. Then he steepled his fingers beneath his chin and regarded me soberly. "And would you blame him for it, Daisy? He's in terrible shape, he's in constant pain,

172

and he can scarcely breathe."

There went my chin again, trembling like one of our occasional earthquakes. "But. . . ."

The doctor sighed heavily. "I know you love him, Daisy. And I know he loves you. But consider his condition before you condemn him for contemplating relief from a life he evidently considers unbearable."

"Even with me trying to help?" My voice squeaked, and I guess I sounded as pathetic as I felt.

Dr. Benjamin's eyes half closed, and he didn't speak for a moment. Then he said, "Do you remember what Billy was like before he went to war, Daisy?"

"Yes. Of course, I do."

"He was young and strong and fit, and he was young enough to believe that he could get through the war and come home to you a hero."

"He is a hero to me," I muttered. It sounded stupid, but I meant it.

"I know he is, Daisy. But his dreams and his spirit were shattered in France. It wasn't just his body that suffered. His entire life was turned upside down. If he'd only been wounded, he probably would have recovered his spirit sooner or later, but that gas . . . well, you know what it did to him. And he was one of the lucky ones. I've seen the lungs of young men who were gassed to death." He shook his head and shuddered. "You wouldn't believe what those lungs look like, Daisy."

I didn't ask him where he'd seen those lungs. For all I knew, he performed autopsies every day. I think I nodded, but I'm not sure. I was too busy trying not to cry some more.

"I'm afraid you're not the first young couple to find out that love isn't everything in this mean old world we live in, my dear. Billy may not use that stock of morphine syrup. I've heard other people with painful physical problems claim that just *knowing* they have a way out of this life if it gets too hard for them is what keeps them from going beyond a certain point."

Brightening minimally, I said, "Really?"

"Yes. Really." He shook his head and appeared genuinely unhappy for a moment. "Believe me, Daisy, Billy's not the only young man whose health was ruined by that blasted mustard gas. Nor is he in the worst shape of the patients I see."

Boy, that was hard to imagine.

He went on, "I also have to treat several young men who are sound physically, but who suffer from terrible shell shock. Even worse than Billy's, if you can believe me — and you can. Some of them aren't far from being frightened, babbling babes. The worst of their symptoms is that they can't forgive themselves for having been so badly affected by the horrors they saw that they can't get over them, can't work, and can barely live with themselves. One young man I see has to live in an honest-to-God bunker in his parents' backyard. Fortunately, his parents have the wherewithal to accommodate him, because he assuredly can't maintain any sort of job of work."

"Oh, dear," I whispered. Poor Billy was still apt to cry out at night after dreaming he was being shelled by the German army. Was it General Sherman who said war was hell? Well, he was right. It's hell on everyone, even those left behind.

"I don't know how to advise you," Dr. Benjamin continued. "If he got hold of one supply of morphine, I presume he can always get more if you dispose of this batch."

"He told me as much," I admitted. "And he wouldn't tell me where he got the one in the closet."

"Well, then, my dear, it's up to you. Unfortunately, I have no sage, fatherly advice to dispense on this issue. I suspect your Billy won't kill himself, but if he does, just remember that it's not your fault. The fault lies, as it always does when it comes to war, with the people who started it in the first place. The fault lies with the old men who refuse to talk out their troubles, and who send young men to fight in their stead after filling their heads with patriotic songs and heroic music. 'Over There,' indeed. Men like your Billy are only cannon fodder, more's the pity. Why, it positively makes me angry."

I could see it did. Boy, what a depressing conversation. I nodded, seeing his point and wishing I could write to President Wilson, Clemenceau of France, Nicholas II of Russia, the King of Serbia, the guy who assassinated Archduke Ferdinand, Prime Minister Asquith and the Kaiser and everyone else who'd started the cursed bloody conflict. Better yet, I'd like to turn them loose in a field, arm them, and let them have at each other and leave my darling Billy and all the other young men at home, safe and sound.

As with so much else in my life, it was too late for that now — and I was only twenty-one! I rose from my chair. "Thank you, Dr. Benjamin. I appreciate your willingness to talk to me about this."

He rose too, and extended his hand.

"Anytime, Daisy. I can't tell you how sorry I am that you and Billy have to endure these problems. I've known you both all your lives, and you're like my own children in many ways."

I knew that to be true. Doc Benjamin had delivered us both, in fact, and he was invited to all our family functions. Since just about every other family in Pasadena and Alta-dena also invited him to the same functions, he didn't always come to ours, but he and his wife had attended many a Christmas dinner at our humble bungalow on Marengo.

"Don't forget, Daisy, that if ever Billy goes — and he will, one way or another — you've done everything you could to help him."

"Sometimes I wonder about that."

He gave me a saddish smile. "I know you do, but you're being too hard on yourself, just as Billy is too hard on himself."

With that, he ushered me out of his office, and I still had no idea how to help my husband.

It then occurred to me to talk to Sam Ro-tondo. Billy and Sam were fast friends. Surely Sam would want to help me out in this instance, even though he didn't like me. Because I didn't want to discuss Billy's problems over the phone, particularly with

the nosy Mrs. Barrow as a party-line neighbor and Billy sitting in the same room with
me, I decided to see Sam in person.

So I headed to the Pasadena Police Department directly after I left Dr. Benjamin's
office. At that time the Pasadena Police
Department occupied space in the back part
of our city hall on the corner of Fair Oaks
Avenue and Union Street. I'd been there
before — seldom because I'd wanted to be
— and I recognized the policeman at the
front desk. I think he recognized me, too.

It then occurred to me that maybe this
wasn't such a bright idea. I mean, I sure
didn't want any rumors to start circulating
about Sam and me! But the policeman up
front only nodded and told me I could go
up to Sam's office, so I did. When I opened
the door, all the people inside turned to see
who'd invaded their space, my face went
hot, and Sam frowned at me. How typical.

Uncomfortably enduring the men's stares,
I walked over to Sam's desk and sat in the
chair beside it. He continued to frown.
"What are you doing here, Daisy?"

Oh, boy. This didn't sound like an auspicious opening line to me. Nevertheless, I
was there, and I knew good and well that
Sam cared about Billy's welfare, even if he
wasn't happy to see me. Therefore, I said,

"There's something I'd like to talk to you about, Sam."

His expression didn't lighten when he said, "Go ahead."

Darn him! "Not here," I whispered. "I need to talk to you in private."

"Now?"

How unhelpful could the man get? "Yes, now. It's important. It's. . . ." I glanced around the room. All the other fellows in it had gone back to their work, so I lowered my voice. "It's about Billy."

Sam gazed at me, his heavy eyebrows lowered for a couple of seconds. Then he stood suddenly, grabbed his suit coat from the back of his chair, started shrugging it on, and said, "Let's go outside. Have you had lunch?"

"Lunch?" I rose too. "What time is it?"

"Lunchtime. Let's go to the Crown City Chop Suey joint."

Did I want to have lunch with Sam? No. I did not. But I had to admit that the Crown City Chop Suey Palace would be a better place to talk than a crowded office full of police detectives. And it wasn't far to walk, being on Fair Oaks and all. I trailed after Sam, as he headed to the door and snatched his hat from the tree residing nearby, and we went downstairs out into the day, which was, as I may already have mentioned, brisk.

We didn't speak until we'd walked about half a block. Then Sam said, "What's this all about, Daisy? You don't generally seek out my wise counsel."

He was being sarcastic. "I know, but I thought you might have a suggestion in this case."

"Huh. Well, we'll talk about it over some chop suey or something."

"Very well," I said meekly, wishing Sam were an easier person for me to talk to. I couldn't fathom why Billy and my father liked him so much. *They* didn't have trouble talking to him. Of course, *they* hadn't been treated like a criminal by him, either. Or arrested by him.

By that time I'd decided this had been a foolish notion.

But it was too late now. Sam held the door for me when we got to the Crown City, as delicious Chinese food smells wafted out to greet us. A Chinese waiter led us to a table tucked away in a far corner, which was a good choice, since it was dark and kind of secluded.

Sam politely held my chair for me. It always surprised me when Sam behaved appropriately, although I'm not sure why. I guess it's because we'd met under somewhat

180

inauspicious circumstances. Well, it was also because he thought I was basically a crook, which definitely cast a pall over our relationship. I freely admit, and always have done, that what I did for a living was bunkum. But I wasn't a crook. I didn't take money under false pretenses. Well . . . oh . . . all right, so maybe I did. But I only worked for people who wanted to be fooled. I never tried to convince anyone who didn't want to be convinced.

But enough of that. Sam and I both ordered from the menu, and the waiter brought us some egg-flower soup. As Sam sipped, I explained my predicament. His brows lowered as I spoke.

"He's never mentioned committing suicide to me," he said at last, after I'd been silent for a minute or so.

"He'd never mentioned it to me, either. But I found that box crammed full of morphine syrup bottles and asked him about it." A wave of sadness washed over me, and I stopped talking for fear I'd start crying again. Blast my oversensitive tear ducts!

Sam pushed away his soup bowl. "I don't like the sound of that."

"I don't, either. That's why I decided to talk to you. You and Billy are good friends. I

181

thought maybe you might be able to suggest something I could do to help him feel less desperate."

Sam gazed at me for so long, I began to fidget in my chair. Before I lost my nerve entirely and bolted from the restaurant, the waiter brought our food. Darned if I didn't realize I was hungry! I'd kind of toyed with my food at breakfast, because I was feeling so baffled and distraught about Billy, so this food idea of Sam's had turned out to be a good one. First time *that* had happened. As a rule, I didn't care for Sam's suggestions, mainly because they generally meant some kind of discomfort for yours truly.

We both dug in — politely, of course — while Sam thought. At least I presume he was thinking. After munching on a shrimp, he looked up at me, his face a study in contemplation. "In a way, I wouldn't blame him if he killed himself."

I almost dropped my fork. "Sam! What are you saying?"

"I'm saying I wouldn't much blame Billy if he drank that syrup. Do you have any idea what he has to go through every day?"

Before I could respond indignantly that I certainly *did* have an idea, Sam surprised me again by saying, "But of course, you do.

182

You live with him and do everything for him."

Merciful heaven, that's the first time Sam had ever admitted I was good for anything at all. I appreciated his words.

"That's one of the main reasons he feels so desperate, I suspect," he said.

"I'm afraid it is," I admitted bleakly. "He hates being helpless."

"I know he does. But no matter what you do for him, you can't do anything about his health or the pain he's in all the time."

My spirits sagged once more. "No, I can't. Wish I could."

"Yeah. So do I."

I couldn't think of anything to say, so I kept eating. The food was really good, although I discovered I wasn't as hungry as I'd thought I was. I think worry has that effect on a person. Sam remained silent, too, as he consumed his lunch.

After several minutes of chewing and swallowing, he set his fork down on his plate and looked at me from across the table. "Listen, Daisy, what I'm going to say probably isn't anything you want to hear, but I'm going to say it anyway."

I lifted my eyebrows but remained silent.

"Billy will do what he has to do. He always has, and he always will. He didn't have to volunteer to go fight the Kaiser and his crew, but he did, and he's still paying for it. He's a good man, and you're lucky to have him."

My eyes began to threaten tears again. Blast!

"He's in a lot of physical pain. You know that as well as I do. Probably better. He feels useless. He can't get out and do things or earn a living for the two of you. But I think the main problem is the pain and the feeling of hopelessness he has. He knows he'll never get better, as well as you do. If he ever does decide to use that morphine syrup, don't get angry with him. Try to understand that he just couldn't take it any longer."

Numbly, I nodded, unable to speak. To my utter astonishment, Sam reached across the table and took my hand.

"Billy's a good man, Daisy. You're lucky to have each other. Try to understand that whatever he ends up doing, he'll do it for a reason. A good reason."

I had to swallow the lump in my throat before I whispered, "Do you really think so?"

"Yes. I. . . . When my wife died, I blamed myself. I thought she'd passed on because I didn't get her out of the climate back East soon enough. But after talking to several doctors and other people about tuberculosis, I realized that there really wasn't much I could have done about her condition. You're even less at fault for Billy's problems than I was for Margaret's."

Goodness. Sam had never revealed so much of himself to me before. So his wife's name had been Margaret. I do believe this was the first time I'd felt anything more than slight — or great — resentment toward Sam.

"As soon as we got Margaret's diagnosis, I applied for positions across the country in areas that were warm and dry. I had been going to join the US Army, believe it or not, but I scotched that idea when she got sick."

Goodness. I hadn't known that before. Sam was one of the men I tended to look at askance because they'd been young and healthy when the United States entered the war and hadn't served. Shows how much I knew about anything. Now I felt guilty about Sam as well as Billy.

"The mail was so dratted slow," Sam said. "It was months before the detective slot in the Pasadena Police Department opened up. I applied for it instantly, but by the time they hired me, it was too late. Margaret died less than a year after we moved out here."

"There's nothing much anyone can do

about TB," I said after an awkward pause. It was probably a stupid thing to say, but it was true. They called tuberculosis the "white plague" for a reason, and Dr. Benjamin had told me how little anyone could do to treat the dreaded disease. The only progress anyone had made so far was to discover it was caused by a bacillus. I said, "As soon as she was diagnosed, it was too late, I reckon."

"That's right," said Sam. "And there's even less you can do about the state of Billy's health than I could do about Margaret's. Unfortunately, both Margaret and Billy were victims of forces larger than they were."

He was sure right about that.

Then he squeezed my hand, rose, paid our bill, and we walked back to the police station. I didn't know what to say, so when we parted at the door to City Hall, I merely said, "Thanks, Sam."

I felt him watching me as I walked back to the Chevrolet.

CHAPTER NINE

While I was out, Mrs. Kincaid had left yet
another frantic message for me. I guess she
didn't want to wait until Wednesday at ten
o'clock. How typical of her. She always
demonstrated every evidence of sympathetic
understanding about other people's problems, but *nobody's* problems overrode her
own, and I personally considered her problems minor. The woman was rich and
healthy, had two hearty children, and was
engaged to a rich man who was not only
friendly and kind but who doted on her.

Oh, well. Ours is not to ask why, I guess.
At any rate, I returned her call when I got
back home. Billy didn't ask me where I'd
been, and I didn't volunteer any information.

"Oh, Daisy!" wailed Mrs. Kincaid. I
believe I've mentioned that she's a first-class
wailer.

"Yes, Mrs. Kincaid?" I said in my sooth-

187

ing spiritualist voice. I wanted to shriek at her to shut up and be still, and tell her that I had more problems than she'd ever see in her entire life, and that I considered her a vain, silly woman who was totally ridiculous. Naturally, I didn't.

"Can you please come over here now, dear? I know you had to visit the doctor about your poor husband and we'd scheduled an appointment for Wednesday, but I'm just so upset!"

"Yes, I can tell." I fear my voice wasn't as soft and gentle as it should have been.

"I feel *such* a need to have Rolly communicate via the Ouija board!"

Suppressing my sigh, I said, "I'll be there in forty-five minutes, Mrs. Kincaid. Will that be all right with you?"

"Yes, dear, that would be wonderful. Thank you *so* much!"

"You're quite welcome."

Oh, brother.

But when I turned from the telephone, I saw Billy grinning at me and I felt a trifle better about working for idiotic people who actually believed the guff I fed them.

"I guess you figured out that was Mrs. Kincaid," I said, trying to sound lively. I wanted to lie down and sleep for a month or two, just to get away from Billy's problems and my own fears. Dream on, Daisy Majesty.

"Yeah. In a tizzy again, is she?"

"Oh my, yes." I gazed at my husband for a moment or two, wishing for all sorts of things that couldn't be. "I just talked to her this morning, too. God knows what happened between then and now. She seemed fine when I talked to her earlier. Well, as fine as she ever is. I'll change clothes and go over there. It's easy money, anyhow."

"I don't know how you keep getting away with it," said Billy. But he was still smiling, so I didn't get angry.

I merely said, "I don't either," and went into our bedroom. There I selected a nice, refined Ouija-board-manipulating outfit of soft wool jersey in a dark brown that went well with the season, my hair, and my wintery mood, and did my best to forget about the box full of morphine syrup residing just underneath Billy's clothes in the same closet.

Dealing with Mrs. Kincaid was both frustrating and as simple as it always was. I never did find out what had set her off, but when I left her, she'd calmed down considerably. She also gave me a most generous gratuity for responding so promptly to her sudden request and begged me to keep the appointment we had for Wednesday. She really was a kindhearted person. She just didn't have anything substantive to worry about, especially since her daughter had joined the Salvation Army, so she worried about nothing. But I shouldn't complain. Heck, she darned near supported my whole family.

I thought about going to the kitchen to visit with Vi, but I was in too gloomy a mood for conversation with my aunt. Anyhow, I'd see Vi at home soon. So I just left.

As I drove away through the heavy wrought-iron gate, guarded as ever by Mrs. Kincaid's gatekeeper, Jackson — who'd taught me many interesting aspects of spiritualism, particularly those dealing with Voodoo, since he'd originally come from Louisiana — I decided there might be one other person to whom I should speak about Billy and my worries: a clergyman. I briefly considered our own pastor at the First Methodist-Episcopal Church, the Reverend Merle Smith, but decided against it. The fellow was a good preacher and had, I'm sure, a willing and helpful spirit, but I didn't know him well enough to discuss my present personal problems. Fortunately, I had an alternative pastor in mind.

Johnny Buckingham was not only a Salvation Army captain, but he was a friend of ours, had gone through school with Billy, and he'd been through hell after the war ended, too. So I tootled our Chevrolet down Fair Oaks and pulled to a stop in front of 51 West Colorado Boulevard, the Salvation Army Headquarters. They called it a headquarters instead of church, I guess to continue the military theme.

Johnny was in his office, and he smiled at me when I tapped on the door. Rising from his chair behind his desk, he said, "How nice to see you, Daisy. And it's not even Saturday." He chuckled. "I've been meaning to tell you how much we appreciate the good job you're doing with your cooking class, by the way."

"It's a miracle," I said, only half joking.

He laughed outright at that. "It must be. God works in mysterious ways."

"He must, if He's got me cooking and not burning down the house."

After peering at me more closely for a bit, Johnny said more soberly, "But you didn't come here to talk about your class, did you?"

Sighing, I sat on a chair in front of his desk. "No. I . . . I'm really worried, Johnny."

He sat, too, and didn't speak for a minute.

When he did, he got right to the point. "Billy?"

I nodded. Then I blurted out the whole of my story, from finding the morphine, to confronting Billy, to talking to Dr. Benjamin and Sam. I ended with "Oh, Johnny, I don't know what to do," giving a fair imitation of Mrs. Kincaid in a wail.

Johnny thought about it for a little bit. Then he said, "I don't know if there's anything you really can do, Daisy. You're already doing it."

"But, Johnny! He said he might kill himself!"

"I know. I heard you." Johnny gave me a patient smile. "Of course, I always recommend prayer when people are at their wits' end."

I hate to admit it, but I hadn't even thought about prayer before Johnny mentioned it. I said, "Of course," because I figured I should, although that wasn't the kind of advice I'd gone there for.

Johnny's grin told me he knew exactly how much praying I did on a daily basis. "You know, Daisy, God answers prayers in His own way and in His own time. Our time and His time don't necessarily correspond."

I thought about arguing: If that is the case, then what good is prayer? But I didn't.

"Don't look so skeptical," he told me, laughing a little. Then he got serious. "Daisy, I've known Billy for even longer than you have."

I nodded. It was true. Johnny and Billy used to play baseball when they were barely old enough to wear long pants and hold bats.

"Ever since that stinking war, your Billy has been in constant pain, both physical and spiritual. I understand all about spiritual pain. Well, you know what I went through before the Salvation Army rescued me. But I was luckier than Billy. I wasn't grievously wounded, as he was, and I didn't get gassed. It might transpire that Billy will take that morphine syrup one day. If he does, then you'll never need to worry about him being in pain again."

His words horrified me. "Johnny! How can you say that? What about the people who love him? What about *our* pain if he kills himself?"

"I should think that the people who love him would want him to have some measure of peace," Johnny said, serious again. "God really does work in mysterious ways, Daisy."

I heaved a gigantic sigh. "But Johnny. . . ." Then I swallowed and blurted out, "I thought committing suicide was a mortal sin."

"Good Lord, Daisy, do you really think God wants Billy to keep suffering if he doesn't have to? Mortal sins are an invention of mankind. God is kinder than we are. Heck, back in the bad old days, clergymen didn't even allow folks in their congregations to go to doctors. They thought pain and suffering were 'from God,' whatever that means."

I stared at him, dumbfounded. Then I asked in a slightly unsteady, very weak voice, "Do you really believe that?"

"Yes, I do," he said firmly.

"But . . . but do you really think suicide is the answer?"

Johnny heaved a huge, heartfelt sigh. "*I* don't think so, no. But we're not talking about me. There were years when I thought my only hope was suicide, Daisy. I don't think you ever saw me when I was at my lowest ebb. And I was nowhere near as bad off as Billy."

"I . . . don't think I did." I'd been too consumed with worry about my husband to think about other folks' problems.

"Well, believe me, I was a hard case. God saved me, but my only problem was the bottle and a brain full of blood and memo-

194

ries." He actually shuddered. "At least I didn't have to contend with the physical pain Billy has to suffer. My only demons were mental."

I said, "Johnny, I. . . ." But I didn't know what to say. That damned war.

Johnny seemed to know what I was feeling. He smiled gently and said, "But I'd like to pray with you, Daisy, if you wouldn't be embarrassed by it."

How kind people were. Even Sam, much to my surprise. I'd always known Johnny possessed a good and generous soul. I nodded, although I felt mighty uncomfortable with Johnny's suggestion. I wasn't accustomed to people praying with me. I probably wouldn't have felt as ill at ease if a stranger, rather than a friend, had asked me to pray with him, oddly enough. But there weren't any strangers present and Johnny was, so when he held out his hand, I took it and bowed my head.

Johnny's prayer was short and practical. "Lord, please give Daisy and Billy a measure of Your grace. They're going through some really hard times, as You well know. You know how to fix their problems, which are truly severe, better than we do. If it's Your will that Billy leave this earth, protect and save him, and take care of Daisy, who loves her husband dearly. Even if she can't cook very well."

"Thank you, Johnnie."

He would have to add that last part.

Nevertheless, I appreciated Johnny Buckingham at that moment more than I ever expected to, even though I'd known him for a kindly man for years. I drove back home feeling — not contented, exactly, but a little more peaceful. Less harried. And I also knew I had to apologize to Billy for blowing up at him. The poor man deserved a better wife than I.

So I did exactly that as soon as I got home.

Billy said, "I'm sorry, too, Daisy. I know you don't like it when I talk about doing away with myself."

"No, I don't. But I understand why you might want to one day. At least . . . I think I do." Because I couldn't help myself, I added, "But I hope you never do it, Billy. I don't know what I'd do without you."

He gave a short, mocking laugh. "You'd be better off."

I stared at him, and I'm sure he could see the denial and sadness in my expression. "No, I wouldn't. You might want to think that, but it's not true. I love you, Billy."

He'd have heaved a sigh if he'd been able. Instead, he said, "I know it, Daisy. I love you, too."

So much for that.

The following day, after breakfast, I picked out one of my better costumes to wear. After all, I was headed into the rarified atmosphere of the Castleton residence in San Marino. I selected a dark-blue serge frock with a long, braid-trimmed roll collar that continued beneath the belt. The only ornamentation were five buttons on the bodice. It was quite fetching, and I believed it was also sober and appropriate for my meeting with Miss Emmaline Castleton. I plopped my recently updated-for-fall black hat on my bobbed hair, drew on a pair of dark stockings, and fetched the pretty pumps that I'd bought on sale at Nash's.

See, this is what's so great about sewing for yourself. I'm sure that entire outfit didn't cost more than four dollars, and that included the shoes and hat!

Anyway, I felt properly dressed and was eager to discover what important subject Miss Castleton wanted to talk to me about.

Billy looked up from his Tarzan novel when I walked across the living room. I executed a little pirouette in front of him and Spike, who sat on his lap. "Do I look good enough to appear at the Castleton mansion in San Marino?"

His eyebrows soaring, Billy said, "Castleton? You're going to the *Castletons'*? Good Lord, don't tell me old man Castleton wants you to conduct a séance there."

I laughed, although it took a bit of playacting, since I still felt kind of blue. "No. His daughter, Emmaline, asked me to meet her there for luncheon. I met her at Mrs. Bissell's séance, and I'm honestly not sure what she wants to talk to me about. She said she isn't interested in getting in touch with her late fiancé." Recalling my wifely duties, I said, "There are leftovers from last night's dinner in the icebox for you and Pa."

"Good. I like leftovers. Especially Vi's." Billy's grin did a good deal to make me feel better about life in general. "Well, you'll have to tell me all about this latest conquest of yours when you get home."

"I certainly will." I gave him a kiss and Spike a pat, and Billy held on to Spike so I could escape the house without him.

The drive to the Castletons' took me through a lovely part of Pasadena. My favorite street down that way is, I think, San Pasqual, which has huge houses and beautiful yards and even a prestigious university. The Throop Institute had just been renamed the California Institute of Technology, and was reputed to have the biggest scientific brains in the nation on its faculty. It had been situated in the middle of Pasadena before moving to this location, on California Boulevard. The campus was quite pretty, but it couldn't hold a candle to the magnificent homes around it.

Miss Castleton had prepared Stickley well. As soon as I drove up to the gate, a buzzing noise sounded from a speaker on a pole next to my window, and a tinny voice said, "Mrs. Majesty?"

"Yes."

"Please come in."

And darned if the gate didn't swing open and allow me to enter the hallowed Castleton grounds! I slowly drove through the gates, and a man held up a hand for me to halt. So I did.

The man came to my window. "Miss Castleton asked me to give you directions," said he.

"Thank you."

So he did. My goodness, but this place was big! It's a good thing he gave me directions. Otherwise, I'd never have found the house. If you can call such a gigantic building a house. I'd read about Mr. Castleton's art collection, and was kind of prepared when Emmaline met me on the massive front porch. She hurried over to the car as soon as I brought it to a stop beside an elaborate portico.

"Oh, I'm so glad you could come!" she said, sounding as excited as I was.

I considered that kind of strange. I mean, I'm just me, and she was a Castleton. Still, I'd learned a long time before then that people are an odd lot. "Happy to help," I said, meaning it. In truth, I was dying to find out what was so important to her that she'd had to set up a private meeting.

"Let Jones park your car. Here, let me take your keys."

Startled, I handed her the keys, and she instantly handed them over to a man, whose name, I assumed, was Jones. He wore a uniform, by gum. Shoot, I guess the woman really was serious about this visit of ours.

"I've asked Caruthers to serve us luncheon on the front veranda."

I took an unintentional glimpse at the sky. It wasn't cloudy, and this was Southern California, but still. . . .

"Don't worry. There's an electric heater that Caruthers will set up so we don't get cold. I really want to speak to you in private."

"I see. Well, that's very nice," I said, although I really wanted to see inside the house. What the heck, did she not think I was good enough to set foot in her famous abode? I tried not to resent it.

And then she said, "But before we eat, you must see inside," and I felt better. "The place is truly fantastic. My father spared no expense, as you'll see. Well, he had all the money in the world, so why should he?"

Why indeed? Her attitude puzzled me. She seemed fond of her father, yet she spoke of his millions as if they didn't mean much to her. I could have educated her to the perils of poverty, but didn't think it would be politic to do so. "I'd love to see inside," I said mildly.

She looked at me keenly. I got the impression Miss Emmaline Castleton was no dummy. "You're wondering why I talk like that about my father and his money, aren't you?"

"Well . . . yes, I guess so."

"Follow me." She walked to a huge, carved mahogany door, which was instantly opened for her by another uniformed personage. Jeez, the Castletons must have employed half the people in Pasadena!

After we'd walked inside, she led me to a gigantic staircase that split halfway up so that you could go either right or left, I guess depending on which room you wanted to visit. She spoke softly. "You see, my father truly is a wonderful man, but he and my uncle used some mighty dirty tactics to make their vast wealth. I guess I've always felt a little guilty about it. Although," she admitted next, "not enough to live on my own." She heaved a huge sigh. "Anyhow, now they're both philanthropists. Kind of like Andrew Carnegie. After he made his millions by running down the little people, he became a philanthropist, too."

I understood her dilemma. Principles were fine, but they didn't put food on the table. Heck, look at me. I was a total fraud. "Believe me, I understand exactly what you mean."

Again her gaze pierced me. "Yes. I think you do. That's one of the reasons I wanted to talk to you. I think you'll understand why, too. After the grand tour."

It was a grand tour, all right. I'd never seen anything like the place. The artwork alone nearly overwhelmed me. Gorgeous stuff. And the servants! I swear, there were servants *everywhere.*

At one point, Emmaline — she told me to call her Emmaline — said, "Father insisted on having a cat. He said there's nothing quite like a cat to make a house a home."

"Hmm," I said. "Maybe he's right, although I think it would take more than a cat to make this place into a home." Then I could have slapped a hand over my too-ready mouth.

Fortunately for me, Emmaline laughed. "You're right about that! It's just too big. Too grand."

"But it's beautiful," I said as a sop.

"It is that. Wait until you see the grounds and the sculpture garden."

"Sculpture garden?"

"Yes. Father had a whole lot of statues imported from . . . I don't know. Greece? Well, they look like a row of Greek gods, anyhow."

"My goodness."

Actually, they looked like two rows of Greek gods. The grounds were as fantastic as the house. I'd have been stricken speechless except that I'm virtually never speechless, and Emmaline was so down-to-earth and . . . well, I guess the word I want is *fun*. Isn't that strange? But she had a wonderful sense of humor and no pretensions at all. When I compared this daughter of wealth to Stacy Kincaid, another daughter of wealth, Stacy sank even farther in my esteem, although before it happened I wouldn't have thought it possible.

"But you must be starving," Emmaline

203

said after we'd wandered around in what, to me, seemed like Wonderland for an hour or so. "I know I am. I'm sure Caruthers has our luncheon ready. I hope you like chicken à la king."

"I'm sure I will," I said, hoping for the best. Chicken à la king was another thing Aunt Vi never made for the family. Too delicate for us Gumms, I suppose.

I did like it. In fact, it was delicious. I said so.

"Thank you. I thought it might be nice to have something a little lighter for luncheon than a big, heavy meal. We always eat . . . well in the evening."

"So do we, thank goodness. My aunt cooks for us. She's a marvelous cook."

"I've heard Harold Kincaid say the same thing. You're fortunate to have such a clever relation who lives with you."

"Yes, we are fortunate." Because I didn't want her to get the wrong idea about Vi, I added, "Of course, if it weren't for the war, Vi would still be living in her own home and cooking for her family, but her son died in the war, and her husband got sick during the influenza pandemic. He died of pneumonia, as so many others did. She hasn't had the best of times these past few years."

To my horror, Emmaline's eyes welled

with tears. Impulsively, I put out a hand to her. "Oh, I'm so sorry! I know you suffered terribly from that awful war, too. I . . . I guess we all did."

"Oh, don't mind me, Daisy." I'd told her to call me Daisy. Turnabout's fair play, after all. "I just get a little teary when I think about all the fine young men who lost everything in that damned war."

Oh, my. I wasn't accustomed to young women saying words like *damn* out loud. I thought it sometimes, and have even written the word a time or two in these journals, but I don't drop it into casual conversations.

Emmaline wiped her eyes with her handkerchief. "Actually, that's the reason I asked you to come here today."

"It is?" I think I gaped at her. "I thought you wanted to talk to me about the Salvation Army's program to help people in distress."

"Yes, yes, I do. But it's all connected to that blasted war."

"Oh. Um . . . I don't think I understand."

"Of course you don't. I haven't told you yet. You see, I'm hoping you can advise me about a young man who suffered terribly in the conflict, and who helped my Stephen and made his last days much brighter than they might have been. He carried him from the battlefield, you see, and tended him as well as he could until he died."

"Good Lord."

Emmaline nodded. "He brought me a letter Stephen had written right before he subsided into unconsciousness. I know it was written by Stephen, because it was his handwriting, and he wrote about things nobody but the two of us would know about." She looked at me earnestly. "This man is a genuine hero, Daisy. At least he's the hero of my life."

"It sounds like it," I said, since I couldn't think of anything more refined to say.

She nodded again. "He is." Firmly. She spoke firmly.

"Um . . . I presume this fellow has had some hard times since the war ended?"

"You wouldn't believe what he went through. He was reprimanded severely for helping Stephen, for one thing, and was even imprisoned for a while. He couldn't get work, and he finally had to escape. I sent him money to get to South America, and he stayed in Mexico for several months. He was ill, you see. Very ill. He had that influenza, too. Plus, he'd been wounded in the same battle that took Stephen."

I held up a hand to stop the flow of her words, because they didn't make any sense to me. "Wait a minute, please. Did you just say he was *reprimanded* for helping Mr. Allison? And was actually *imprisoned* for helping him?"

Gripping her hankie tightly in both of her hands, Emmaline said, "Yes. Severely reprimanded and jailed."

"But . . . but I don't understand. Why ever would anyone reprimand someone for trying to save someone else's life? That doesn't make any sense."

She sucked in a deep breath and let it out slowly. "It *will* make sense to you, trust me."

I lifted my eyebrows and said, "Oh?"

"Yes. You see, the young man who tried to save Stephen's life was a German."

CHAPTER TEN

My mouth fell open and stayed that way until I snapped it shut and rose to my feet. Astounded doesn't half describe the state I was in at that time.

Emmaline held out a hand to me. "Daisy? What's the matter? I know Germany was our enemy during the war, but this fellow. . . ."

I regret to say I raised my voice. "Do you know what those people did to my husband? Do you? Do you have any idea what they did?"

Emmaline shut her eyes and looked miserable.

"They shot my Billy, Emmaline! And that wasn't enough for them. They gassed him! They *gassed* him! With that filthy mustard gas. Only my Billy didn't die. No, he's only suffered every single day of his life since that battle! He's going to die one of these days, because they used that putrid gas on him! Before I'd help a German, I'd cut off my own hand!"

And then, as if I hadn't already made enough of a fool of myself, I collapsed onto the chair in which I'd eaten such a delightful luncheon, folded my arms on the little table Caruthers had set up, buried my face in my arms, and burst into tears. They weren't dainty, delicate tears, either, but huge gasping sobs.

Poor Emmaline didn't know what to do with me. Fortunately for me, her nature is sympathetic and she's got an open and understanding heart. She knelt beside me, put an arm over my shoulders and crooned. I don't remember what all she said, but it was something like, "I know, Daisy. I understand completely. It was Germans who killed my Stephen, too. But this young man tried to save his life, and he was punished for it. I'd like to help him if I can, and the only program I can think of that might help him assimilate is the one offered by the Salvation Army."

"I hate G-Germans," sobbed I. Not a pretty picture, I know.

"I understand, Daisy. Believe me, I understand."

Wiping my cheeks with my hands — I was too upset to reach for a hankie — I said,

"Do you know that my poor husband has stocked a whole lot of morphine syrup in order to kill himself when the pain of his life gets to be too much for him? Well, he has! Because of those damned Germans!"

Emmaline closed her eyes again and looked as if she were in as much emotional agony as I, although hers was quieter. Breeding shows, I guess.

I began to calm down after a few minutes. Then I started feeling like a total fool. Sniffling pitifully, I said, "I'm . . . sorry. I just . . . I don't. . . ." But there was no need to go on. Emmaline understood.

"There's no need to apologize, Daisy. If it weren't for the circumstances surrounding my request, I wouldn't help a German cross the street. Not awfully forgiving, I guess, but it's the truth. But this fellow — his name is Kurt Grünfeld, by the way — only joined the German army because he had to. He didn't believe in the Kaiser's cause any more than we did."

My spate of tears had made my nose stuffy, so I sounded like I had a cold when I said, "How do you know he's the genuine article? I mean, how do you . . . ?"

"How do I know he's the man who tried to save Stephen's life?"

I nodded.

"Because Stephen told me so in the letters he wrote to me."

Skeptical, I asked, "And you say you're sure the letters were really from Stephen?"

"Yes." She reached into the bodice of her gown — which, by the way, was perfectly gorgeous. No homemade frocks for Miss Emmaline Castleton. Unless, of course, she had a seamstress on the staff at the residence, which was quite likely — and pulled out an envelope.

The envelope was relatively tidy, considering she must have had it for years, but when she withdrew its contents, I saw a tattered sheet of what looked like paper torn from a book or something. The paper had brown-red spots on it, and I feared I knew what those spots were.

"Kurt said he mailed this and another couple of letters to me after the Armistice. He'd kept them for a year and a half before he was able to get them into the post. I didn't receive them until last year. But this is the message I want you to read." She handed me the raggedy piece of paper.

It was torn from a book, and the book had evidently been published in Germany, since it was written in German. I read:

My darling Emmaline,

I don't think I'm going to be here much longer. My wound is severe. Kurt isn't able to tend it properly, because we're hiding in the loft of a barn. Please know that I love you. If you ever have the opportunity, please try to assist Kurt. He's going to catch hell for helping me and for deserting in order to do so. He's going to try to get out of the country, but neither of us thinks he'll make it. It will be a miracle if you ever read this letter.

I can't write any more now. I'm losing this battle, darling, and I'm sorry we won't be able to see each other again. Remember me always.

Love,
Stephen

Naturally, by the time I came to the end of the letter, I was sniffling again. Without speaking, I handed the letter back to Emmaline.

She sucked in a deep breath and let it out slowly. "You're the only person I've ever shown this letter to," she said at last.

"Why?"

"You're the only one I've trusted to understand."

Good Lord. Me? Who earned my living as

a total fraud? It occurred to me then and there that Emmaline must have great depth of perception to look past the trappings of my profession and see the me inside.

"Why in the world do you trust me?" I asked, genuinely puzzled. It then occurred to me that maybe this was a setup. Could Sam Rotondo, in an effort to get me to desist in my career as a phony spiritualist, actually. . . .

No. Not even Sam would pull a stunt like this. I hoped.

She sat down in the chair that she had vacated to stifle my tantrum, and she thought for a moment in silence. I didn't pressure her.

After what seemed like forever, she said, "I'll tell you why I trust you, Daisy, and I hope you won't take my words amiss."

Shoot. But I determined to behave with dignity for the remainder of our time together. I nodded at her to let her know I was listening. I wasn't sure about the *taking her words amiss* part yet. We'd see about that.

"I . . . don't believe in spiritualism, and I have a feeling you don't, either."

I only blinked at her, too startled to speak.

"But you're so wonderful at your job, and so . . . so *good* at it. . . . I mean, you don't promise people anything they couldn't figure out on their own if they had any sense, you know? And you don't try to tell them more than you can deliver. Telling someone to live happily in this world until called to the next because the deceased loved one wants him to is, in my opinion, a brilliant ploy."

Good heavens! Still, I didn't speak.

She went on, a little desperately, I thought. "And I've talked to Harold and Mrs. Kincaid and Mrs. Bissell and other people about you. They all say the same thing. You're the best at what you do. And you never, ever tell other people what folks tell you in private sessions."

Finally I felt compelled to whisper, "Thank you."

"But you don't honestly believe you're communicating with spirits from beyond, do you? I mean, do you *really?*"

Talk about a struggle! Did I want to tell the truth to this woman, who had just revealed a deep, dark secret to me? Well, what the heck. Why not? I got the feeling what we said at this little meeting wouldn't go any farther than her father's grand front porch. After heaving a huge sigh, I told the truth.

"Of course not." And then, because I felt

compelled to do so, I told her the total, *unvarnished* truth. "I began playing with the Ouija board because, back when I was ten, Mrs. Kincaid gave her old one to my aunt Vi. I made Rolly up at a family get-together when everyone else was afraid of — or pretended to be afraid of — the board. I had a grand time pretending for my family. Then Vi told Mrs. Kincaid how 'talented' I was with the board, Mrs. Kincaid asked me to work a party she was having, and that was it." I hesitated for a moment and went on, kind of bitterly, "When Billy finally came home from the war, he was unable to work because he was so badly injured. So I began reading tarot cards and palms for people. I could make ever so much more money doing that than I ever could as a clerk at a dry-goods store or as an elevator operator."

Emmaline nodded. "Yes. I see. It's as I suspected. I can't begin to tell you how much I admire you, Daisy."

She admired me? Mercy sakes. "Well, I don't think there's really much to admire. I'm . . . well, I'm a fake."

"But you're so good at it. And you're never cruel. And you tell people the truth." She reached across the table and took my hand. "Don't you see? I went to Mrs. Bis-

215

sell's to see if what I suspected about you was the truth, and discovered it was. And you . . . you have such a strong connection with the German issue. . . ."

"I should think that would have put you off." Feeling stupid, I added, "After the scene I just played for you, I'm surprised you still trusted me enough to tell about your German."

She shook her head hard. "No. Don't you see? You're totally honest."

Totally honest. After I admitted I earned my living as a phony. Well, I never claimed to understand rich people. I could only gaze at her in wonder.

"You and your husband have suffered so horribly from that war. You understand what I've been through."

"I know lots of people who lost loved ones, including my aunt. She lost her only son."

I saw tears well in her eyes again, and they surprised me.

"The Kaiser is a devil," she said. I got the impression she meant it.

"I agree."

"But, you see, it wasn't only France, Belgium, England and we who suffered under his hand. His own people have endured dreadful hardships. They were just

216

his toys in the whole mess, and now they're being punished for it."

With a grimmish sort of half smile, I said, "Yes. That's just about exactly what my husband says."

"I'm surprised he's so . . . so generous."

"Billy's always been a levelheaded sort of fellow." Yet another deep sigh preceded my next difficult confession. "And I guess you're both right. It's just . . . it's just that I'm so resentful of what the Germans did to him, it's difficult for me to be fair."

"I know. They killed the only man I've ever loved."

We both sat there, staring across the magnificent lawns surrounding us that were interspersed every now and then with a piece of statuary or a grand tree or what have you.

Emmaline broke the silence. "But I truly would like to help Kurt if I can. In order to do that, of course, I'll have to sponsor him."

"Yes. I understand immigrants to this country require sponsors."

"It's terribly difficult for Germans to get into the United States, even with sponsorship. Providing I can manage that part, then I'd have to find him employment somewhere. That's when I thought of the Salvation Army. I've supported the organization for years now. They're about the only religious entity I respect, because they behave the way Christians are supposed to behave — at least, they behave the way Christ behaved."

"I agree," said I, rather surprised, since I'm a lifelong Methodist. Still, I admire the Salvation Army because they really *are* like Jesus in that they don't turn up their noses at people who are poor and hungry — or even drunks or dope fiends. Maybe even if they're Germans. And when Harold told me you were teaching a class there, I thought you might be willing to speak to the captain about Kurt."

"Kurt is in Mexico now?"

"Yes. I doubt he'll be able to enter the country legally unless I can get my father to write strongly worded letters to the immigration folks and to his congressman and have my sponsorship and the Salvation Army back up my claims that Kurt is both employable and has a job waiting for him after he completes the Salvation Army's program. Then he can become a United States citizen and be safe. He's not safe in Germany, and he's totally alone in Mexico."

"What sort of job do you have for him?"

"I figure he can be my chauffeur or something."

And then, as if I didn't already have enough on my enfeebled mind, I thought of Hilda Schwartz. I sat up straighter in my chair and said, "Oh!" I didn't mean to. The word just slipped out.

"What?"

"I just thought of a woman in my cooking class."

"Oh?"

Clearly, Emmaline didn't have a notion in the world why I'd changed the subject. But I hadn't changed it at all, and I enlightened her.

"I think she's German, although she says she's from Switzerland. If she is German, I'm sure she's in the country illegally. If . . . I hate to ask you this."

"Go ahead. If you want me to sponsor her, I'd have to meet her first, but I don't see why I couldn't do that."

"And get your father to write a letter, too," I said, greatly daring.

She eyed me and grinned a little. "I thought you hated Germans."

"I do. But I don't hate Hilda." I shook my head and actually chuckled. "Very well, I'm inconsistent. But Hilda seems like a lovely woman, and I get the feeling she's scared and lonely and needs help. Just like your Kurt."

"He's Stephen's Kurt," Emmaline corrected me gently. "Although I've met him." Then, as if she couldn't keep the emotion contained any longer, she burst out, "Oh, Daisy! He's a *boy!* Even today, with nineteen twenty-one almost over, he can't be more than nineteen years old! I don't know how old he was when the war started, but he must have been an *infant* when he enlisted."

"The Kaiser is a devil," I said, echoing Emmaline's sentiments.

We parted on the friendliest of terms, and I hoped we'd remain friendly. You never know about these things. Sometimes you'll meet someone and hit it off, and you never make contact with that person again. Then again, sometimes you'll meet someone like Harold Kincaid, who becomes a fast friend. I had to admit that I hoped Emmaline and I would stay in touch. I liked her very well. Of course, we'd have to be in touch in the near future because of our aims regarding Hilda and Kurt.

I could scarcely believe I was actually going to help a couple of Germans become United States citizens. My mind was boggled.

In my still-boggled state, I drove directly to the Salvation Army and found Johnny Buckingham in his office. He looked up and frowned, which took me aback for a moment, until he said, "Is Billy all right, Daisy? I meant to visit him, but I got busy. That's no excuse. I'll visit him this afternoon."

See? I told you he was a good man.

"Billy's as fine as he ever is, Johnny. I'm here about something else."

His eyebrows rose inquisitively. "Have a seat." He gestured at the chair in front of his desk.

So I did, and then got right to the point. "Johnny, I just had a meeting with Miss Emmaline Castleton —"

"Shoot, Daisy, you're traveling in exalted company these days." He grinned to let me know he didn't fault me for it.

"Yeah. I know. And it's not necessarily a wonderful thing, either."

"Oh? Does your visit today have something to do with Miss Castleton?"

"Yes, it does. And Hilda Schwartz, too."

"Hilda Schwartz? Isn't she one of the ladies we're sponsoring?"

"Yes, she is. And she claims to be from Switzerland, but I'm pretty sure she's a German."

"Oh?"

Johnny rose and walked around his desk to the door, which he closed gently. I guess he didn't want anyone to overhear the rest of our conversation.

"Yes. I've spoken to her several times, and I'm . . . well, as I said, I'm pretty sure she's from Germany and not Switzerland."

He sat at his desk again and folded his hands on some papers scattered there. "Is this because you don't want to have a German lady in your class, Daisy?" He looked so disappointed in me, I practically leaped to correct his impression.

"No! I mean, yes, it's true I told you I hated Germans, and I do." Frowning, I amended my statement. "I mean, I did. I still do, in general. But Hilda is a nice lady, and I'd like to know her story and, if it turns out she's worth it, I'd like to help her become a citizen."

"And you think you can determine who's worth it and who's not?"

The question was asked gently, but I knew Johnny meant to teach me a lesson. I sighed heavily. "No. Well, I mean yes. Oh, blast it, Johnny! Just listen to me, will you?"

He nodded, so I told him Kurt's story.

"So you see," I concluded, "we've got Kurt Grünfeld on the one hand and Hilda Schwartz on the other, and Miss Castleton wants to help Kurt, and I want to help Hilda."

"If she's worth it," said Johnny rather dryly.

"Well, you know what I mean."

"I think I do."

"Well? What do you think?"

He didn't speak for at least a minute. I was getting a little anxious in the prolonged silence, but I didn't want to interrupt it, as I expected Johnny was considering all aspects of the situation. After a couple of moments he said, "Miss Castleton truly believes her father will write letters for these people?"

"She says so. I got the feeling she doesn't anticipate that he'll be easy to convince, but I don't think she'll give up until he does. She's a very persuasive woman."

He grinned at last. "She must be, if she's got you helping a couple of Germans."

I primmed my mouth but didn't say anything nasty.

"Let me pray about this, Daisy. Is that all right with you?"

"Sure," I said. I'd forgotten that Johnny always prayed about things before he made decisions. Maybe I should try the same path, although I doubted I'd do it. Too impatient, I suppose.

I made as if to rise, but he stopped me with another gesture. I remained in my seat.

"Do you really think Miss Schwartz is German?"

"Well . . . yes, I do."

"How did you come to that conclusion? She came here as a Swiss immigrant. At least she said she was, and the Salvation Army in Mexico City believed her. Why don't you?"

So I told him.

"You think she's German because she likes dachshunds and doesn't yodel?" Johnny sounded incredulous, drat him.

"It's not just that! I've talked to her, Johnny. She doesn't know any more about Switzerland than I do, and I don't know anything. Except about the cuckoo clocks."

"Oh, dear. This may prove to be a problem if you're right."

"I suppose it might. But you'll think about it, right? You'll let me know?"

"I'll pray about it," he repeated, grinning to let me know he understood my own hesitation to use that word. "And I'll be in touch with you when God and I reach a decision."

This time he let me get up from my seat. "Thank you, Johnny. I really appreciate this, you know."

"I know you do." He rose, too, because he's a gentleman, and went to open the door for me. "Anyhow, I expect I owe you one for helping Flossie and me out with the cooking class."

Believe it or not, I hadn't even thought about that aspect of the situation. Now that Johnny had pointed it out to me, however, I told the truth. "You owe me considerably more than one, Johnny Buckingham!"

His laughter followed me down the hall and out the building.

CHAPTER ELEVEN

The rest of that week went as normal. I worked a couple of séances, although not for anyone interesting. Well, that's not entirely true, since séances are, by their very nature, kind of interesting. Nevertheless, nothing eventful occurred. Rolly showed up, like the helpful chap he is, and everyone thought he and I were both wonderful. Gee, I wish my family thought as the people I worked for did. I didn't hear from either Emmaline Castleton or Johnny Buckingham, and I wished Johnny, at least, would call and give me a progress report so that if Emmaline did call me, I could tell her something.

No such luck.

Aunt Vi and I had discussed what I should teach my students at class that day, and eventually, we'd decided upon scalloped meat.

You know, before I began teaching that

stupid class, I'd always thought scallops came from the ocean. I never did figure out why cookbook makers had decided things prepared with bread crumbs should be called "scalloped." Since chickens were the cheapest meat available at that time, Johnny said he'd get some and Flossie would cook and debone them. Thank God for that, since I'd never deboned a chicken in my entire life. But you had to use chopped cooked meat in the recipe, you see, so we figured we'd be better off if that part of the process was done early, just as we'd done when we'd prepared the chicken croquettes. Otherwise, with my talent, we might have been there for days, burning chickens. This time, moreover, I aimed to chop the stupid chickens *during* the class. Poor Flossie had already done enough. I was supposed to be the teacher; it was time I learned how to chop a chicken. As I've already said several times, thank God for Aunt Vi.

I'd just parked the Chevrolet in front of the Salvation Army and was making my way to the fellowship hall when Gertrude Minneke leaped out at me from behind a pillar. I nearly dropped my copy of *Sixty-Five Delicious Dishes.* Unfortunately, the book would assuredly have remained undamaged. "Good heavens, Miss Minneke! You scared

227

me to death."

She appeared suitably abashed. "I'm so sorry, Mrs. Majesty, but I was desperate to talk to you before the class started."

That didn't sound good. "Oh?" I said cautiously. "Why is that?"

She actually, really and truly, wrung her hands! I'd never seen anyone do that except on a motion-picture screen. "I need to talk to you," she whispered. "Desperately."

There was that word again. I didn't like it. If there was one thing I really didn't need right then, it was to get involved in another person's problems. I already had plenty of my own to worry about, and had been handed another, and a whopper at that, by Miss Emmaline Castleton. "Um . . . can this chat wait until after the class is over? It's about time for it to begin."

"Yes. I suppose so. But *please* don't leave before I have a chance to speak with you. Please, Mrs. Majesty. It's *so* important."

Gertrude's tone of voice, which clearly expressed the desperation she'd already mentioned twice, made my blood run cold. Every now and then I wished people would take care of their own problems and leave me to my own. Her problems were important to her, I had no doubt; I wasn't so sure they would turn out to be important to me.

That however, was, I'm sure, a totally unchristian attitude, and I told myself I should be ashamed of myself. Scolding didn't help, and neither did it help when I reminded myself that Johnny Buckingham relied on prayer and I should probably do likewise. I still wished Gertrude would find herself another confidante.

The class went pretty well, in spite of the looming threat of Gertrude's conversation in which I didn't want to participate.

"Let's all turn to page ten, ladies," said I in the teacherish voice I'd cultivated, much as I'd cultivated my Rolly voice years earlier in my career.

"Today we're going to prepare scalloped meat. The first thing we need to do in this case is prepare approximately one cup of breadcrumbs. In order to do that, we will use stale bread and prepare the crumbs as we did when we made the chicken croquettes. This is yet another case in which stale bread need not be wasted." Did I sound like an authoritative cooking expert, or did I not?

After we've prepared our breadcrumbs by placing stale bread between two pieces of paper (each) pounding them into submission with whatever heavy object was at hand — I used a hymnal I'd confiscated from the sanctuary — Flossie passed out the cooked chicken.

"We need to chop our chicken now," I said with feigned confidence. This was the only part of the operation that frightened me, even though I'd managed to chop chicken in our kitchen at home. Still, there's not much a slice of stale bread can do to one if one wants to crush it. The chicken, however, needed to be chopped into little bits via the use of a large, sharp knife or cleaver. Aunt Vi had drilled me in the art, which she performed with the ease of long practice. I feared I'd chop off a finger or something worse. The knife was very sharp. And that sapient point needed to be conveyed to my students.

"I know we've discussed this before, ladies, but it's worth another mention. In order to chop meat safely," I said, quoting my aunt, "you need to make sure your knife is the proper size and very well honed. A dull knife is the worst implement you can use for this task. Even though it might sound as if it would be safer to use a blunt knife, it isn't. Dull knives can slip, and they can still, being knives and all, inflict severe wounds." I only knew that, of course, because Aunt Vi had told me so. Well, I'd always known that knives could cut one, but

I hadn't realized that dull knives were more dangerous than sharp ones, until Vi told me. The notion still didn't make a whole lot of sense to me, but I trusted my aunt.

"Mrs. Buckingham has secured the proper cutting utensils for each of you to use." I eyed Gertrude during this speech, hoping she didn't aim to stab me with her long, sharp knife — or cleaver — after class.

But that was silly. The poor thing was worried, not homicidal. Every now and then, I wished my imagination didn't take off and soar as much as it liked to do.

"And," I went on, "it's always best to use a wooden cutting board." Flossie passed out wooden cutting boards to the students. "Then you need to place your piece of meat on the board and, holding the knife like this" — I demonstrated, hoping I'd correctly remembered Aunt Vi's directions, which she'd given me several times over the past few days — "and chop like this."

It worked! I've seldom been so surprised in my life. Why, I could have chopped a whole side of beef if I'd been asked to do so. At least that's what it felt like at the time. God bless Vi. She was such a trooper to teach me this stuff. I held down that piece of chicken and chopped it up like a pro.

"Of course, tastes vary," I said, as if I knew

231

what I was talking about. "Some folks like their chicken chopped into fine little pieces, and others prefer a larger dice. I like to use smaller chunks." Actually, as you'd probably already figured out, I didn't care. Vi preferred a smaller dice, and as far as I was concerned at that point in time, Vi was Queen of the Culinary Arts. Therefore, wielding my knife as if I did this sort of thing every day, I chopped and chopped until I had a little mound of chicken bits. Boy, was I ever proud of myself!

"After you get your breadcrumbs ready and have your meat all chopped up, you need to butter your baking dish." At last we'd come to a part of the process I couldn't botch. Probably. Hopefully.

I buttered my baking dish. My students buttered *their* baking dishes.

"After we have our baking dishes prepared, we'll start filling them. Begin with a layer of chopped meat followed by a layer of breadcrumbs. You'll need to salt and pepper each layer as you go along, and drop dabs of butter on top of each layer. Keep layering until your dish is full. Your last layer should be breadcrumbs."

We layered and layered until our dishes were full. Lord, I loved these women. They were so good to me, and they all followed my directions as if they trusted me. Even Hilda did. Her attention and precision troubled me slightly, since I continued to believe she was German and not Swiss. Since I had a reputation as a German-hater to maintain, I really wanted to find fault with her. Unfortunately for me, I was unable to find a single character flaw to pounce upon and detest.

"When your dish is filled, beat an egg in a little bowl and add a cup of milk." I demonstrated, and the ladies followed my instructions like the good students they were.

"Then pour the milk-and-egg mixture over your scalloped meat, dab it with more dots of butter, and bake in a moderate oven for approximately one half hour."

When we all got our dishes into the big oven in the back of the room, preheated by the ever-helpful and vigilant Flossie Buckingham, we returned to our places and discussed yet more uses for dried bread. Fortunately, the students and the book were resourceful in that regard, since I definitely wasn't. We covered bread rusks, how to resuscitate stale bread, milk toast, and sprinkling the bottom layer of pie crust with breadcrumbs to ensure the bottom crust didn't get soggy. As if I'd ever made a pie in my life — or intended to make one in the future. Well, why should I, when we had Vi to cook for us?

After half an hour or so, having pursued the issue of what to do with stale bread, we traipsed back to the stove and withdrew our dishes. By gum, they looked quite nice! They smelled as if they tasted good, too. Another triumph brought to you by Daisy Gumm Majesty, the worst cook in the world. When people say wonders never cease, I think they mean me.

We sampled our scalloped meat (quite palatable, if not up to Vi's standards) and as we said our good-byes until the next Saturday, I braced myself to receive more confidences from Gertrude Minneke.

She remained behind while the other ladies filed out. They all thanked me and looked happy. When I glanced Gertrude's way after the last student left the room, she appeared troubled. Oh, goody. If she told me Eugene had been falsely accused of yet another murder, I was going to tell Sam, darn it. I don't care if I promised her I wouldn't. Flossie and I chatted for a bit at the door, and then Flossie, too, left the hall. Gathering my courage, I turned and smiled at Gertrude. She didn't smile back.

"Would you like to chat now?" I asked pleasantly.

"Yes, please," she said, her voice a subdued muffle.

"Would you like to sit here?" I gestured at two of the desks.

"Let's go outside to talk. Is that all right with you? I don't want anyone to overhear us."

Oh, dear. "Of course." Inwardly, I heaved a big sigh.

But I walked with her outside, where the Salvation Army had a little courtyard. Two benches had been set out there under a couple of big old oak trees, and we sat on one of the benches. It wasn't an especially comfortable place to sit, what with the seats being hard and cold, oak leaves plopping down on us and the wind picking up, but I didn't complain. What I wanted was to get this over with.

"Now, Miss Minneke, what can I do for you?"

"Get Eugene and me out of Pasadena."

My eyebrows soared and I gawked at her. "Do *what?*"

"Oh, Mrs. Majesty!" She burst into tears. Have I mentioned how much I dislike having people cry at me? Well, I do.

"But . . . but, Miss Minneke, how do you expect me to do that?"

She wiped her eyes with a hankie. "You

have an automobile, don't you?"

"Yes. It belongs to my entire family, though. It's not just mine."

"But you *have* one. That's the important point."

For her, maybe. "Um . . . I think I need to know a little more about what seems so important to you that you need to flee the city where you're getting so much help from Mr. and Mrs. Buckingham and the Salvation Army. It doesn't seem right to me that you should just up and go away. They took you on and sponsored you," I reminded her. "And you agreed to the deal they offered."

"I know. I know." She sounded miserable. As well she might. "But, you see, some of the awful people Eugene got mixed up with back East have suddenly shown up in Pasadena. Eugene is sure he saw the leader of the gang in town the other day."

The leader of the gang? Just who were these people Eugene used to hang around with, anyhow? I decided to ask. "Just who are these people, Miss Minneke? If Eugene is afraid of them, he ought to go to the police and make a clean breast of things."

"No! He can't do that. He'd be arrested if he went to the police, and then we'd never be able to prove he didn't do what they're saying he did."

So we were back to that scenario, were we? With Eugene and Gertrude trying to clear Eugene's name of a crime he was believed to have committed in New Jersey. From all the way across the country, in my fair city of Pasadena. That part of her story still didn't make any sense to me.

"Are you absolutely sure your brother had nothing to do with the . . . crime?" *Murder* sounded so ugly.

"Of course, I'm sure!"

Now she looked offended, which I considered nonsensical. "Miss Minneke, I can truly sympathize with your troubles, but you must understand my reservations. You may well be sure that your brother is an innocent man, but I have no way of knowing that."

"But I *told* you he didn't do it!"

"Yes, yes, I know you did. But your saying so doesn't necessarily make it so."

Her expression changed dramatically. Now she gazed upon me as she might have if I'd kicked her kitten. "You don't believe me?"

This time my sigh was entirely audible. "Listen to me, Miss Minneke. I believe *you* believe your brother is innocent of the heinous crime of which he is accused. But I don't know him the way you do. For all I know, you, a loyal sister, are looking at him

237

through rose-colored glasses. I've read about people who have refused to believe their loved ones committed terrible acts, yet their loved ones have been proven to have done the deeds of which they'd been accused. You might well be one of those people. I don't have any way of knowing the truth one way or the other."

She began to whimper softly.

"Besides," I went on, "my time isn't really my own. I have an invalid husband to care for, and a living to earn for the both of us. He was seriously wounded in the war and is unable to work, and my father has a bad heart condition, and *he* can't work. I can't just take off if I feel like it. I have too many people depending on me."

Silence descended upon us, much as those pointy oak leaves continued to do. At least she stopped whimpering.

At last Gertrude said, "Well . . . I guess I understand your reservations — although I *know* Eugene didn't kill anyone. I'm not looking at him through rose-colored glasses, believe me. I'm too much of a realist to do that."

Hmm. I didn't buy that one for an instant. I didn't say so, however.

"But . . . well, if you can't drive us to Los Angeles or San Diego, could you possibly

238

lend us some money?"

Good Lord. This was almost worse than driving the two of them out of the city to elude the coppers and New Jersey goons.

She began wringing her hands again. Shoot. "*Please*, Mrs. Majesty. It would mean so much to Eugene and me. And we'd pay you back. Truly, we would."

I was getting tired of this, darn it. My voice was a trifle tart when next I spoke. "I'm sure you would, and I'm also sure it would mean a good deal to you and your brother. But it would also mean breaking your agreement with the Salvation Army and with two of my own dear friends. It's not a matter of paying me back. If you didn't think you'd be able to abide by the contract you signed with the Salvation Army, you shouldn't have signed it in the first place."

"But it was the only chance we had. We learned of the opportunity through the Salvation Army in Trenton. They paid our way out here on the train, and we never *ever* guessed people would come after us."

"Then it's doubly important for you to keep your word," I said in my severest tone of voice.

She whimpered again. "I know. I hate deceiving people."

We sat there silently for a few moments, Gertrude biting her lower lip and me wishing myself elsewhere before she spoke again. "If . . . if I could get hold of some money from someone else, would you be willing to purchase train tickets for us?"

"Train tickets? Where would you go?"

"Oh, I don't know!" She sounded as desperate as she claimed to be. "It doesn't matter. We just need to get out of here."

"If you're determined to go — and I still don't think it would be honorable of you to do so — then why can't you buy your own train tickets? Why the elaborate charade?"

"Because they might be watching for us at the train station!" Her tone implied I ought to have known that already.

"Who's 'they,' in this context?" I asked drily.

"The criminals."

"Oh. Well. . . ."

"*Please*, Mrs. Majesty! This may be the only chance Eugene and I have."

Nuts. "The Salvation Army is giving you both a chance at a new life right here in Pasadena," I reminded her.

"I know. I know." She clearly didn't like being prompted to remember where her duty lay.

"They not only paid for your transportation, but they found housing and a job and training for the two of you. I think it would be. . . ." I hesitated, trying to select the right word. I wanted to use *immoral,* but didn't think Gertrude would appreciate my candor. I opted for *dishonest.* I supposed it amounted to the same thing, but it didn't sound quite so severe. "I think it would be dishonest of you to break your agreements with two Salvation Army churches."

Her tears started in earnest once more. "But we didn't *know* those horrid men would come after us, Mrs. Majesty! And Eugene is innocent! You're being terribly unfair."

I was being unfair? *I,* Daisy Majesty, whose only responsibility to this woman was to teach her how to cook with stale bread? I thought not. However, I couldn't find it in my heart to completely crush her. I stood and said, "I don't know, Miss Minneke. This whole scenario makes me very uncomfortable, as much as I'd like to help you. Let me think about it for a while."

She didn't appear happy, but she said, "All right. Thank you for thinking about it, anyway."

I drove home that day feeling pretty darned oppressed.

CHAPTER TWELVE

The next day, Sunday, I took the family for a nice ride up into the foothills after church and dinner. But not before I had to endure much questioning by Lucille Spinks about Sam Rotondo. Shoot.

"Do you know if he ever asks ladies out to movies, Daisy?" Lucy was buttoning up her choir robe as she asked the question.

Pulling my stole over my head, I said, "I don't know. He took my family out to a movie and dinner once. Want me to ask him?" I didn't want to ask Sam if he'd like to better his acquaintance with Lucille Spinks. For some reason, when it came to Sam, I still couldn't help but think of her as a rival. Idiotic, I know.

She blushed, for Pete's sake! "Oh, no! Well . . . would you mind?" She turned around and put her hands over her face. "Oh, I feel so silly!"

Would I mind? Yes, I would. "Of course I

242

wouldn't mind, Lucy."

In a way, it was both unkind and foolish of me to resent Lucy's interest in Sam. The war had deprived us of so many, many young men that there weren't a whole bunch of them left for the ladies who'd been left behind. Then again, some of the men who'd fought in Europe had come home with French or British brides, thus taking even more men away from the crop of females wanting to get married at home. The situation was tough, and I resolved to treat Lucy with compassion, even if she did want to take Sam away from Billy.

Besides that, it was entirely possible that Sam might want to get married again. In fact, when I thought about it, he might well be a lonely person. Why else would he be at our house so often? And at least Lucy was a nice person. If Sam had to marry somebody, Lucy seemed a likely and plausible choice.

She whirled around again and took my hands. "Thank you, Daisy. You know I had thought Marvin Halliday and I would marry, but he. . . ."

Oh, dear goodness. That's right. I finally recalled that Lucy's beloved had also been lost in the war. Cursed war. Cursed Kaiser. I squeezed her hands. "I know, Lucy. What a dismal aftermath, huh?"

Tears filled her eyes. "Dismal is a good word for it." And she let go of me to snatch her handkerchief and wipe her eyes.

Bah.

But it was a crisp, sunny November day, and we endured the church service. Also, everyone was looking forward to Thanksgiving, which was the following Thursday. I think Thanksgiving is one of my favorite holidays. Not only do we always have a wonderful meal, thanks to Aunt Vi, but my birthday would fall on the Wednesday after Thanksgiving. I'd be twenty-two, by gum! And Aunt Vi would bake a delicious meal and a lovely cake, and I'd get presents. I know it sounds childish, but I liked getting presents. Well, who doesn't?

I also appreciate Thanksgiving because it's the one day in the year when we all concentrate on our blessings rather than our burdens, and I regret to say I dwelt a lot on my many responsibilities in those days — more than I should have, I'm sure.

Not only that, but Thanksgiving hymns are some of the loveliest, in my opinion, second only to those dedicated to Christmas. I generally prefer Thanksgiving and Christmas hymns to Easter hymns, which tend to be gloomy because of Good Friday and all. The Sunday of which I write, the choir sang "Come Ye Thankful People, Come," which is one of my very favorites, and the organist truly outdid herself during the collection of the offering with a perfectly gorgeous medley of Thanksgiving music.

And then, after feasting on one of Vi's more delicious meals, we went for our Sunday drive.

In Southern California, we don't get the glorious fall leaves my father speaks of fondly — he's originally from Massachusetts — but the weather sure shone upon us that Sunday, even if our leaves turned more yellowish than red and orange. Except for the evergreens, of course, which remained . . . well, green. Sometimes in November we get horrible winds the newspapers call Santa Anas. They knock the oranges off both of our trees, and sometimes entire branches. More than one of the magnificent pepper trees on our street had been uprooted by a windstorm. I am also prone to get hideous headaches during windstorms. No evil winds marred our Sunday drive that day.

In Altadena, which is a little town just north of Pasadena, there is an extremely charming street called Santa Rosa. It's the town in which Mrs. Bissell, the dachshund breeder, lives, only she's a little north and east of Santa Rosa. The street is lined with great big deodar trees, and every time I drive up it, I think of Rudyard Kipling's *Under the Deodars*. Not that Kipling or his book has anything to do with this saga; I only mention it. Anyway, the long line of deodars on Santa Rosa originally lined the drive of Colonel F. J. Woodbury, who used to have a huge ranch up there and after whom a big east–west street in Altadena was named. Now Santa Rosa is lined not merely with deodars, but with huge, gorgeous houses, and it's still nice to drive up.

So we did. Drive up Santa Rosa Avenue that day, I mean, and we all enjoyed the beautiful fall day. Ma and Pa and Vi sat in the backseat so that Billy and I could sit together in the front street. I doubt that Billy would have cared much one way or the other. What he wanted was to be able to drive the machine himself, but he couldn't. He didn't complain, however, and the day was quite enjoyable. He held Spike on his lap, and Spike had his nose stuck out the window, his ears flapping gloriously in the breeze.

We didn't share a cross word all day long, wonder of wonders, even though I couldn't get the image of that cache of morphine syrup out of my mind's eye. But I didn't bring up the subject again with Billy. Not ever. Perhaps I should have. I don't know, and I suppose it's no good second-guessing oneself.

At any rate, the Monday following that lovely and peaceful Sunday, I got yet another frantic call from Mrs. Kincaid. Her wedding was to take place the following Sunday, and Billy and I were invited. I wanted to go, mainly because I'd get to see Harold Kincaid and Edie Applewood, my old school chum who, as I've already mentioned, worked as lady's maid for Mrs. Kincaid. Billy wasn't so keen on going, but he said he would. I wasn't counting on that, but I determined not to nag him. If he decided to go to the wedding, fine. If he didn't, well, I'd miss him, but that was fine, too. *I* sure intended to go. The reception was going to be held at the Valley Hunt Club, which was a fabulous place, and which I only ever got to see when rich people invited me.

This wedding of Mrs. Kincaid's to Mr. Pinkerton had garnered me oodles of bucks over the past several months, due to her nervousness about embarking on another marriage. I didn't think she needed to worry. Mr. Pinkerton seemed to be a genuinely fine gentleman. Not that one can always tell about things like that, of course.

But I'd known him slightly for years and years, and he'd always been pleasant and kind to me — and to Mrs. Kincaid, too. He was a heck of a lot nicer to her than her previous husband, the dastardly Eustace Kincaid, who was serving time in the state penitentiary — which was a good place for him in my considered opinion — for fraud and theft.

At any rate, after I finished cleaning up the breakfast dishes, I changed into one of my spiritualist outfits and set out for Mrs. Kincaid's, Ouija board in hand in the lovely little traveling bag I'd sewn for it years earlier.

That day, because Mrs. Kincaid had begun to annoy me a little and I didn't feel in the mood for anything perky, I selected a long-sleeved dress of dull gray wool with a dropped waistline and black trim. With my black shoes, handbag and coat, I looked like a widow woman in half-mourning. That was a fine look to achieve for a person in my profession.

Mrs. Kincaid didn't care what I looked like. She probably didn't even see me, she was so involved with her own petty problems. Well, I considered them petty. She certainly didn't. So I sat with her, pulled my Ouija board and accompanying planchette out of their carrying cases, set the board on the lovely mahogany coffee table in the drawing room, we put our fingers lightly on the planchette, and the planchette spelled out answers to Mrs. Kincaid's questions. The answers were the same as ever, mainly because the questions were the same as ever.

Billy has a point about how ridiculous it seems for people to ask the same things over and over and expect to get different answers.

After our session, I decided to see if I could find Edie, so I tiptoed up the back stairs and started looking through the chambers. I felt kind of like I'd broken into a royal castle or something, because there were so many rooms so beautifully furnished, but sure enough, I discovered Edie tidying up Mrs. Kincaid's brushes and combs in a perfectly gorgeous dressing room that led off a sitting room. Mrs. K's bedroom occupied another end of the suite of rooms dedicated to her sleeping and reading pleasure. She also had her own bathroom. I know for a fact, because Harold has told me as much, that there were two other suites of rooms in the upstairs of that house, I guess for Stacy and Harold himself before he moved out.

I'm not sure I'd like to live in a huge

house like that. I'd feel like I should invite another family or four to live with me.

I peeked around the corner and said, "My goodness, Edie, this place is fantastic."

She turned and spied me. "Ain't it grand?" she said with a broad grin. "I wouldn't mind living here."

"I thought you did live here."

"Well, we do, but we have quarters downstairs off the kitchen. Still, they're nice quarters, so I don't mind."

"I remember those quarters. They're like a little apartment, aren't they, with a sitting room and a bathroom and a bedroom. Very nice." I've often wondered why some people have so much and other people, some quite deserving, have so little, but I'm no philosopher and haven't come up with an answer that's satisfied me yet.

"They are very nice, and they're perfect for us. One of these days, Quincy and I want to start a family, but we're going to wait until he's saved up enough money to buy a house."

A family. That sounded so nice. I mean, I had a wonderful family, but it didn't include any children of my own. I had to settle for my siblings' children when they came to visit for holidays — which meant I'd see them the following Thursday. I looked forward to it.

I gave Edie a brief hug. "Is everything crazy around here, what with wedding preparations and everything?"

Edie rolled her eyes. "You have no idea." She hesitated, frowning, and then said, "Actually, you probably do, since she calls you all the time. I'll just be glad when it's all over."

"Are they going anywhere fancy on a honeymoon or something like that?"

"You betcha. They're going to Paris, France, and then they aim to go to Egypt, believe it or not, and take a trip down the Nile. Or maybe it's up the Nile. She told me, but I can't remember. But they're going to see all those old pyramids and stuff. She's bought more clothes than you can ever imagine, and I've hemmed and fitted all of them at least twice. Still, I don't mind. She's very nice to Quincy and me, even if she is a little . . . well, you know."

I did know. That reminded me of something I'd been meaning to ask Edie for a long time. "I thought Quincy was supposed to become a horse trainer for some racing stable or other." Edie's husband, Quincy Applewood, had been born in Nevada and worked on a real, live ranch before he moved to California. He even acted in a cowboy picture, but he broke his leg, which pretty much ended his picture career. He still loved working with horses, however, and Edie'd told me before that he was set to go to work training racehorses.

Edie shook her head. "He decided not to do that after all, when Mr. Pinkerton hired him to tend to his polo ponies."

I'm sure my eyes bulged. "Mr. Pinkerton plays *polo?*" I couldn't quite feature the plump, pleasant, pink Algernon Pinkerton swinging a mallet, or whatever those polo stick things are called, from the back of a galloping horse.

"He doesn't, but his sons do."

"He has *sons?*" Goodness gracious, I hadn't known that! Talk about wonders never ceasing!

"Two of 'em. They're kind of nice, like him, only taller and not so round."

"Well, I'll be darned. I didn't even know he'd been married before."

"Oh, sure. Mrs. Kincaid told me all about it. His wife died young, and he didn't remarry because he was so crushed at her passing. Well, until now, I mean."

"I'll be darned. How long will this trip to France and Egypt take, do you know?"

"A couple of months. She's putting me on board wages, but Quincy will keep getting paid his usual salary because he'll still tend Mr. Pinkerton's horses."

I'd read about board wages in detective novels set in England, but I didn't know we had them here in the United States, which is probably stupid of me. "It's good that you won't be without an income."

"Yeah, it is. Not that it matters a whole lot. We eat here and your aunt prepares the meals, so we won't starve, even if the meals won't be quite as elaborate during those two months as they are now." Edie grinned at me. "I'm trying to learn how to cook from your aunt, Daisy."

"You are? Me, too."

It was Edie's turn to have bulged-out eyeballs. "*You?* Good heavens, Daisy, I remember when you almost flunked that home-economics class because your hard-boiled eggs burned."

"So do I," I admitted glumly. "It's even worse than that, unfortunately, because Johnny Buckingham has me teaching a cooking class at the Salvation Army."

Edie's mouth dropped open and stayed that way until she started to laugh. And laugh. And laugh. I finally got sick of her amusement at my expense, so I said, "Well, I'm going down to see Vi. Maybe she'll have another hot cooking tip for me."

By this time, Edie's eyes had begun to drip with the power of her hilarity and she could only give me a feeble wave, so I hotfooted it down the back stairs, the same way I'd come up — the servants' stairs, that is to say — and on into the kitchen. My aunt was there, all right, patting some kind of dough around a big slab of what looked like roasted beef.

"Whatcha doing, Aunt Vi?"

"Good afternoon, Daisy. I'm preparing beef Wellington for dinner tonight."

Gee, she'd never prepared beef Wellington for us. "Oh? How come it's called beef Wellington?"

"I have no idea. I think it's named after some famous English statesmen or soldier or something like that."

"The Duke of Wellington? I remember reading about him in a history class. Isn't he the one who defeated Napoleon?"

"I have no idea whom he defeated, but it sounds like he's probably the one."

"What exactly makes up a beef Wellington, Vi?" I eyed her preparations with misgiving. "It looks like it might be too complicated for my cooking class."

Chuckling, she said, "It definitely is. And it's far too expensive for your cooking class, too. It's a sirloin of beef, roasted and smeared with liver pate, mushrooms and onions, then wrapped in a puff pastry crust, baked until the crust is done and served with horseradish sauce. I'm fixing asparagus to go with it, along with a clear soup, tomato aspic and roasted potatoes."

"Sounds yummy."

"Oh, it is." She shaped her dough some more and frowned. "Perhaps I should make it for the family one of these days. Perhaps at Easter."

That notion perked me right up. "Sounds like a good plan to me."

She gave me a small, ironic smile. "Anything you don't have to cook sounds good to you, Daisy Majesty."

"I sure can't deny that, although I haven't erred too terribly in my cooking class so far, thanks to you."

"I'm happy to help, dear. I think you'd be a good cook if you concentrated more."

That was what I loved best about my family. They were always happy to help anyone who needed help, and they always thought the best of everyone, even when it was me. "Thanks, Vi," I said humbly and meant it sincerely.

She frowned down at her dough. "I don't know, though. Beef Wellington is pretty expensive. I don't think we could afford to feed the entire family, including Daphne and Walter and their spouses and children, if I served beef Wellington."

I had what I considered a brilliant idea. "You could make it for my birthday." Then I grinned slyly at her.

She laughed again. "Maybe I'll do that."

"I'll pay for the sirloin of beef," I told her as an encouragement.

"You shouldn't have to pay for your own birthday dinner, Daisy Majesty."

"Heck, I don't mind. It'll be my birthday present to myself."

Vi smiled, although I noticed a little sadness lurking around the edges of the smile. Because her only son had been killed in the war, she'd be alone in the world if it weren't for the fact that she had us. That war had done so much damage to so many people. But I didn't want to dwell on it. Instead, I watched my aunt.

She'd finished wrapping the roast in the pastry and picked up her rolling pin. She rolled out another hunk of dough and began cutting leafy shapes from the rolled dough with a sharp little knife and setting them aside.

"What are those for?"

"I'm going to decorate the roast with a vine pattern. It'll look pretty that way."

"Oh, my, that sounds very fancy." I squinted at the dough leaves and back at the rolled roast. "Do they stick all by themselves?"

"With a little help from a dab of water. Then I'm going to brush an egg wash over the whole thing right before I bake it."

"An egg wash? What's an egg wash?"

"An egg beaten with a little water and brushed over the pastry. Cooks use egg washes on lots of pastries."

Good grief. That sounded like a whole lot of work for something that was going to be carved up and eaten in probably a matter of minutes. This demonstrates yet one more way in which rich folks are different from the rest of us. I mean, I don't mind spending a lot of time sewing for my family and myself, but when you sew something, it lasts for more than a single wearing. I aimed to make Christmas shirts for all of us beginning as soon as Thanksgiving was over. It was fun, when we got together on Christmas Eve, to have everyone wearing the same patterned shirt. At least it was fun for me, and the family didn't complain. Well, Billy did, but he always complained about everything, so his opinion didn't count.

"Did you get a call from Mrs. Kincaid to do a reading today?" Aunt Vi asked as she started pasting leaves onto the dough clinging to the beef.

"Yes." I sighed. "She's sure in a state about her wedding, isn't she?"

"She is indeed. Marriage is a big step for her. You know how her first one ended."

Boy, did I ever. "I remember all too well."

Aunt Vi shook her head. "Once bitten, twice shy, I guess is the expression to describe poor Mrs. Kincaid's nerves these days."

"But Mr. Pinkerton is nothing at all like Mr. Kincaid."

"And thank the good Lord for that," said Vi firmly.

I added my own "Amen" to her sentiment and moseyed out the back door to climb into our Chevrolet and head to the library to return my family's crop of last week's books and check out some more.

Because I was wildly curious about Gertrude Minneke and her brother, even though I wasn't longing to see her again anytime soon because I'd have to disappoint her about the money and train-ticket thing, I set out to search for her after I'd selected my books — *Dark Hollow* and *The House of Whispering Pines,* by Anna Katharine Green and *The Sleuth of St. James's Square,* by Melville Davisson Post. I actually wanted to pick up some more books before I left the library. Billy had asked me to look for some more Westerns, even if they weren't by Zane Grey, and Pa was finished with *The Beautiful and the Damned.* With a grimace of distaste, he had given it to me to return to the library and asked me to pick up something more compatible with his view of the world.

Which brings up an interesting point. Well, I think it's interesting. Probably other people won't, but I'm going to say it here anyway. We Gumms stick together on our dislike of shallow people with more money than sense and no awareness of social responsibility. I can stand working for Mrs. Kincaid and Mrs. Bissell, both of whom probably had more money than was good for them, because they were good-hearted people who did their best to help other people, even if they didn't quite understand how the rest of the world actually got on. For instance, Mrs. Bissell was a big supporter of the Humane Society in Pasadena, and Mrs. Kincaid gave lots of money and other stuff to the poor, even if she didn't understand how anyone could be poor.

F. Scott Fitzgerald's people, who are well set up in the world as a rule, all seemed to be suffering from massive cases of ennui for no good reason that I could discern. Heck, our next-door neighbors' boy, Pudge Wilson, had a bigger sense of responsibility to his fellow beings than the people in Fitzgerald's books. At least he did a good deed every day for the sake of his scouting group. Generally he tried to get it out of the way early so he didn't have to worry about being good for the rest of the day, but at least he tried.

Where was I? Oh, yes. I aimed to pick up some more books, in other words, but the ones I already had were heavy enough to be lugging all over the library, so I decided to look for Westerns and stuff after I'd found Gertrude.

But I didn't find her. Because I was still curious, I asked Miss Petrie if she knew where Gertrude was.

"Gertrude Minneke?" Miss Petrie said, looking a little startled that anyone would be asking her about a library page. "I believe Miss Minneke is out for the day. Someone said she telephoned to say she was sick."

"Oh, I'm sorry to hear that."

"What's your interest in Miss Minneke, Mrs. Majesty? Do you know her from somewhere?"

Was it my imagination, or did Miss Petrie have a certain look on her face? I couldn't quite place it, but it seemed to me that it was a combination of suspicion and dislike. It was, as usual, probably my imagination. "No, I don't really know her well. I'm helping out a friend on Saturdays at the Salvation Army, and Miss Minneke is one of my . . . er, she's one of the people who joins in the effort."

For the life of me, I couldn't take one more person laughing at me for telling her I taught a cooking class. And Miss Petrie didn't even know what a terror I was in the kitchen.

I swear, her expression cleared. "Ah. I see. Yes, I understand Miss Minneke has taken advantage of a program offered by the Salvation Army. The library has hired, I believe, three people through their auspices."

"The Salvation Army is a great organization," I said loyally.

"Indeed."

Miss Petrie didn't seem as thrilled with the Salvation Army's good works as I. Curious, I asked, "You don't seem to care much for Miss Minneke, Miss Petrie. Or am I wrong about that?"

She hesitated for a moment or two, then said slowly, "It's not so much that I don't care for her. I . . . just get a funny feeling from her."

A funny feeling? "Um, I'm not sure I understand."

Miss Petrie heaved a sigh. "I'm not sure I do, either. Miss Minneke is always polite, and she does her work well. Perhaps it's that brother of hers. He comes in to fetch her after work sometimes, and he doesn't appear to be an upright individual to me. Although, really, I suppose I shouldn't say that, since I don't know the young man at all, and it's not right to judge people if you don't know them."

"I suppose it isn't, although I understand what you mean." Perhaps Eugene wasn't as innocent as Gertrude wanted to believe him. Miss Petrie had always seemed a logical, eminently sane person to me; I doubt that she made unfavorable snap judgments about people very often.

Since I couldn't very well tell her about Gertrude and Eugene's problems, I toddled off to search out more books and tried to forget about Gertrude.

Such blessed forgetfulness was not to be mine. I kept picturing Gertrude in my mind's eye, sneaking in disguise to the train station on South Raymond Avenue and being captured, tied up and flung into the rear seat of a big black car by a bunch of big, burly thugs from back East. Shoot.

As I was running through that, and similar scenarios in my mind's eye, all having to do with Gertrude being punished for her brother's sins, I managed to get my hands on *Main Street* by Sinclair Lewis — which I suspected Pa wouldn't like much, either — *Tarzan the Untamed, A Princess of Mars* and *The Gods of Mars,* by Edgar Rice Burroughs for Billy. Then, because I didn't think Pa was going to care for the Sinclair Lewis book, I poked around on the shelves until I found *The Path of the King* and *The Thirty-Nine Steps* by John Buchan. For myself, I added *The Man in Grey* by Baroness Orczy, and *The Devil's Paw* by E. Phillips Oppenheim, and I left the library burdened, but happy with my choices.

Chapter Thirteen

I was right about Pa and *Main Street,* but he really liked *The Thirty-Nine Steps.* Billy was pleased with the Edgar Rice Burroughs books, too. He loved *Tarzan* in particular, probably because Tarzan could do all sorts of things Billy couldn't do any longer. Poor Billy. Then there was my cooking class. I honestly don't think I had an easy moment for the entire seven weeks that class lasted. But there were only two classes left, thank God.

For next Saturday's lesson, I decided to prepare a dessert. We hadn't made a dessert before. Unfortunately, most of the recipes in *Sixty-Five Delicious Dishes* required that the desserts, mainly puddings, be steamed for hours, and we didn't have hours to use the Salvation Army's stove. We had one hour, and I sure as anything didn't want to prolong my own agony. I don't know if my students felt the same way.

Anyhow, I decided on a recipe even though I didn't know how to pronounce it, and still don't: Arme Ritter. I decided, for no particular reason, that it was French, so I pronounced it with a French accent. It was basically French toast — which I knew about because Aunt Vi served it for breakfast every now and then — but spiced up with cinnamon and sugar, and served with fruit preserves. I thought I probably couldn't kill that one, even with a stick. Vi agreed with me.

So, that decision made, I called Flossie to tell her to provide eggs, milk, cinnamon, sugar and fruit preserves and then thought some more.

In fact, I wracked my brain (which hurt) to think of a bang-up dish for my cooking students to fix on our last — hallelujah! — class together. Then I took a deep breath and decided to tackle the pea castle. One of the students had asked if we could make it, and I saw no *real* reason not to, as long as Vi could help me figure out what a bread croute was, and show me how to build the castle. There's supposed to be a little upside-down V over the u in that word, but I don't know why. The recipe didn't really require a whole lot of cooking, since I could ask Flossie to boil up some eggs and have them ready for the class on that final Saturday along with some milk, butter, peas and flour. It occurred to me to write the Fleischmann Company and ask them why they'd named such an elegant-looking dish something as prosaic as Eggs and Green Peas.

To be on the safe side, I asked Vi to help me a couple of weeks in advance. No sense taking chances, after all. Bless Vi's heart, she did.

After several attempts, Aunt Vi finally managed to teach me the rudiments of making a bread croute, which is a lump of bread that's been hollowed out and then cut around the upper edges with a sharp knife so that it resembles a castle's crenellations. If that makes any sense. Once you've turned the bread lump into a castle tower, you fry it in hot fat until it's golden brown. That was the hard part for me, since almost everything I fry burns to a crisp.

"All you need to do is concentrate, Daisy," Vi told me sternly. "The reason you burn things is that you lose interest and your mind wanders. You have to keep your mind on your work."

"My mind never wanders when I'm sewing," I said meekly in my own defense.

"Exactly. That's what I'm telling you. What you need to do is expend the same concentration on cooking as you do on sewing."

But I liked to sew. I *hated* to cook. Cooking bored the socks off me. I thought about pointing that out to Vi, but figured I'd be better off not doing so.

"Just keep your mind on what you're doing, and you'll be fine. See?" Vi said, happily pointing at our frying bread croute. "It's turning a beautiful golden brown." She turned it with some kitchen tongs she used, and by gum, she was right.

The silly thing truly *was* turning a beautiful golden brown. With luck, maybe Vi's lesson in creating bread castles would remain with me for two weeks, until that longed-for last Saturday class, although I expected I'd have to take several more lessons from her to finally entrench the technique in my thickish head.

Sam had come over during my lesson. I learned that obnoxious fact when he rolled Billy and his chair into the kitchen.

"Whatcha doing, Daisy?" Billy asked. He never sounded that cheerful when it was just me in the room with him. I was used to it.

Sam just stood there, frowning. As usual.

"Vi's teaching me how to make a bread croute for my last class at the Salvation

267

Army. After the croute's made, we'll fill it with eggs and peas and top it off with a white sauce." Whatever a white sauce was. Vi hadn't come to that part yet.

"A what?"

"A white sauce."

"No, I meant that other word."

"A croute? I think it's a French word."

"What's it mean?"

Billy would have to ask, wouldn't he?

"I don't know. Fried-bread pea holder?"

"It means crust, Daisy," said Vi, laughing.

"Oh." I felt really silly.

"I thought you took French in high school," she added, to put the crown on my discomfort.

"Spanish," I said. And I had retained a very little bit of Spanish, too. I'd had a grudge against French ever since my cousin Eula took it in high school and paraded all over the place spouting French phrases as if she were something special and the rest of us were stupid. That's the reason I took Spanish in school. Which reminded me of something. "Do you know how to fix Mexican food, Vi?"

She frowned as she again turned our croute in the fat so it wouldn't burn on any particular side. "I've never tried to fix Mexican food, but I don't think it's complicated to do."

"I love going to Mijares," I said, feeling slightly dreamy. Not having to cook the food I eat does that to me. Mijares was a fairly new Mexican restaurant located on Palmetto Drive, not too far from our house, and they served really tasty stuff. Mind you, I didn't eat there often, since I didn't throw my hard-earned money away. Besides, with Vi to cook for us, why would we dine out?

Still frowning, Vi said, "I think you need special ingredients for Mexican cooking, Daisy. Like chili peppers and so forth. I don't know where one would get those sorts of things in Pasadena."

Gee, the Mijares people sure seemed to find them, and probably nearby. I didn't say so. Restaurateurs probably had access to stuff the rest of humanity didn't. Kind of like rich people.

Sam said, "How'd you all like to go to Mijares with me one of these days?"

We all turned to look at him, and he smiled. He had a nice smile when he used it, which wasn't often.

"Hey, Sam, that would be great," said Billy enthusiastically. The only time he was enthusiastic was when Sam suggested something. I tried not to take it personally, although it was hard not to.

269

"But . . ." I started, but Sam interrupted me.

"We could go to dinner and a movie," Sam suggested. "Like we did last time."

"Better and better," said Billy. Crumb.

Several months earlier, Sam had taken us all to eat Chinese and then to a movie. We'd all had a good time. Even me, by gum, although we'd been Sam's company. Nevertheless, I didn't think it was a good idea.

"I've wanted to try that Mexican place for a long time," said Sam.

"But . . ." I tried again.

"How about this week?" asked Sam.

"I'd love it," said my husband.

I cleared my throat. "But wouldn't it be awfully expensive, Sam?" I was always thinking about money in those days. Everyone was. We were pretty comfortable, thanks to Aunt Vi and Ma and me, who all worked, but as I've already mentioned, we didn't toss money around by going out to eat very often.

"I don't have anyone else to spend money on," said Sam, and he shrugged. "And I like the company."

It was one of the few times I'd felt a modicum of sympathy for Sam Rotondo. But he was right. He didn't have any family. His wife was dead, his folks were still in

New York and, basically, about all he had in the way of friends were Billy and Pa.

Which reminded me of Lucille Spinks. My better and bitter feelings warred with each other for a few seconds and, much against my will, my better feelings won the battle. Therefore, I said, "Say, Sam, would you be interested in letting Lucille Spinks come along with us?" Then it occurred to me that it wasn't nice to invite people to somebody else's party, and I said hastily, "I'll be happy to pay for her meal and movie."

Sam squinted at me. "Who's Lucille Spinks?"

Oh, brother. Attempting to keep my temper, I said, "You've met her several times now, Sam. She's the lady I sang the duet with at church a few weeks ago, and she's come to our house a couple of times while you were here."

He thought about it for a minute, then said, "Oh, yes. I think I remember her."

Sheesh. This didn't sound good for Lucy. Unless Sam was playing some sort of deep game. I eyed him hard for a minute, but didn't notice any trace of cunning on his features. But then, no one ever noticed a trace of anything on Sam's countenance. The Great Stone Face. That was Sam Rotondo.

Sam went on, "You don't need to pay for her. I'll be happy to treat the bunch. Sort of a pre-Thanksgiving feast. After all, you're always feeding me."

Well, that was true.

"That would be so kind of you!" Vi exclaimed. Poor Vi *never* got to eat out.

I steeled my nerves. "Yes, Sam, it is. Thank you. When would you like to do this?"

He shrugged again. "Well, since Thanksgiving is Thursday, and most restaurants are closed on Monday, which is today, how about tomorrow? Tuesday?"

I looked at Vi. She looked back at me. I glanced at Billy. He nodded. Pa was out walking Spike, but Pa was always agreeable to just about anything, and Ma would just be glad she didn't have to wash dishes.

"Well . . . sure. Thanks, Sam. I'll call Lucy. Maybe she can come over here, so we don't have to pick her up."

Sam had begun to frown. After about five seconds, I thought I knew why.

"Oh, I forgot about how many of us there are!" I slapped my forehead. "How about we take two cars? We don't need to take Billy's chair." I eyed my husband with misgiving. The last time we'd gone out, Sam and Pa had helped Billy walk into the Chinese restaurant, but that was before his illness last February. He was a good deal weaker now.

Billy understood my thoughts. "I'm sure Sam and Pa can help me get into the restaurant, Daisy." He didn't sound angry or even resigned. He just sounded as though it was a logical idea. Which it was, but generally Billy's logic was clouded by bitterness. Not that I blamed him. I'd be bitter too, if I were in his shoes. Or his wheelchair.

"Sure we can," Sam said heartily. "Tomorrow it is, then. Should be fun." He looked at me. "Can you think of a movie for us to go to after dinner?"

"I'll be happy to, Sam. Thank you. This is very nice of you." I hated thanking Sam Rotondo for anything, but he was being awfully generous now, and I appreciated it.

In fact, I decided on the spot, I'd reward him by having Lucille get to the restaurant in his car and take my family in ours. Especially if we didn't take Billy's wheelchair, we could all squeeze into the Chevrolet. My heart gave a small spasm. I think that was because of the Billy–Sam connection.

But, heck, even if Sam and Lucy did fall in love and get married, he wouldn't desert Billy. I think I've mentioned before that I didn't give Sam credit for much, but I did know that he was a true and loyal friend to my Billy.

Therefore, after we'd dined on chicken and little pea castles — which were quite tasty and filling — and Ma and I had washed and dried the dishes, I picked up the day's *Pasadena Star News* and browsed the moving pictures. By the way, Ma was ecstatic about our promised treat. She loved going to the flickers.

Oh, boy, there was a lot to choose from. We could see *The Kid,* with Charlie Chaplin, which would be fun. Or we could see *The Four Horsemen of the Apocalypse,* which had Rudolph Valentino in it. Everyone was talking about Rudolph Valentino, and I'd kind of wanted to see him dance the tango with that French lady he was supposed to be having the affair with — in the movie, not in real life — but the picture took place during the war, and I didn't want to remind Billy of that accursed time. Harold Kincaid told me that Valentino dies a hero's death in the picture, which in some ways seemed a kinder fate than my Billy suffered from that conflict.

Harold had cried at the end, he told me, and that was enough for me. I nixed *The Four Horsemen of the Apocalypse.*

Hmmm. What else was there? Ooooh.

There was a new Valentino picture showing at the Academy: *The Sheik.* Oh, boy, wouldn't I like to see *that!* But it would probably be better to see that one with Lucy or Edie. Except Edie was married now and never went anywhere without Quincy. She might make an exception for Rudolph Valentino. I decided to shelve *The Sheik,* too.

That left *The Kid* at the Crown. Well, that was all right. It was supposed to be a good picture, and the theater was relatively close to the restaurant. I glanced up from the newspaper. Billy, Pa and Sam were playing their ten-thousandth game of gin rummy, Ma had her nose stuck in Billy's Tarzan book, and Vi snoozed in a chair in front of the fire that Sam had kindled for us. He could be helpful when he wanted to be, I guess.

I cleared my throat. Everyone turned to look at me — except Vi, who continued to snooze. "Is *The Kid,* with Charlie Chaplin, all right with everyone?"

"Sounds great to me," said Billy. It was one of the few times he'd agreed with me for weeks and weeks.

"Okay by me," said Sam.

"Sounds good," said Pa.

"That sounds lovely, dear," said Ma. She

gave me a happy smile. "I do enjoy a good comedy."

"What time does the movie start?" asked Sam. It was a sensible question and one I should have thought of myself.

"Let me look." I buried my head once more in the paper, and looked up again. "Seven o'clock."

Sam cocked his head to one side for a minute. "Then why don't I pick you up at five. We'll have an early dinner, and be out in time to catch the picture. Then nobody will be up too late, since some of us have to work the next day."

Boy, that was almost tactful! I'd never given Sam Rotondo credit for tact before. He was sure never tactful to me. "That's great, Sam. I'll go call Lucy."

So I hied myself to the kitchen and dialed Lucille Spinks's number. She was overjoyed with the notion of going to dinner and a picture with Sam, even though we Gumms and Majestys were going to tag along.

"Thank you so much, Daisy!"

"You're welcome, Lucy." Because I couldn't seem to help myself, I added, "But remember that Detective Rotondo might not be fully recovered from his wife's death yet." Gee, just a month or so ago, I was telling Lucy exactly the opposite. I was beginning to think there was something seriously wrong with me.

She sobered instantly. "I know, Daisy. I'll be kind to him."

Kind to him? Good heavens. "Fine, then. Say, could you get over here at maybe four-thirty? Then you can ride with Sam to the restaurant, and I can drive my family in our car."

"Oh, Daisy, would you really do that for me?" She was positively breathless.

"Sure," said I, feeling noble for no good reason.

So the next afternoon, Lucille Spinks arrived at our house at precisely four-thirty. The afternoon was a chilly one, and she wore a smart skirt-and-shirtwaist ensemble of prunella cloth, which was all the rage at the time. Her coat looked new, and I wondered if she'd bought it especially for the evening. Except that she was still kind of tall, skinny and rangy and had rabbity teeth, she looked swell, and I told her so. Well, I didn't mention the tall and rabbity part.

She executed a little twirl in the living room. "Thanks, Daisy. You always wear the most wonderful clothes. I thought I'd try to look good, too."

I did? Interesting. "I make all my clothes,

Lucy. Thanks for thinking they're wonderful."

"Do you really? I guess I didn't know that." She eyed me speculatively. "You know, if you ever give up spiritualism, you can go in for dressmaking. I could keep you busy all by myself."

Good heavens. "Thanks for the flattering offer, Lucy, but I think spiritualism pays better."

She heaved a huge sigh. "I suppose it does. I make my clothes, too, for the most part, but when it comes to anything fancy, I'm afraid I have to hire someone."

"Doesn't your father mind spending the money?" I asked, perhaps not tactfully, but I was curious.

"Not really. He says he's happy to support me until I get married." She heaved a huge sigh this time, and her face took on a glum aspect. "If I *ever* get married. There are so few men our age left."

My sigh joined hers. "Too true."

She brightened. "But you look swell, Daisy. I love your frock."

"Thank you." It was an old dress I'd worn a couple of hundred times, a dark-blue jersey, but it was comfy and warm, and went well enough with my black coat and other accoutrements.

She leaned toward me and whispered, "Is he here yet?"

"Who? Oh, Sam?"

She rolled her eyes. "Yes, dear. Detective Rotondo. Isn't that a queer name, though?"

"Sam?"

"No! Rotondo, for heaven's sake."

"Oh." I thought about it as I hung Lucy's coat on the coat tree.

Did I forget to mention that this conversation was constantly being interrupted by shrill, rapturous barks from Spike? Well, it was. Fortunately, Lucy liked dogs, so she didn't mind. However, in order to shut him up, after I hung her coat, I picked him up. He was ecstatic and Lucy petted him, so that was all right.

"Well?" Lucy prodded.

"I don't suppose it's terribly odd, at least not for a person from New York City, where there are lots of other Italians. We don't have so many of them out here, I guess." I mused for another second and a half. "I suppose it does sort of bring to mind the word *rotund,* which Sam isn't."

"Yes, it does, and no, he isn't."

I could practically hear her little heart pitter-pattering in her bosom. Poor Lucy. I didn't tell her that Sam kept forgetting who she was, and that I truly didn't hold out much hope for her making a match of it with him, although the notion of such a match still worried me some.

However, a knock came at the door just then, Spike tried to leap out of my arms — I didn't let him — and I went to answer the knock. Sam. I stepped back, and he entered our house to see Lucille Spinks simpering at him.

After a moment, which I could swear he spent trying to figure out who she was, he said, "Good evening, Miss . . . uh. . . ."

"Lucille Spinks," I hissed as close to his ear as I could get.

"Of course. Good evening, Miss Spinks. How nice that you could join us."

"Thank you," said Lucy, a note of worship in her voice.

I feared for the evening. Or at least for Lucy.

"Is that Sam?" came a voice from the hall, and Billy rolled himself into the living room. "Hey, Sam, I'm really looking forward to this." He spotted Lucille. "How-do, Miss Spinks."

"Good evening, Mr. Majesty."

"Gee, guys, when did you become so formal?" I asked, astonished at the Mister-and-Miss thing. We'd gone all through school together, for Pete's sake. Neither of them answered.

"Hey, Billy. How are you doing?" Sam asked my spouse.

"Pretty good, all things considered."

I surveyed my husband as the rest of my family crowded into the living room, ready for a night of fun and fellowship — which worked out nicely, the season being one for thanksgiving and all.

As far as I could tell, Billy didn't look pretty good. He still looked pale and pasty and unhealthy, which he was. My heart gave one of its gigantic spasms. Oh, how I wished I could help him.

Since I couldn't, I decided to do my best for Lucy. "Say, Lucy, could you ride with Sam? Our car isn't big enough for all of us."

"I think I can fit everyone in my Hudson," Sam said, frowning. He would. As uncooperative as ever, Sam Rotondo.

"Oh, it would be such a tight fit," I said lightly. "Let's take both machines."

He eyed me suspiciously. "Well. . . ."

"Good," I said. "Then it's settled."

It took some maneuvering to get Billy into the automobile without his chair, but we managed. Sam helped him, then turned and said in a low voice, "What are you trying to do, Daisy? If you're trying to set me up with —"

281

Bother. I honestly didn't think he'd catch on, since I'd never believed him to be a man of particularly keen perception. On the other hand, he was a detective, so perhaps I was wrong. "I'm not trying to do anything, Sam Rotondo, except get us all to the movies."

"I don't even know that woman."

"For heaven's sake, you've met her three or four times now!"

"Cripes," he muttered, and stomped over to his Hudson.

I did notice, however, that he was courtesy itself to Lucille. He opened the door for her, smiled, and said something to whatever she'd said to him, and then he went to the driver's side. He shot me one last severe glance before climbing into his car and slamming the door.

So I got into our machine. Billy said, "It'll never work, Daisy. I don't think Lucille is Sam's type."

"Oh," I said. "Well, at least I tried."

Billy shook his head. Ma said something about not interfering in other people's business. Vi said she hadn't realized what a matchmaker I was. Pa only laughed.

God bless my father.

CHAPTER FOURTEEN

Dinner at Mijares was wonderful. I had something called tamales, which were . . . well, I'm not sure what they were, but they were very tasty. I'm also not sure what everyone else ate, but they all seemed to enjoy whatever it was. I noticed Vi inspecting her meal closely, as if she were trying to discern what went into the various dishes, and it occurred to me that I needed to drop in at Grenville's Books and see if I could find a book on Mexican cookery for her. I'd never seen one there, but as you must have guessed by this time, I didn't look for cookbooks on a regular basis.

I did suffer a start, though, when I saw Eugene Minneke busing tables. I almost said something to my dining companions, but recalled Sam's interest in the ever-vanishing Gertrude in time to stop myself. I did offer Eugene a sweet smile from across the room, but he only scowled back. Hmm.

What, if anything, did that unpleasant expression mean? Probably nothing, although I could discern no reason to be scowled at by the fellow. Shoot, I hadn't yet even told his sister I wasn't going to help them escape from Pasadena. That jolly task would be mine on Saturday. Oh, joy.

Anyhow, I no longer felt the least bit guilty about not attempting to assist the Minneke siblings to run away from their responsibilities and/or the people who chased them. I'd begun to harbor severe doubts about Gertrude and her brother. Anyway, their problems were in no way mine, even when I considered assisting them in the most altruistic light possible. If I abetted them in their flight from Pasadena, I'd be helping them turn their backs on an obligation, not merely to the Salvation Army, but to my dear friends Johnny and Flossie Buckingham.

So there. I had a mad urge to stick my tongue out at Eugene, but quelled it, thank God.

However, I didn't allow Eugene to spoil my evening. Dinner was delicious, and the flicker was funny, and we all had a very good time. Even Billy.

I don't think Sam was elated at having to drive Lucy home all by himself, but I figured he was a big boy and could handle the job. Heck, he dealt with criminals all the time, didn't he? How difficult could it be to deal with a nice young lady for one tiny little evening?

Before I climbed into bed, Billy said, "I don't think your devious plot worked, Daisy. I got the feeling Sam was unimpressed with Lucy."

"I'm afraid you're right," I said upon a sigh. Maybe it was a yawn. "I did it as a favor to Lucy. She fancies Sam. Or thinks she does."

"Poor Lucy," said Billy, snuggling under the blankets and getting as comfortable as it was possible for him to get.

"Poor Lucy," I agreed. "She was really hoping Sam was the fellow for her."

I was asleep as soon my head hit the pillow.

Thanksgiving Day turned out to be perfect. My sister Daphne and her two little girls (and her husband Daniel) drove all the way from Arcadia, and Walter and his wife Jeanette made the trip from Los Angeles, which took them a long time. They aimed to spend the night, since it would take them so long to get home again after dinner. As his family virtually no longer existed, Billy had adopted mine as his, and he seemed to enjoy himself with my siblings and Polly and Peggy, my sister's girls, who were five and seven respectively. Fortunately for Daphne, Daniel's family lived in the state of Washington, so there was no quibbling about at whose house holidays were celebrated.

The dinner itself was, as you can well imagine, perfectly splendid. If there's anything I like better than turkey, stuffing, potatoes, gravy and all the trimmings, I don't know what it is. Well, except for the rest of the stuff Vi cooks. We were so very fortunate to have her living with us!

Naturally, Sam Rotondo had been invited to dine at our house. He arrived with a big bouquet of flowers for Ma and Aunt Vi, which even I had to admit was a nice gesture on his part. He got along like a house on fire with Walter, who had flown airplanes during the war. They traded stories, and Billy joined in, and so did Pa, and they laughed and laughed. I don't have any idea what they found to laugh at about that hideous conflict, but they were men, and men are an odd lot.

I was in the kitchen with Ma, Daphne, Jeanette and Aunt Vi, madly whipping cream for the two pumpkin pies Vi had baked for dessert, when I heard a perfect uproar coming from the living room, where everyone had retired after eating too much turkey and so forth.

"What on earth are they doing now?" asked Ma. She had an indulgent smile on her face, so I could tell she was glad the family was having an enjoyable holiday. I agreed. As far as I was concerned, laughter beat the other stuff hollow.

"I don't know," said I truthfully.

And then Walter, laughing as if he were about to bust, staggered into the kitchen, holding his stomach, tears streaming from his eyes. We all looked at him in alarm.

"Tell me it isn't true!" said he, still hooting with revelry.

"Tell you what isn't true?" I asked, although I was getting a glimmer. And I aimed to pound whoever had told on me.

"Tell me *you're* not teaching a cooking class!"

He couldn't contain his mirth and remain standing, so he flopped into one of the kitchen chairs, covered his face with his hands, and darned near howled with glee.

Still beating the heavy cream, I frowned one of the biggest frowns of my life at my once-adored brother. "It's not funny," I grumbled. I'm sure he couldn't hear me.

"*You!* Good gravy, Daisy, I remember

when you tried to make breakfast for me after I came back from the war!" Again, he collapsed in merriment.

"At least I tried," I said with whatever remnants of dignity I could summon.

"Stop it, Walter. You're being terribly unkind."

I knew I liked Jeanette for a reason. I smiled at her to let her know I appreciated her support.

Walter threw out an arm and drew his wife onto his lap. "You don't know Daisy's history with the art of cooking," he said, after he gained a modicum of control over his hilarity.

Darn it, I was tired of people laughing at me for teaching that stupid class! "So far," I said, aiming a deadly glare at my brother, "the class has been quite successful. We haven't ruined a single dish we've made. And *I'm* the teacher." I felt like adding "So there" to my speech, but restrained myself.

"That's right, Walter. You're being most unfair to Daisy. She's trying very hard to make this class a success, both for herself and for her students, who are all ladies in need of a helping hand."

Have I mentioned how much I love my aunt Vi? Well, I do.

I nodded.

Ma added some powdered sugar and a dash of vanilla to the cream, and I continued beating it. I'd rather have taken a baseball bat to my brother and beat him, so I was glad my hands were busy beating the cream.

"Yes, Walter," Ma said. "Daisy's class has been very successful so far, and all the dishes she's brought home have been more than tasty. They've been wonderful."

I love my mother, too.

Jeanette, who was blushing rosily after such an overt display of affection from her husband, struggled to release herself from his grip. "Yes, Walter. You're not being fair to Daisy. Even if she isn't the world's best cook, she's trying awfully hard. Besides, she has so many other talents, you really shouldn't tease her about cooking. Why, she sews like a master seamstress! Even you said that's a beautiful gown she made for my birthday."

I gave her another huge smile and said, "That's right, Walter, you rat." I probably should have left out the *rat* part.

Finally, his amusement spent, Walter released Jeanette, wiped his eyes, sucked in a huge breath and said, "Oh, my. I'm sorry, Daisy. But even you have to admit the notion of you teaching a cooking class is . . . funny."

"Huh," said I. "I don't think it's the least bit funny. I didn't think it was funny when Stacy Kincaid called and bullied me into doing it, and I don't think it's funny now." In a burst of honesty, I added, "It's a miracle that everything's worked out all right so far."

Walter's eyes went round. "Kincaid. *Stacy* Kincaid? The one you think is an evil changeling?"

"That's the one," I said upon a weary sigh. My arms were strong from helping to support Billy when he walked and restraining the ever-ebullient Spike, but I was getting tired of whipping cream. Fortunately, it looked done to me, and Vi nodded to tell me I could quit. So I did.

"I thought you didn't even speak to each other."

I eyed my brother and decided he was going to behave from now on. "We didn't used to. I still don't like her, but she got religion and joined the Salvation Army. That's the only reason she called. Well, that, and because Johnny probably told her to. Well, I know he did."

"How is Johnny?" asked Walter, who knew Johnny slightly.

"He's fine. He got married a few months ago to a lovely woman named Flossie."

My mother gave a refined sort of snort. She knew all about Flossie. Still, she didn't hold Flossie's background against her.

"Did he? Well, that's nice. I'm all for the married state."

The look that passed between my brother and his wife was embarrassing to behold. Still, I was happy for them both.

Because I'm a nice aunt, I took the eggbeater to the door of the kitchen and hollered, "Who wants to lick the beaters?"

It sounded like a herd of wild zebras stampeding toward the kitchen in answer to my query. Polly and Peggy stopped short in front of me, both beaming up, their faces cherubic. I handed over the eggbeater. "Share nicely, children."

They did.

I'm embarrassed to admit it, but I cried the next morning when Walter and Jeanette left us to drive back to Los Angeles. I hated seeing my family go away after they'd come. And we wouldn't see Walter and Jeanette again until Christmas Eve, which they planned to spend with us. They'd spend Christmas day at her sister's place in Los Angeles. I guess that was fair, but I sure missed Walter when he was gone. Even if he did laugh at me for teaching that wretched class. Heck, everyone else did, too. Why

291

should he be any different?

There wasn't time to miss him for long, however, because I had to teach a class that Saturday. Naturally, since she was to be married on the day after my class, Mrs. Kincaid called in her regular tizzy, asking me to please go to her house and read the tarot cards for her. So I did that before the class began.

When I was shown to the drawing room by Featherstone, Mr. Pinkerton was holding her hand, and Harold hovered in the background. He winked at me and rolled his eyes, so I knew this was a large tizzy and not just a normal-sized one.

I wafted gently toward Mrs. Kincaid. "Whatever is the matter, Mrs. Kincaid? All your problems will be over tomorrow, you know."

She lifted her eyes, which were glassy with tears, to me. "Will they, Daisy? Oh, will they *really?*"

I thought about Stacy and decided to backpedal a bit. Since Mr. Pinkerton had risen and offered me his seat next to his bride-to-be, I floated gracefully down onto the sofa and took her hand, which was still warm from having been held by him. "You know, Mrs. Kincaid, that everyone has little troubles now and then. That's the nature of life itself. If we didn't have the rough patches, we'd be hard pressed to enjoy the smooth times. But tomorrow you'll be marrying a wonderful gentleman who loves you dearly." I prayed that was so. Mr. Pinkerton was nodding hard, so I guess it was. "And you have a loving son and a daughter who. . . ." Oh, dear. Whatever could I say about Stacy? "Who has seen the error of her ways and straightened up." I prayed for that one, too.

Harold rolled his eyes again, but I didn't acknowledge the gesture.

"Oh, Daisy, you always make me feel so much better," Mrs. Kincaid said, hiccupping slightly in her distress. Or maybe it was relief.

Sometimes I wondered about Mrs. Kincaid. Surely the woman must understand that she was better off than most of the citizens of the world. But you'd sure never know it if you just judged by her hysterics. After I finished reading the cards for her, I then decided to wonder about Mr. Pinkerton. Did the man know what he was getting himself into? Well, of course, he did. He'd known the woman for years. Decades, probably. Besides, just because *I* wouldn't want to marry a woman who was prone to hysterics and who had an evil daughter, didn't

293

mean *everyone* wouldn't. If you know what I mean.

At any rate, I barely got out of there in time to dash to the Salvation Army and conduct my class. I was grateful that Gertrude didn't waylay me on my way to fellowship hall, although she did look upon me with an expression not unlike Spike when he thinks I'm going to give him a bone after supper. Well, I'd deal with her after class.

All my students were in their places, eager looks on their faces — except for Gertrude, whose expression I've already described. Flossie smiled warmly at me. Gee, I was lucky in my friends. They made up for a lot of the other, less pleasant things in my life.

"Good afternoon, ladies," I said, hurrying to the front of the room and panting slightly. "I'm sorry to be so rushed. I had a job to do before coming here." I beamed at them to let them know it didn't matter, and that they were more important than any old job.

They beamed back.

"We're making a simple recipe today, ladies, because we've all probably had too much food lately, and we're going to lighten things up a bit."

That might have been a mistake. For all I knew, these poor dears, who, I deduced, had no family connections nearby, had spent a lonely miserable Thanksgiving alone. I glanced at Flossie.

She must have read my mind, because she said brightly, "That's right, Mrs. Majesty. We had a lovely Thanksgiving Day here at the church. All the church ladies brought covered dishes, and Johnny and I cooked two turkeys."

I eyed her speculatively. It seemed to me that she was becoming more comfortable in her role as the captain's wife. She should be able to teach the next class, should there be one. Thank God. Life wasn't all bad, I reckoned. "That sounds wonderful, Mrs. Buckingham. I'm so glad you all had a festive holiday." I sighed, remembering my family and the lovely time I'd had with them.

Then I shook myself out of my reminiscent mood. "Anyhow, as I said, we're preparing a simple dish today, ladies. It's on page thirty-one of your booklets. Arme Ritter." I probably massacred the pronunciation, but Vi had helped me with it.

They all turned to the proper page.

"As you can tell, this is not at all unlike regular old French toast, but it has a twist, in that we're going to put some cinnamon into the egg batter. As the recipe tells you,

you can put some preserves on the eggy pieces of bread after you fry them in hot fat, and they're most tasty." I knew this for a fact, because Vi had prepared some for breakfast that very morning, so I'd not be unprepared for this afternoon's class.

Class that day didn't take very long, and we packed up fairly early. Flossie came up to me as I was packing my leftover arme ritters into paper bags. "They don't stay crisp very long," I said, eyeing the soggy lumps in my bag.

She laughed. "I know. Mine are already soft. But Johnny never minds that sort of thing. He's so good to me, Daisy."

Her dreamy expression warmed my heart. "I'm so glad, Flossie!" Impulsively, I gave her a little hug.

"And we owe it all to you," she said, hugging me back.

"Well, I don't know about that, but I'm happy I was able to help a little bit."

"You helped more than a little bit," she declared firmly. "I've never been so happy in my life, Daisy. What with the holidays coming and all . . . well, I just can't thank you enough."

She wiped away a tear, and I was terribly embarrassed. But happy, too, if you know what I mean. "Gee, Flossie, I can't tell you how glad I am that you and Johnny found each other."

"We didn't just find each other, Daisy. *You* introduced us!"

"Well. . . ."

"Um . . . Mrs. Majesty?"

I'd known it couldn't last. Flossie and I stepped apart, and sure enough, there was Gertrude, looking nervous. She always looked nervous, except when she was crying. Then she only looked miserable. I sighed heavily. "Yes, Miss Minneke. I suppose we need to chat, don't we?"

Flossie eyed us both with a good deal of surprise. I only smiled to let her know everything was all right. She said, "Well, I'd better see what Johnny's up to." And she left us alone in the cavernous fellowship hall.

Gertrude clasped her hands to her bosom, and I felt a pang of compunction. Then I recalled the consternation a defection by her and her brother would cause many good people, and I hardened my heart. "Come over here, Miss Minneke. I'm sure we don't want others to overhear our conversation."

"No. We don't."

She came over to where I stood, and I revised my plan slightly. I wanted to be as near to my escape route as I could be when I delivered the bad news. "On the other

297

hand, perhaps we should go out into the courtyard."

"Very well."

The wind had started blowing, and leaves were flying everywhere when we exited the hall. I clapped a hand to my hat so it wouldn't blow away, and used my other hand to clutch my handbag, paper bag and cookbook.

"Have you thought about what I asked?" Gertrude asked, when we got to the Chevrolet.

This was it. I took a deep breath. "Yes, Miss Minneke. I have thought. Long and hard. And, as much as I wish you and your brother both well, I'm afraid I can't assist you to run away from your responsibilities to the Salvation Army and my friends, Captain and Mrs. Buckingham."

She sagged. "I was afraid of this." She looked at me pleadingly, reminding me of Spike again. "And you can't lend us any money?"

"I'm afraid not. I support my husband and family, you know. I'm afraid I can't spare money to assist people to cheat other people."

My words seemed to shock her for some reason. "Cheat? We don't want to cheat anyone! Oh, Mrs. Majesty, you don't believe

298

me, do you?"

I don't like the fall winds in our fair city, but that day I was more glad for them than not, since Gertrude's howl was almost as loud as the wind. "I believe you mean what you say, Miss Minneke. But I can't assume responsibility for you and your brother. What you do is up to you. I think you owe the Buckinghams and the Salvation Army a good deal, however, and I won't assist you in escaping your duties to them. I'm sorry if that seems harsh to you."

"It does." Now she sounded sulky.

"I'm sorry about that. I hope to see you in class next week."

And with that, I left her on the sidewalk. I could hardly *wait* to press the starter and get the heck away from her. I looked in the rear mirror, and saw her glumly staring after my retreating automobile until I turned the corner on Fair Oaks and drove north. Nuts to the Minnekes!

I'm ashamed to say that my family didn't eat the leftover arme ritters. Really, they were too much like leftover breakfast, and soggy, to boot. So I wasted all that effort and threw the leftovers away. Well, I gave Spike a couple. He didn't care how soggy they were. Anyhow, Aunt Vi had made floating island, which was an ever so much more tasty dessert after a dinner of beef loaf, lima beans and Saratoga chips. I know lots of people don't like lima beans, but I do. And Saratoga chips are my very favorite way to eat potatoes.

But that's neither here nor there. We all went to bed early that night, because tomorrow was the big day — and I don't mean merely church in the morning, either.

CHAPTER FIFTEEN

Billy surprised me and didn't make a fuss about going to Mrs. Kincaid's house for the wedding that Sunday afternoon.

He looked very handsome, in a pale and interesting sort of way, in his black suit and white tie, when we arrived at the Kincaid mansion. Quincy Applewood helped him out of the Chevrolet and assisted me to get him indoors and to the scene of the crime, which was the ballroom on the second floor. Fortunately for us, Mrs. Kincaid's first husband had installed an elevator, since he'd pretended to be wheelchair-bound. He turned out to be a faker at that, as he was at everything else, but the elevator was a godsend for Billy and me.

"I thought you were working for Mr. Pinkerton, Quincy," I mentioned as we negotiated our way into the elevator, where Edie had been stationed to help guests who chose not to climb the stairs to the ballroom.

"I am, but Edie and I are both working the wedding today."

"Good show," I said, smiling at both Applewoods.

"You're looking fit, Billy," Quincy said brightly. He didn't mean it. Billy looked sick.

But Billy didn't bridle at Quincy's falsehood. He took it for what it was: a nice fabrication in honor of the day and the affection everyone had for my husband. Billy used to be sociability itself back in the old days, before the Germans got at him.

"Thanks, Quincy," Billy said, smiling his beautiful smile. "You're a good liar."

Quincy chuckled. Edie said, "Did you make that gown, Daisy? It's absolutely gorgeous."

I glanced down at my rust-colored creation. I'd have rather made it in a rose crepe Maxine's had on sale, but I have reddish hair, and my hair and that rose wouldn't have been friendly together. So I'd made it of a rust-colored wool crepe and, I have to admit, I was darned proud of it. I'd copied it from a Worth creation I'd seen in a ladies' magazine and adapted a pattern all by myself. I'd also sewn on all those darned beads, but the result was worth it. It was, as Edie said, gorgeous. Modestly, I said,

"Thanks, Edie. Yes, I made it myself."

She shook her head, as if in awe and wonder. "You're amazing, Daisy. I wish I could sew as well as you do."

"She even made a scarf for the dog," said Billy, laughing as well as he could. "I told her he already has a fur coat, but she insisted he needed a scarf. For windy days, she said."

"Even dogs can get cold," I said, grinning. "Besides, he looks adorable in it."

"He looks like a girl," said my loving spouse.

We were all laughing when the elevator creaked to a stop at the second floor. "You know where the ballroom is, don't you, Daisy?"

"Yes. I've never been in it, but I know where it is."

"It's all decorated for the wedding," said Edie upon a romantic sigh. "It looks so pretty."

She was right. When Quincy and I negotiated Billy into the room, we saw that it had been decorated in very Christmassy reds, greens, and silvers, with garlands and so forth draped all over the place.

"Shoot," said Billy. "This place looks real classy."

"It sure does."

I wasn't altogether sure where we were supposed to sit, but fortunately, Harold had been watching for us. He dashed over as soon as he saw us, grinning like a jack-o'-lantern. "Daisy!" he cried. "And Billy! I'm so glad you could join us for this happy occasion."

"Thanks, Harold." I gave him a kiss on the cheek. Billy shook his hand and didn't even frown, which was a concession neither Harold nor I had anticipated. But Billy could behave when the situation called for it.

"Quincy," said Harold, "will you help get the Majestys settled? Over here." He gestured to a row of seats about in the middle of the room, close to the door we'd entered. "Take the outer seats, so you won't have to climb over anyone. I'd sit with you, but I have to give my mother away." He rolled his eyes and trotted off.

"Hey, that was nice of him," said Quincy, gazing after Harold. "His mother is probably having conniption fits, but he must have come out here in order to see that you could get good seats."

"He's a good friend," I said, meaning it sincerely.

Billy remained silent. No surprise there.

We settled into our seats and looked at

the gathering throng. There were sure a lot of people in attendance, and everyone was dressed to the nines. I smiled at several of the folks I'd met over the years through my business as a spiritualist, and was kind of surprised when Miss Emmaline Castleton entered the room, paused, looked around, spotted me, and walked over, leaving her escort — I think it was her father, although I'm not sure — to fend for himself. He didn't seem to mind, as he evidently knew just about everyone there. He was jovially greeting friends and acquaintances when Emmaline slipped into the chair next to mine.

"I'm so glad you're here, Daisy," she said. Then she glanced at Billy, so I made the introductions.

"How do you do, Miss Castleton?" Billy said politely as they shook hands. He'd risen at her approach, noble soul that he was. It wasn't easy for him to get into and out of chairs.

"I'm well, thank you. And you?" Then she appeared flustered, as if she hadn't meant to ask that of a man in Billy's condition.

I wished she'd kept her poise a little better, since her losing it meant Billy would know we'd discussed him when I went to her home for luncheon.

But Billy didn't react to her clear uneasiness. He only smiled blandly and said, "Fine, thank you."

I loved my Billy so much. It was times like that when I forgot all the unhappiness and bitterness in our relationship and remembered why I'd fallen in love with him and married him.

"It's so nice to see you here, Emmaline," I said in order to divert attention from Billy to me. That was my duty, after all.

"Yes, I really felt I ought to come. Harold and I have known each other for years now." She eyed me speculatively. "Have you given any consideration to our discussion, Daisy?"

"Oh my, yes," I said. "But I'm not entirely sure how to go about part of it, although I have spoken to one of the people you asked about." What with Billy sitting right next to us, I didn't want to get into Hilda's having probably illegally entered the country. Not that he'd have done anything about it, but . . . well, I just didn't want to talk about it in a crowded room, I guess.

"You've spoken to . . . ?" Emmaline let her sentence die out. I guess she didn't want to talk about the matter in a crowded room, either.

"Yes. I did. He's. . . ." Oh, boy. If I told Emmaline that Johnny Buckingham said he'd pray about it, Billy would know something funny was going on. "He's going to get back with me on the matter."

"I see. Yes, that's fine. Thank you."

"I know you're in a hurry about it, but. . . ."

"No. That's all right, Daisy. Yes, I'm impatient, but being impatient in this situation won't do a bit of good. I know that. I just hoped things would move . . . smoothly. That's probably asking too much."

"I wouldn't mind, myself, if things went smoothly every now and then," I said, aiming for a light tone and not achieving it.

She smiled, and I got the feeling she knew exactly what I was thinking. With a sigh, she rose. "Well, I'd best go find Father. Mother was ill and couldn't come, so I have to keep my eye on him." Turning to Billy, she said, "It was such a pleasure to meet you, Mr. Majesty. Daisy has told me so much about you. You're lucky to have each other."

And with that, she left us, loping off to find her father in the crowd. I noticed Billy's lifted eyebrows, and said, "She lost her fiancé in the war. A fellow named Stephen Allison." I heaved a deep sigh. "So many people lost so much."

"Yeah," said Billy. "That's for sure."

We subsided into silence for several moments, both of us glancing around at the decorations and the people, most of whom were also quite decorative. I've seldom seen so many magnificent gowns in one room, with the exception of some of the parties for which I'd been hired to perform — you know, read tarot cards and palms and stuff like that.

After quite a while, Billy said, "Do you really feel comfortable with these people, Daisy? Most of them are so rich, and we're so . . . not rich."

"Oddly enough, I do, Billy. I guess it's because I'm used to being around them. When you think about it, people are really pretty much all alike, except that some of them have money and some don't. Mind you, I know darned well that the rich and the poor are different from each other, mainly because the rich have more op-portunities than the rest of us. But . . . well, we're all human, if you know what I mean."

He grinned, which I took as a good sign. "And if the rich folks hire you, I guess that means we're all gullible, too."

I laughed a little, although I didn't think the comment particularly amusing. "I guess so."

The organist began to play then, and everyone who still stood found places to sit.

The music was glorious. Sounded just like church, actually. Father Frederick, Mrs. Kincaid's priest (Episcopal variety) entered the room at the front, where a platform had been set up with an altar and all the normal church-type stuff that goes along with weddings. The setting was fabulous, and I suspected Harold, who was quite artistic, and his . . . um, gentleman friend, I guess is what you'd call him . . . Del Farrington had arranged for most of the decorations.

The groomsmen, who'd been put to work seating everyone, were, I presumed, Mr. Pinkerton's sons. They were a good-looking pair. So was Del, who, oddly enough, seemed to be Mr. Pinkerton's best man. I'm not sure why that was, but he was standing up front with Mr. Pinkerton and Father Frederick.

And then the best part of the ceremony began. I don't know who the little boy and little girl were whom they'd got to act as ring bearer and flower girl, but they were adorable, and they did their jobs beautifully. Stacy came next, looking actually quite nice. She hadn't attempted to do anything outrageous with her makeup or hair, and she wore a simple, stylish gown. Then came Mrs. Kincaid's sister, whom I'd met the year before, and who had also lost a son in the war. She was matron of honor, I guess.

The organist began playing Mendelssohn's "Wedding March." We all stood up — including Billy — and in came Harold with his mother on his arm. Mrs. Kincaid looked as good as I've ever seen her look. She was around fiftyish, I guess, and a little round, but her light-blue gown and veil were very lovely. And she didn't flutter or fidget! That amazed me almost more than Stacy behaving herself.

The ceremony was beautiful, and Billy agreed that he'd go to the Valley Hunt Club for the reception with me. "It's probably the only time I'll ever get to see the place."

"Me, too, come to think of it." The Valley Hunt Club was a *most* exclusive club. It didn't cater to the likes of the Majestys and Gumms.

I'd just started worrying about how to get Billy out of the ballroom and into the elevator when Quincy showed up. I suspected he'd received Harold's instruction in that regard. Whatever had prompted Quincy to act, his assistance was greatly appreciated by Billy and me.

"Did you enjoy the show?" asked Quincy as he guided Billy to the elevator.

Billy chuckled. "It was a show, all right."

"It's going to be difficult for me to think

of Mrs. Kincaid as Mrs. Pinkerton," I said, adding my bit to the conversation. "She's been Mrs. Kincaid for so long, you know?"

By that time, we'd reached the elevator, and Edie, still working as the operator thereof, joined in. "Me, too. But I like Mr. Pinkerton ever so much better than Mr. Kincaid." She gave a theatrical shudder, and I didn't blame her. Mr. Kincaid used to try to trap Edie with his wheelchair and pinch her bottom. Awful man!

The Valley Hunt Club was as elegant as we expected it to be. After I seated Billy at a table where our name cards resided, I made it through the reception line, and both Mr. Pinkerton and Mrs. Kincaid — I mean Mrs. Pinkerton — hugged me. It was nice to be appreciated. Emmaline Castleton and I spoke briefly once more, but again, we weren't able to discuss our mutual problems. She said she'd 'phone me once she got her father to "cooperate with me on writing the letters. First, of course, I need to meet your . . . friend."

Hilda. Hmm. No friend of mine, really. Yet I didn't dislike her. In fact, I felt rather sorry for her. Mrs. Bissell had told me she was the best maid she'd ever had working for her — and she'd employed tons of maids over the years. So it seemed Hilda was willing to work, and work hard, for her keep. It seemed a shame that Hilda should suffer because of the wretched Kaiser and our stuffy immigration laws.

We didn't stay awfully long at the reception, primarily because Billy began fading fast after the meal was served. We ate a perfectly lavish dinner, and then we made our excuses and escaped. Mrs. Pinkerton said she understood completely when I told her Billy's health prevented us from staying for the rest of the evening. Heck, even if he'd felt better than he did, what was the point? We sure couldn't dance together, and I wouldn't have trotted off with some other dance partner and leave Billy by himself. Not even Harold, who assisted us to the car.

"Thanks, Harold. You're a true friend," I told him as he helped Billy into his seat.

"Happy to help, Daisy. Lord knows, you've helped my mother and me often enough."

"Your mother, maybe. You, never. I only ever got you into trouble."

"But I was a willing participant," Harold said, laughing. He glanced back at the club and sighed. "But I'd better go back in there and continue to do my duty. Got to dance with all of Mother's friends, God save me."

"Thanks, Harold," said Billy. I think he

meant it.

"You're more than welcome," said Harold. And he left us to rejoin the festivities.

"What friend of yours was Miss Castleton talking about? Why does she have to meet her?" asked Billy once we got settled in the Chevrolet. When I glanced over at him, I noticed he appeared really ill. His skin was more pasty than ever, and he had the sheen of perspiration on his brow. It occurred to me that he might be missing his morphine syrup, and my heart gave another of its huge, painful spasms. What a hideous fate to befall so wonderful a man as my Billy. Naturally, I didn't ask him if he was suffering some kind of withdrawal symptoms. I'd pretty much closed the door to his communicating with me about his problems. My fault, and I felt it deeply.

"There's a woman in my cooking class whom I suspect is a German lady here in the United States illegally."

"Really? Is that the one who keeps running away when Sam shows up?"

I heaved a sigh. "No. That's another one. She's got other problems."

"Oh?"

He appeared interested, and I found myself almost blabbing the truth to him about the Minneke siblings. I recalled my promise to Gertrude in time to shut my mouth on total revelation, although I had another painful spasm, this one more of resentment than sympathy for my Billy. I didn't care to be the recipient of such morbid secrets as the one Gertrude and Eugene had thrust upon me. Help to get them out of Pasadena and welsh on their promises, indeed.

Pooh. I didn't want to talk about this stuff. "She's worried about her brother, who's in some sort of trouble." There. That didn't reveal too much.

"Oh? What kind of trouble?"

Rats. "I think it's of the criminal variety, actually. But I told her I couldn't help her."

"Good." He hesitated for a moment, then said, "Gee, Daisy, this is one of the first times you've not stuck your nose into someone else's business when you had the opportunity. I'm proud of you."

I shot Billy a glare, but he only grinned back at me. Unfortunately, he was right, but most of the rather unfortunate things I'd become entangled in hadn't been my fault. Not really. And most of the time my motives had been purely benevolent. It wasn't my fault that things went a bit awry from time to time. Billy had never been able to appreciate that, and I guessed there was no use fighting with him now. We'd covered that territory what seemed like millions of times, and both of our opinions had remained unchanged. What was the point?

"So why does Miss Castleton need to meet this German lady?"

It seemed Billy wasn't going to give up questioning me today. Maybe chatting kept his mind off his unpleasant physical symptoms. "She's trying to assist another German to enter the country legally: she's writing letters to congressmen and getting her father to intervene and that sort of thing. When she told me about that German, she reminded me of Hilda, one of the ladies from my cooking class, and I asked if perhaps she could assist Hilda in gaining legal status here. Providing Hilda ever admits she's German, because she claims she's Swiss, but I don't believe her." I glanced again at my husband. "Did that make any sense?"

He scratched his head. "I guess so. Why are you interested in helping this Hilda person? I thought you hated all Germans."

Another sigh. "I thought I did, too. But I guess you're right, Billy. People are people the world over, and we're all victims of brutes like the Kaiser." I recalled Dr. Benjamin's words regarding war and young

315

men fighting for old men's misdeeds, but didn't think Billy would like to know that I'd been talking to others about his problems.

"Ha. Well, I'm glad to hear it. I guess you feel about rich people the way I feel about Germans. About their being just people and all."

"I guess so. I have to admit that sometimes I resent the Mrs. Kincaids of this world —"

"The Mrs. Pinkertons," Billy said, interrupting.

"Oh, dear, that's right. I must try to remember her new last name. She's been Mrs. Kincaid for so long now. Anyway, sometimes I resent that people like Mrs. Pinkerton, who are nice but silly and rather unintelligent, should have loads of money and people like you and Ma and Pa and Aunt Vi don't."

Billy only shrugged. "The world's never been fair to its denizens, Daisy. You should have learned that by this time."

"Oh, believe me, I know." How could I help but know about the world's unfairness when I was faced with the results thereof every day of my life? Poor Billy.

"Yeah," he said. "I guess you do."

In terms of geography, our house wasn't far from Mrs. Pinkerton's, although it was miles away in terms of status. Still and all, I loved it as a refuge from the world's woes. We arrived home about that time, so we stopped talking about the problems of my various students and the vagaries. I was glad about the former, since I wasn't keen on discussing them with my family.

Pa had anticipated Billy's need for his wheelchair, bless his heart. When I pulled the Chevrolet up in front of the house, Pa rolled the chair down the ramp he'd built, Spike cavorting at his heels, yelping in ecstasy that his humans had returned home again.

"Thanks, Joe," Billy said as he subsided into the chair. He looked perfectly dreadful. "I was wearing out fast."

"I figured you'd be exhausted, son. But Vi's got a nice supper prepared, and you'll soon perk up."

After he downed another long gulp of morphine syrup. I didn't say that. "Good deal, Pa. But Billy and I ate pretty well at the reception."

"Speak for yourself," said Billy, smiling. "I prefer Vi's homemade stuff to all that fancy food."

"I don't know," said I, pushing my beloved's chair back up the ramp — Spike had leaped onto Billy's lap. "I kind of liked that lobster Newberg thing."

"Lobster!" Pa exclaimed. "La-di-da." He polished his nails on his shirt front.

"It was tasty," Billy admitted.

"And the roast beef was swell, too," I added.

"Roast beef *and* lobster?" Pa's eyebrows lifted.

"I know. That would be two or three meals for us, but those rich folks eat them all at the same time," Billy said. "And don't forget the duck thing."

"Oh, yes. I forgot the pressed duck. And the pâté. And don't forget all the salads and side dishes." I smiled at my father. "Billy's right, Pa. Rich folks eat too much. Heck, our whole family could have eaten for a week on what Mr. and Mrs. Pinkerton expected their guests to eat at one meal."

"Well, I reckon it's nice to see how the other half lives every now and then," said Pa.

"I guess," said Billy.

I was pretty sure he didn't mean it. But that was all right. We were together, and we were home, and we were back in the bosom of my ever-wonderful family.

CHAPTER SIXTEEN

Naturally, the topic of conversation for the remainder of that Sunday was the wedding. Ma and Aunt Vi oohed and aahed about the food and the decorations and the clothes. Billy had gone in to our room to lie down for an hour or so — and, of course, to consume some morphine syrup — right after I rolled him into the house, but he joined us later. Turned out he and Pa had invited Sam Rotondo over for a friendly game of gin rummy that evening. As ever.

Oddly enough, in recent days I had begun feeling a little less annoyed about Sam constantly showing up at our house. Perhaps the change in my attitude began when he listened to my tale of woe about Billy and that cursed cache of morphine. Perhaps not. I wasn't about to let down my guard around him, but I was glad he was there for Billy and Pa, both of whose health was about as bad as it could be.

I thought about asking him if he'd telephoned Lucille Spinks, but decided it would probably be better not to. Anyhow, I'd see Lucy at choir practice on Thursday. I'd ask her.

The rest of the week was uneventful. Actually, it was positively dull. Mr. and Mrs. Pinkerton were on their honeymoon, so I didn't get one single hysterical call from that source. A few other folks called to ask me to conduct séances or read tarot cards, but other than that, I might as well have slept through it. Well, except for my birthday, which was swell. Not only did I become a young woman of twenty-two years, but Aunt Vi made beef Wellington for the family. Boy, was *that* a success! Naturally, Sam came to dinner that night, but I didn't really mind. Plus he brought me a very nice bouquet of flowers that he'd picked up at a flower shop. They were pretty, too, and I thanked him graciously.

Billy gave me a lovely gold necklace with a very pretty pendant with a topaz in the middle. Topaz is November's birthstone, and I appreciated his thoughtfulness a lot. It was very difficult for him to do any shopping, given the state of his health and his inability to walk much. I suspected either Pa or Sam had driven him to Arnold's

Jewelers. Come to think of it, it was probably Sam who'd done so, since Pa wasn't
supposed to drive anymore because of his
bum heart. Anyhow, Pa and Billy would
have had to go when I wasn't using the car
for my work, and then I'd have been home
and known all about their errand, wouldn't
I? Another gold star for Sam Rotondo.

I wasn't sure I could stand having Sam
turn into a friend. I'd enjoyed disliking him
for so long. Well, he'd probably annoy me
again soon. I held that thought to my heart.

Not really. I'm honestly not that small-
minded. At least I hope I'm not.

That Thursday, talking with Lucy Spinks,
I cautiously probed the topic of Sam Rotondo. She gave me a sad little smile and
shook her head.

"No, I'm afraid Mr. Rotondo doesn't
return my interest, Daisy."

"He wasn't unkind to you, was he?" I
asked, instantly suspecting Sam of having
been horrid to poor love-struck Lucy.

"Oh, no. He was a perfect gentleman, but
a girl can tell, can't she?"

Could she? I didn't know, never having
been in Lucy's situation. Heck, I knew I
was going to marry Billy when I was five
years old. Mind you, Billy didn't know my

plans back then, but that didn't matter to me.

"Are you sure?" I asked, feeling kind of bad for Lucy.

"I'm afraid so. He was very kind and spoke gently and generally behaved as if he considered me some kind of younger sister whom he'd been given responsibility for and whom he'd tucked under his wing until he could deposit me back at the nest."

Mercy. That was quite a poetical flight of verbiage from the generally prosaic Lucy. "Well, perhaps he thinks he's too old for you," I suggested in an attempt to cheer her up. "He is somewhat older than we are, I think."

"He's twenty-seven," said Lucy.

I blinked at her.

She shrugged. "I asked him. Couldn't see any reason not to. I don't think five years is that much of an age gap, do you?"

"Well . . . no, I guess it isn't. How funny. I thought he was much older than that."

"He is kind of a sobersides."

Sam? A sobersides? Hmm. Maybe he was. In a fit of uncharacteristic charity, I said, "Perhaps the loss of his wife has made him behave in a stuffier manner than he used to. Or something like that."

"Maybe."

Lucy and I sat side by side in the front row of the choir. She was at the end of the sopranos, and I was at the beginning of the altos, but I think the main reason Mr. Hostetter had us sit together was because when we sang duets, our exit from the choir to the microphones wouldn't cause a big upheaval in the ranks. If you know what I mean.

"I did find him fascinating, though," Lucy said upon a mournful sigh. "And where am I going to find anybody else?"

Good question, and one to which I had no answer, good or otherwise. I thought nasty thoughts about the Kaiser while Mr. Hostetter explained the night's agenda to us. We were at the beginning of the Christmas season, which I loved because of all the beautiful carols. The choir generally sang Handel's "Hallelujah Chorus" on Christmas Eve, and both Lucy and I got solos. Solos were scary, but we both enjoyed performing.

The rest of the week was absolutely boring. It was so boring, in fact, that I was almost glad when Saturday rolled around and I had to teach that stupid class. The last class. Talk about hallelujahs! However, this was the fateful class in which I was going to teach my students how to create and fill pea-and-egg castles. Thanks to Vi, I'd had lots of practice creating the little castle-like holders. Naturally, we didn't always fill them with peas and eggs and cover them with cream sauce. Heck, mainly, we ate the croutes as rather fancy pieces of fried toast for breakfast.

As I set out in the Chevrolet, I figured I was as prepared as I'd ever get. That didn't prevent me from praying throughout the drive to the Salvation Army. Actually, it occurred to me that if I was willing to pray over a stupid bread croute, I probably ought to be willing to pray about something as important as my husband's problems. It was, therefore, a very guilty-feeling Daisy Gumm Majesty who parked her automobile and shambled toward the fellowship hall that day.

All the students were there, perky as ever, and Flossie greeted me with a cheerful embrace and yet another bouquet of flowers! My goodness, nobody ever gave me flowers, and here I'd had two bouquets in a single week.

"We all appreciate so much what you've done for us, Mrs. Majesty," said Flossie in her newly refined accent. "The class got together and decided to present you with a token of their esteem."

324

Naturally, I cried. I swear, I'm hopeless. However, I didn't cry for long, and after brushing away my few tears, I thanked Flossie and my students warmly. "Truly, I've learned more by teaching this class than you folks have." I'm sure they thought I was kidding. I wasn't.

At any rate, I put the bouquet in a little vase I found in the church's kitchen and returned to the front of the class.

"Today, ladies, we're going to prepare the dish pictured on the cover of our cook booklet." I beamed at them, trying my level best to portray the confidence of a genuine cooking teacher. What a sham! Truly, I considered myself a pretty honest person until I remembered that I earned my living as a spiritualist, and how honest is that? But I felt better about spiritualism, which I do well, than I did about that silly class.

But my students all showed evidence of delight that we'd be fixing the pea castle, so that made me happy. Except for Gertrude, who seemed to be slightly sulky. Ah, well.

"Let's all turn to page seventeen, ladies." We did.

"Mrs. Buckingham has brought bread for us to use, and she's already boiled the eggs we'll need. Therefore, the first thing we need to do is cut our bread to fit our serving dishes." I don't know if you're old enough to remember, but in those days, one didn't go to a store and buy sliced bread. One first baked loaves of bread and then sliced it as needed. Therefore, we were dealing with big hunks of bread during that class.

One of my students raised her hand. "How big should the piece of bread be?"

According to Vi, it should be any size you wanted it to be, so I said, "That's up to you. If you're going to be serving several people, you'll want to make it tall. For our purposes today, I suggest perhaps five or six inches is a good size." I demonstrated and they followed suit.

"Now," I continued, positively reeking of confidence, "we need to scoop out our bread, leaving approximately a quarter to a half inch of bread around the edges and at the bottom. And save the bread you scoop out, and use it to make breadcrumbs." Ah, breadcrumbs. Until I got pressured into teaching this class, I'd had no idea how useful breadcrumbs were. And here I used to think they were merely bird food. "You see, by scooping out the bread, we're creating a case in which to place our eggs and green peas."

I scooped out my piece of bread, working very carefully, because a couple of times I'd managed to poke a hole in the castle wall. I'd done so, according to Vi, because I wasn't concentrating. Believe me, that day I concentrated extremely hard.

"Once you've got your bread scooped out, a fun thing to do is to cut notches in the top, like the booklet shows, so that it looks like a little castle. Of course, you don't need to do that part, but it makes the case very pretty." Sort of. I mean, we were just going to eat the stupid thing. How pretty did it have to look? I guess this was kind of a poor man's version of beef Wellington, *sans* the beef.

We notched our bread.

"And now, ladies, let us carry our bread croutes to the kitchen, where we'll fry them in hot fat until they're golden brown while we're cooking our peas and making our white sauce. That way, we won't waste any time."

So, like a line of good little soldiers, we carried our bread castles to the kitchen.

"While we take turns frying our bread, ladies," I said once we were all gathered around the stove, "let's put our peas on to cook. Mrs. Buckingham has kindly shelled enough peas for our use."

It turned out that, after lots and lots of practice at home, even I could cook peas, which requires putting water in a pot, peas in the water, a little salt for luck, and a hot fire underneath the filled pot. However, since I was the teacher, I offered to allow one of my students to do the honors. Hilda volunteered.

The skillet we were offered for use in the kitchen was huge, so we were able to fry two castles at a time in it.

"First we shall melt some fat in the bottom of the skillet. Then, using these handy kitchen tongs, we can make sure our bread fries crisply but does not burn."

Clever devil that I am, I allowed my students to do that part, as well. Two at a time, they fried their castles.

"And, while the bread is turning a lovely golden brown" — I hoped — "we can begin making our white sauce."

This part was kind of tricky, but Vi had pointed out to me before I left the house that it was past time I began to rely on my students to follow the instructions printed in the book. Therefore, I selected Gertrude and Maria to begin making the white sauce, and Margaret and Wilma to begin peeling and slicing the hardboiled eggs. That way, if anything went wrong and the sauce turned lumpy or the shells stuck to the eggs, I wouldn't necessarily have to take the blame.

Cowardly, I know, but it sounded good to me.

In fact, we worked as a sort of assembly line. Henry Ford would have been proud of us. The students all fried their bread, taking turns; the sauce-makers took their turns; and the egg slicers took *their* turns. By the time we had all of our bread castles fried to a relatively golden brown, give or take a few light or dark spots, the sauce was ready, the peas were cooked, and the eggs were all sliced. I was quite proud of our teamwork.

So pleased was I, in fact, that I virtually beamed at my students, most of whom beamed back at me. Gertrude still appeared kind of sulky. Well, pooh on her.

"As long as we're here and so are all of our ingredients, ladies. . . ." I paused for a minute because several of them laughed. Either they were extremely polite, or I was funnier than I thought. "As long as everything's here, why don't we finish our dishes in the kitchen? What you need to do is place your bread croutes on your small serving platter, put a layer of peas in the bottom of the croutes, then put a layer of eggs and sauce on top of the peas. Continue layering until your croute is filled, ending with a layer of peas. Then you can artfully arrange some white sauce on top and sprinkle some peas around the base of the croute to add an air of festivity to the dish." Well, it sounded good, anyway. I'm not sure how festive the finished products looked, but they were honestly kind of pretty.

"And there you have it!" I waved my arms in a flourish at all our nice, tidy little pea castles. It amazes me to this day to admit it, but I was impressed. *We,* a bunch of ladies of wildly disparate backgrounds, some of whom hardly spoke English, had actually created edible foodstuffs through *my* tutelage! The latter part of that scenario is what astonished me the most. Naturally, as I've said many times before, and will say many times again, my success was due entirely to my aunt Vi: without her, the dishes I tried to teach my class would have been toast. Literally. And probably the Salvation Army, too. I've never underestimated my ability to demolish things when I attempt cookery.

Johnny came into the classroom right before we were to disband for the final time. He made a lovely speech about how the Salvation Army's goal is to rescue people in need, both spiritually and physically, and he hoped that in a small way, his particular church had helped this clutch of ladies. All the ladies assured him they had, indeed, been helped by him and his organization.

He then led us in prayer, said a fond farewell to the cooking ladies, and they all filed past Flossie, Johnny and yours truly, most of them smiling and with tears in their eyes. They all thanked us effusively for our help. Talk about feeling humbled. Boy, I'd just as soon not go through that again, primarily because I'd felt like a total fraud the whole time I was in that room attempting to impart the art of cooking to those poor women.

And that's something else that's kind of odd. Pretending to be a spiritualist doesn't bother me the least little bit, but pretending to be an adept cook bothered me *a whole lot.* I suspect it has something to do with me being good at the one and abysmal at the other.

After hugs all around and fond farewells, Flossie and Johnny walked me out of fellowship hall. They'd probably have walked me to the Chevrolet, but I told them I could handle my accoutrements, which consisted of my pea castle, my handbag, my bouquet of flowers and my cook booklet, all by my lonesome.

As you've probably already guessed, I should have known better.

I had just about made it to the machine

when I heard a soft "Mrs. Majesty?" behind me.

Turning, I beheld Gertrude Minneke. She no longer looked surly. She looked only kind of . . . well, bland, I guess is the best word to describe her expression. She stood there in her plain print frock with her hands clasped, or so I supposed, behind her back.

My heart was by then brimming with benevolence, primarily because I'd never have to see her or any of my other students again in this lifetime — well, except maybe Hilda, depending on how things worked out.

I smiled at Gertrude. "Yes, Miss Minneke?" I said in my sweetest voice.

She licked her lips nervously, although I'm sure I couldn't figure out why she should be nervous. "Um . . . is your decision not to assist Eugene and me final? I mean . . . you haven't had a change of heart or anything? You won't help us leave Pasadena? The class is over now, after all."

"True, but your obligation to the Salvation Army doesn't end with the class, Miss Minneke. You know that. You still have your jobs to consider, and your eventual placement with companies that will hire you when you complete your training. I really don't believe I could, in good conscience, assist you in breaking your promise to the organization. I do wish you well in all your future endeavors, however."

"I see. And that's your final answer on the matter?"

Strange way to put it, but I'd already decided Gertrude was strange. "Well . . . yes, it is. I'm sorry I can't help you."

She heaved a big sigh. "Well, then, I guess we'll just have to move along to our next option."

And I'll be hornswoggled (my father likes to say that) if she didn't haul her hand out from behind her back. In it was probably the biggest gun I'd ever seen! Not that I've seen very many guns in my life, and I certainly don't know one type of gun from another, but this one was either a pistol or a revolver. A *big* pistol or revolver. I know that much because it wasn't a rifle or a shotgun, which are both a lot longer that Gertrude's gun.

"Get in the car, lady," ordered a masculine voice from behind me. In spite of Gertrude's gun, I was so shocked, I whirled around, and who should be there but none other than Eugene Minneke! Also carrying a firearm! You could have knocked me over with the proverbial feather.

Then, as if two people interfering with my well-being weren't enough, yet another voice, high and piercing, shattered the afternoon air.

"Halt! Halt! Was tust du, Schwein? Nein, nein! Das geht nicht! Halt!"

And darned if Hilda, like a Valkyrie out of one of Wagner's more dramatic operas, didn't come charging at us from the side. I shrieked, "Hilda! They have guns! Be careful!" But either she didn't understand my English or she didn't give a care. She plowed into Gertrude much like I've seen football players plow into opposing players. Gertrude plowed into me, and we both hit the ground with a thump and Gertrude with an extremely profane curse. Undaunted, darn it, she leapt to her feet, grabbed poor Hilda by her hair, which was flying out of its normally tidy braids by that time, and pulled her off her feet. Hilda went sprawling, Eugene yanked me up by the arm, and with Gertrude shoving me on an indelicate portion of my anatomy, I plopped across the front seat of the Chevrolet.

Growling like a bear, Eugene leaped into the tonneau and said, "Get the hell over to the driver's side and drive, dammit!" He jammed that cursed gun into my back, and I knew I'd have a bruise and a half if I got out of this alive.

"And hurry it up! We don't have all day,"

said Gertrude, shoving me as she, too, climbed into the front seat.

My heart gave a gigantic lurch when I saw Hilda grab for the door handle, because I feared Gertrude or her evil brother might shoot her. Instead, Gertrude whacked Hilda's hand with the gun, prompting a loud Germanic expletive from her. I heard a wail from Hilda behind us, and then more German. *"Halt! Halt! Wast tust du, Schwein!"*

Oh, Lord, I didn't want them to start shooting at poor Hilda, who was trying to help me. "But what about —"

"Damn it, *go!*" hollered Eugene. And he did as I feared he'd do, and fired a shot at Hilda. I couldn't see if he'd hit her, but I prayed like mad that his aim was as lousy as his character.

So I did as they demanded. As the Chevrolet shrieked away from the curb, leaving skid marks that would probably remain until the street was repaved, I did manage to glance back to see if Hilda was still alive. Right before the Chevrolet screamed around the corner onto Fair Oaks Avenue, I thought I saw Johnny and Flossie racing toward the commotion. And I saw Hilda! Thank God, she was on her hands and knees, trying to rise, so I guess the evil duo didn't kill her, at least.

We'd just have to wait and see about me,
I reckoned.

CHAPTER SEVENTEEN

"But I don't understand," said I, although I thought I did. I was all scratched up from my tumble on the asphalt, but I didn't worry about my wounds at that point. Guns seemed ever so much more important then.

Evidently, Gertrude shared my opinion. "If you haven't figured it out by this time, you're a lot stupider than I figured."

"Keep driving, damn it," growled Eugene, who didn't want us to become sidetracked by irrelevancies.

"Drive where?" I asked. It sounded like a reasonable question to me, but he didn't seem to share my opinion. From the tonneau he tapped me on the side of my head with the gun. Boy, did that hurt!

"Don't hurt her yet, Gene. She has to drive us to San Diego first."

Yet? San Diego? Oh, dear, although I guess that answered one of my questions. "Are you going to try to escape into

Mexico?" It seemed as if all the crooks in my life so far had tried to escape to Mexico. Mr. Kincaid didn't make it, and I hoped to heaven these two wouldn't, either.

"That's none of your damned business," Eugene snarled. He certainly wasn't a very polite young man, and he had an execrably good handle on profanity.

"Oh, hell, Gene, it doesn't matter anymore," said Gertrude. She continued, sneering at me, "If you'd helped us, you know, you could have stayed alive. But no. You had to be Miss Goody Two-shoes, didn't you? You wouldn't help us get the hell out of Pasadena, would you? Wouldn't even buy the damned train tickets for us, would you? That would have saved you all of this damned bother."

Gertrude did all right in the profanity game herself. I'd said it before, but I figured it wouldn't hurt to say it again. "Mr. and Mrs. Buckingham are my friends. I couldn't very well assist you to run out on your contract with them, could I?"

"If you knew what was good for you, you would have," Eugene said.

Right. This wasn't the first time my basically honorable nature — if you discount my profession — got me into trouble.

"But I don't want to listen to you whine.

338

Just shut up and drive, damn you," said the ever-sweet Eugene.

So I figured it was time I did as he commanded. No point in pushing things, after all. As we drove through Pasadena, there was quite a bit of traffic on the road. The farther south we went, the scarcer the automobiles became, and farming wagons and horses started showing up. This area was all over farms and orange groves.

After about an hour, we were well past Pasadena, and we were encountering no traffic at all, which I might have considered unusual had I been thinking about traffic. I wasn't. What I was doing was coming up with and rejecting schemes to get me out of this pickle. Even if I drove the Chevrolet into a ditch, thereby ruining our lovely new car, there was no guarantee I'd survive the crash. Or that Gertrude and Eugene wouldn't. Automobile accidents were unpredictable at best.

Not only that, but I was beginning to worry about gasoline. I couldn't recall when I'd last refilled the fuel tank. Mind you, it might be best merely to let the machine run out of fuel. That would bring us to a definite halt. I got the impression, however, doing that would also bring me to a halt, since I couldn't figure Gertrude and Eugene needing me any longer if I no longer had the use of an automobile.

Therefore, summoning my courage in both hands and sending a heartfelt prayer heavenward, I dared ask a question. "Um . . . I think we're going to have to refuel pretty soon."

"Huh," said Eugene. "How much gasoline do you have in this thing?"

"I don't know."

I think, although I'm not positive, that Eugene made as if to hit me with his gun again, because Gertrude's hand shot out, and my flinch proved unnecessary.

"Let her talk, Eugene. We don't want to run dry." She squinted at the innards of my lovely new auto. "How can you tell when you need gasoline? Is there a gauge in here somewhere?"

"I'll have to stop the car and use the dipstick," I told her. "It's marked in gallons, but it's been quite a while since I got gasoline."

"Goddamned women," said Eugene. "Why the devil didn't you get a machine with a float and a marker?"

I didn't even know what a float or a marker was, so I couldn't answer that question. Not that I sensed he wanted an answer.

"Well, pull over to the side of the road,"

he grumbled. "I'll check the level of the gas. Where the devil are we, anyway?"

"Um . . . I'm not sure. I think we're either in or near El Monte. Or maybe Monrovia."

"Do they got gas stations in El Monte or Monrovia?"

As Eugene himself might say, *How the devil should I know?* Recalling my manners, not to mention my desire to cling to life a little bit longer, I said, "I'm not sure, but they use a lot of farm equipment, like trucks and stuff, so I imagine they do."

"Shit. Well, pull over."

I did as he requested. I kind of hoped the two Minnekes would allow me to get out and stretch my legs, but I didn't expect such cooperation from them. I wasn't disappointed. Gertrude said, "Just stay right there and don't move. I've got my gun on you."

Oh, goody.

I'm sure you've already figured out long since that I saw Billy's best pal Sam Rotondo a good deal more often than I wanted to. That particular day, however, I would have given anything to have Sam show up with a squad of policemen. Unfortunately, the police are never around when you need them.

Eugene yanked the hood of the auto up,

making me wince, since I didn't want him to mark the lovely black finish. After all, the machine was less than a year old and, since we Gumms and Majestys weren't rolling in wealth, it was going to have to last us a long time. I heard him snatch the dipstick from its little metal holder and unscrew the cap of the gasoline tank. Then we all heard a *clink.* Whoops. That didn't sound like a good thing. Perhaps I waited a little too long to remember about fuel.

"God damn son of a bitch!" hollered Eugene, from which I gathered I was correct in my suspicion.

"Is it empty?" Gertrude asked, leaning out the window, her gun hand wavering in a way that made me quite nervous.

"No, it's not empty, but it might as well be. Where the hell are we, anyhow?"

When I leaned out my own window — mainly because I didn't like to see that gun waving at me — I discovered I still couldn't enlighten him. We seemed to be on a paved road that was winding through a lovely grove of orange trees. Oranges were certainly not uncommon in Pasadena and the vicinity at the time. Heck, they were all over the place. But under Eugene's stern, not to say nasty directions, I'd driven and not asked questions. As I'd already told the man, I thought we were maybe in Monrovia or El Monte, although I didn't know for sure.

"You got any ideas?" he asked his sister, to whom he was no more polite than he was to me.

"How should I know?" asked Gertrude, sounding exasperated.

"And you?" Eugene said to me. He stomped to my side of the car. "What the devil were those towns you mentioned?"

I jerked my head inside, not wanting another tap from his gun. Oh, boy. If I said the wrong thing, I'd probably get more than tapped. Therefore, I sucked in a very deep breath and said, "I'm not sure, but we might be in El Monte. I saw some cows a ways back, and El Monte has some dairies. We've been driving for about an hour, haven't we, or maybe a little more?"

Without answering my question, Eugene reached into an inner coat pocket and hauled out a watch, at which he squinted. "Yeah. It's been about an hour and a quarter." He stuffed the watch back into its pocket. "Why the devil didn't you say something about gasoline before?"

Because he'd scared the words out of me, of course! What an idiot. Naturally, I didn't say that. I shrugged, which was the wrong thing to do, as I might have known it would be. Anything at all would have been the wrong thing to do.

Eugene proceeded to stamp and stomp up and down the road. Gertrude said to me, "Wait here. Move, and I'll shoot you," and she got out, too.

If I'd had more courage — or more gasoline — I might well have gunned the engine and taken off, leaving the two miscreants in my dust. Of course, they'd certainly have shot at me, and I had no way of knowing if they were as proficient with their weapons as they were with profanity. Or I might have run off into the orange grove. Unfortunately, orange groves are planted in neat little rows, and I'd be very easy to spot and, as mentioned before, shot.

Therefore, I sat in the Chevrolet, trying my hardest to figure out what to do.

As it turned out, I didn't have to figure out anything after all, which was a good thing, since my brain was abnormally empty at the time. The two Minneke siblings stormed back to the automobile, shouting at each other as if they hated one another's guts. Mind you, I didn't blame either one of them for their sentiments, but I sensed they might be going to have an uneasy alliance in their future criminal career together. I was sure glad I had my Billy. He might be grouchy a good deal of the time, but at least he wasn't a Minneke.

As soon as Eugene got into the tonneau, he growled, "Start the damned car and drive slow. It'll use less gas that way, and then stop at the nearest farmhouse or service station you see."

That made sense, since lots of farmers kept stores of gasoline and oil and so forth in their barns to use with their equipment. I nodded my assent, pressed the self-starter, and let out the clutch. We inched along for a moment or two before Eugene snapped, "You can go faster than that, dammit! If we do run dry, we can push the damned car!"

Yes, sir. I sped up a bit, his previous words making me feel the tiniest bit optimistic. Surely, if we stopped at a farmhouse, I could somehow or other convey my distress to a resident there. I hoped.

And then, as if God were out to get me for my many sins, darned if one of my tires didn't blow! It made a *pow!* sound as if somebody'd shot the silly thing with a bullet. Although we weren't going fast, the automobile swerved like mad for a second or three before we ended up perilously close to one of those orange trees. And the right front wheel was sunk in a ditch.

"God damn son of a bitch!" screeched Eugene, as ever with the *mot juste* for any occasion. Provided it was a scary one.

"What happened?" asked Gertrude, sounding shaky. When I glanced over at her, I saw that she'd hit her head against the window frame. Good. I only wished she'd knocked herself out.

And then a miracle occurred. Honest to goodness. To say I was flabbergasted, dumbfounded and struck all of a twitter would be to minimize my feelings.

As if God Himself roared from heaven, a voice shouted — I learned later it shouted from a bullhorn — "Come out of the car with your hands up! Throw your weapons out and climb out! *Now!*"

Well, boy howdy — as a person I knew who came from Texas used to say — I didn't need to be told twice! I also didn't trust my companions, so rather than leaping out and running, I kind of pushed my door open and rolled out of the car. As the car was slanted into the ditch, I unfortunately rolled underneath it.

That, however, didn't turn out to be a bad thing, since Eugene leaped out of the Chevrolet with his gun blazing. It didn't blaze long, and neither did he. He dropped like a rock as soon as the coppers fired back. I didn't see what Gertrude did, but I gather she threw her weapon away. I did hear her scream, "Don't shoot! Don't shoot! It's not my fault!"

A likely story. I couldn't see a whole lot from my vantage point, but as soon as the shooting stopped and people started running toward the machine and I heard a voice holler, "Daisy! Damn it, where are you?" I knew this was rescue and not a rival gang of criminals. Only Sam Rotondo could stir up such a wealth of emotions in my bosom. I was ever so grateful to be rescued, but did the stupid man *have* to swear at me as he did it?

Well, never mind. I crawled out of the ditch — evidently the orange trees had been irrigated recently, because I was all over mud — and the first words out of *my* mouth were "She is, too, at fault!" I regret to say that the next words were "Curse you, Sam Rotondo, if you'd only told me why you were interested in Gertrude Minneke, maybe I could have *helped* you. But *no!* Not *you!* You always have to — umph!"

The umph was occasioned by Sam grabbing me and shaking me as if I were a sheet he aimed to hang out on the line to dry. "Shut up! Tell me what happened! All I know is that your friend Buckingham called the Pasadena Police Department with some wild story about a Swiss girl claiming you'd been abducted at gunpoint!"

I took a deep, calming breath. I also realized I was really cold. December had just descended upon us, I was wet and muddy, and I was shaking like a leaf in a strong breeze. Part of my shakiness was probably due to nervousness, but it was still darned cold. I opened my mouth to tell Sam the saga, but he yanked off his coat and put it around me.

"Here. You're shivering. Damn it, get out of the cold!"

"Stop swearing at me! And your coat is going to be filthy!"

Naturally, he paid me no mind. He hauled me over to a police car and shoved me inside. It relieved what was left of my mind that he stuck me in the front seat. Evidently this time, at least, he wasn't holding me responsible for the shooting and escaping part of this fiasco. Well, if he didn't care about the state of his wardrobe, why should I? I hugged his coat close to my body, drew up my knees so that they were covered, too, and sat there, staring at the action taking place on the street.

It didn't make my heart swell with relief to see that Eugene was still alive. I guess he

348

was shot in an unimportant part of the body, like maybe a leg or an arm or something. I suppose that makes me a bad person. Or maybe it just makes me human. But I would have been just as happy if he'd been shot dead. As for Gertrude, I aimed to do my level best to make sure she suffered any punishment she deserved. It already appeared that she was going to try to pin everything on her brother, but from my perspective, she was as guilty as he. She, after all, was the one who'd lied to me, told me idiotic stories, and was the first of the siblings to shove a gun at me.

And then there was Hilda. As soon as I could function properly again, I aimed to telephone Miss Emmaline Castleton, tell her of Hilda's heroism, and make sure her father included Hilda in his letter to his congressman or the president, or whoever he aimed to write to regarding Kurt Grünfeld.

It occurred to me then that I'd have to tackle Sam on the Hilda issue, too. That knowledge didn't make my heart sing, but I'd got around Sam Rotondo before, and I'd be darned if I'd let him bamboozle me this time. Hilda had saved my life, and my life was worth something, even if Sam didn't often think so.

And . . . aw, nuts. Billy and my parents were simply going to love this latest attestation to my inability to stay out of trouble. Darn it. None of these things were my fault!

Shoot. I sounded like Gertrude. Perhaps I'd do well to spend the entire ride back to Pasadena making what was truly an innocent involvement in crime sound even more plausible than it really was.

Bother.

CHAPTER EIGHTEEN

"You mean that's the reason there was no traffic on the road?"

My entire family — well, the part of it that lived in Pasadena — Sam Rotondo, another police detective named Ernest Gilchrist, Johnny and Flossie Buckingham, and none other than Miss Emmaline Castleton (I'd called her from the police station to tell her about Hilda's heroism) were sitting around the dining-room table. We were drinking either hot tea or hot cocoa (my choice) and nibbling on sandwiches Vi had put together in a jiffy, since this was an unorthodox time for dining. It was a tight fit, but Pa and Sam found enough chairs so that we could all squeeze in. Kind of. It didn't matter. Nobody cared.

In actual fact, according to what I was told, dinner that evening had barely been touched, since no one could account for my absence, and the family was in a dither. The class I taught at the Salvation Army had lasted a little longer than usual, as it was the last class and there were so many good-byes and so forth to get through. Then I'd been accosted by Gertrude and Eugene Minneke and forced to drive them, they hoped, to San Diego. From there they aimed to cross the border. They told me they'd leave me in our trusty Chevrolet on the California side of the border, but I sensed I'd be the only one of the two remaining in California, and the Chevrolet the only one of the two of us still extant.

Eugene's watch had been wrong — by the way, it turned out the evil duo was from Boston and not New Jersey, if you care — as had my assessment of the time we'd spent in the automobile. I'd actually been driving for an hour and a half by the time the tire blew. By the way, the Minnekes' accostment (is that a word?) of me caused me to drop my egg-and-pea castle, my flowers and my cooking booklet. I didn't care much about the book, having resented it for weeks now, but I was darned proud of that castle and the flowers and hated to see them hit the ground. Ah, well, such is life.

"Yes," said Sam. He wasn't looking aw-fully well. I don't think he was mad about his suit coat, which would have to be cleaned by a dry-process cleaning establishment. After all, he was the one who'd made me wear it. He just looked kind of pale and nervy, if you know what I mean. So did Billy. Even more so than usual. I guess they'd been worried about me. How sweet.

Sam went on. "When we got that call, we didn't know where the . . . um, where they were making you take them, but we figured that since the authorities in New Jersey were after them, too, they'd probably try to get across a border, and Canada's too far away."

I stared at Sam, flummoxed. "You *knew* they were wanted by the police? Why didn't you tell me?" I regret to say my voice was rather shrill. "I *asked* you! You never said a word!"

He held out both of his hands in a please-forgive-me gesture. I continued to glare. "We didn't have any positive identification of the two. All we knew was from a bulletin stating that two people from Boston named Violet and Vernon Rossi were wanted by the police back there for violent anarchic activities. Evidently, they were involved in the robbing of a bank, during which Vernon shot a teller and Violet threw a bomb."

Underlying my shock was the silly notion that the Rossis' parents should have named her Violent rather than Violet. I didn't say so aloud. I was still too mad at Sam. Therefore, what I said was, "I *asked* you, Sam Rotondo, why you were so darned interested in Gertrude . . . Violet . . . whatever her name is. Why didn't you *tell* me at least what you suspected?"

"We had written descriptions of them, and the Boston police sent photographs, but none of our men ever got a clear look at either one of them."

Now this was just ridiculous, and I told Sam so. "How on earth," I said in a measured voice, "could the entire Pasadena Police Department find neither hide nor hair of those two? *I* kept seeing them on the street every time I turned around!"

"Well then, why didn't *you* tell *me? *That might have helped, you know."

"Why should I tell you about them when I didn't know you were interested?"

"Besides," said Sam, "they'd changed their appearance. Both of them."

"Oh, pooh! Nobody can change *that* much!" I argued furiously, "Anyhow, you knew very well that Gertrude — Violet, I mean — came to that stupid cooking class every Saturday afternoon for seven dreadful weeks! You could just have shown up there and had your answer. You could have stared at her to your heart's content. I would have

354

even held her down for you so you could check her from stem to stern."

Sam looked at his uneaten sandwich. "I asked about that. The chief didn't want to chance their finding out we were on to them."

Silence prevailed for several moments. I broke it. "So the Pasadena Police Department, which very kindly rewarded me with a framed certificate of bravery not even a year ago, would rather have me killed than tip the criminals off that you were suspicious of them?"

"Daisy," my mother said.

Unrepentant, I transferred my glare from Sam to her. She gulped and said no more.

"Listen," Sam said after heaving a heavy sigh. "It wasn't my idea. I wanted to warn you, but I wasn't allowed to. You know, Daisy, we policemen are kind of like soldiers. We can't just hare off on our own. We have to work as a team under the direction of a chief."

Still scowling, I pondered that. I still didn't like it, but I guessed I couldn't blame Sam for not breaking the rules of his job, could I? I decided to ask another question. "The machine was almost out of gas. I think we'd have made it to El Monte, but one of the tires blew before we got there. And you fellows were right there, Johnny on the spot. Did you plan the blowout?" Our poor car! Driven into a ditch, and it was practically brand new.

"We had motorcycle police everywhere. When you were spotted on Foothill, heading through Arcadia, we deduced they were making you drive to the border, and that you'd have to continue on that road for some time. So we planted nail-bait on the road and cleared it so that no other traffic could get through. We had barriers on both ends and on the few side streets leading off of Foothill. There was nowhere else you could go but straight ahead or you'd have been stopped by a barricade and armed policemen."

"Oh." I was feeling pretty darned sullen by that time. Not to mention sore. Heck, I'd been thrown to the ground, whacked with a gun and scared out of my mind. I deserved to feel sullen. "Did Hilda call you? They bashed her and shot at her, and I was afraid they might have hurt her."

Sam nodded. "They did hurt her, but she was only scraped up some. She had Captain Buckingham here" — he nodded at Johnny — "call us. We immediately put out an all points bulletin."

Whatever that was. Probably because I

was so traumatized, I said without thinking, "You're not going to do anything to Hilda, are you?"

He blinked at me, and I realized my mistake. To Sam Rotondo, Hilda was a nice immigrant lady from Switzerland. Darn it.

"Why would we do anything to her? She's the heroine of the piece." He hesitated and then added, "And you, of course."

"Of course," I said drily. Very drily.

Being Sam, naturally he wouldn't let the matter drop there. He squinted at me. "Why do you think we'd be interested in doing anything to Miss Schwartz?"

Miss Emmaline Castleton answered the question, even though it had been directed at me. "Because Daisy believes Hilda to be a German in the country illegally. But we're going to —"

She didn't get a chance to tell Sam what we were going to do. He turned red in the face, glowered at me, and said, "*What? What did she just say?*"

Giving me a guilty-but-game look, Emmaline said staunchly, "Miss Schwartz is just as much a victim of the late conflict as is Mr. Majesty." She bowed her head at Billy, and it occurred to me that I hadn't been paying much attention to my dearly beloved. When I glanced at him, he was *grinning!*

"Told you they're all only human," he said to me.

Curse all men. I decided it would behoove me to take over explanations. After giving my husband a brief smile, I said, "Calm down, Sam. I don't know for sure what Hilda's nationality is, although I've questioned her several times and believe she's not Swiss. In fact, I believe she's from Germany originally. However, Miss Castleton is absolutely correct. Poor Hilda was no more responsible for that ghastly conflict than Billy was. She's a victim, just as he is. We — Miss Castleton and I — have conferred, and she is. . . ." Hmm. What was she doing? Begging? Imploring? Those words didn't sound strong enough. I had it: "Miss Castleton is enlisting the assistance of her father to write to our congressmen and any other authorities whose help might be necessary in order to allow Hilda — and another German fellow whom Miss Castleton knows — to reside legally in the United States and eventually become American citizens."

"At the Salvation Army, we'll do anything we can to help," Johnny slipped in.

"Indeed we will," said Flossie. I was kind of surprised at the firmness of her voice, since she tended to be a little shy in company. Especially in the company of coppers. She hadn't lived a precisely meticulous life before she'd married Johnny.

Sam seemed to hold his breath for a long time, I presume so as not to release it in a bellow of rage. At last he said, "I see."

We sat in silence.

Again, he said, "I see." Then he sucked in a huge breath, released it slowly, and said, "Perhaps we at the department can be of some assistance."

I nearly jumped out of my chair. "You *will?*" To say I was astounded would be an understatement.

Giving me a good, hot frown, Sam said, "We're not unjust at the police department, you know. Miss Schwartz performed a noble service to a citizen of this city. We don't punish people for doing things like that. Even if they are illegals."

Illegals. That sounded terrible.

Rather than berate Sam for his crudity, I managed to gather what common sense I had left to me that day and said merely, "Thank you. Both Miss Castleton and I would appreciate that very much."

"Indeed, we would," agreed Emmaline.

We exchanged a smile.

Then I thought of something else. "Gertrude — Oh, blast it! Whatever her name is, she told me that her brother had become involved with some low types back East and they'd come out here, and that's why they wanted to get out of Pasadena. Was that a lie, like everything else she told me?"

Sam seemed relieved to be on safer ground. "Actually, no. She was telling the truth there, although it was in Boston and not in Trenton. I think that's the story she gave you. It appears that these two participated in the bank robbery and bombing and then lit out with all the loot, leaving the rest of the gang back in Boston, wondering where they and the money were. There were definitely fellow anarchists — if that's what they really are, and not your garden-variety crooks and gangsters — who'd tracked them out here. We caught one of them a week or so ago —"

I interrupted. I know that's impolite, but who cared at that point? "You caught one of their gang, but you couldn't catch *them?* How . . . inept."

My mother whispered the word this time. "Daisy."

I didn't even bother to scowl at her. I pursed my lips and glared at Sam, who wasn't pleased at my description of his department.

"Not inept. Remember, we didn't know

exactly who we were looking for."

I said, "Huh."

"We had a good description of the one we caught. But he wouldn't talk. He didn't admit he was looking for the Rossis or why or even who he was. We confronted him with his photograph, and he still wouldn't give anything up. There wasn't much we could do."

"How about the third degree?" I asked. I'd read about the third degree.

He gave me a good frown. "We do not torture prisoners, even murdering, thieving ones, in Pasadena. That's an old New York custom, and one I hope has gone out of style long since."

I gave him another "Huh."

Sam brightened some. "He's talking now, though. When we brought in the Rossis, he opened up like a geyser. He damned — sorry, ladies. He darned near murdered Vernon."

"He was there? In the office?" I asked, wondering how this had come about.

"Oh, yes indeed. We wanted to surprise all of them. We figured a confrontation would garner results, and we were right. Battaglia almost killed Rossi and Rossi almost killed Battaglia before we separated them, and Miss Rossi nearly snatched Battaglia bald.

I've never heard a woman use so much foul language."

"How distressing for you," I said in mock sympathy. I shot a warning glance at my mother. I'd been through too much that day to take any discipline from her about my use of sarcasm on Sam Rotondo. "Didn't you have them in handcuffs?"

"We had them restrained," Sam said in a neutral tone.

"Not well-enough restrained, it would appear," I muttered.

He eyed me coldly. "We wanted to gauge their reactions to each other, remember?"

I didn't even bother with another "huh."

Billy spoke into the next silence to descend upon us that evening. "Is this going to get Daisy another commendation from the PPD?" He grinned at Sam and then at me.

I smiled back. I did so love my husband, even though . . . well, you know. "I don't want another commendation. I only want to get back to my old life. My life without cooking and criminals, I mean." I glanced at Johnny and Flossie. "Not that I don't appreciate everything the Salvation Army does, you understand, but I hope you'll be able to carry on without me from now on. I am, after all," I added, "a Methodist, you know."

Flossie gave me a gentle smile. Boy, before she met Johnny, I wouldn't have guessed she had a gentle smile in her. I was sure wrong about that. "Daisy, you're absolutely wonderful, and we love you. You've done us a huge service. I think I'll be able to take over the cooking classes from now on. I'll carry on in exactly the way you did."

I sincerely hoped she didn't mean that.

Evidently so did Johnny, who said, "Except that Flossie can cook."

Everybody in the entire room laughed. Except me. Truly, I have a good sense of humor. It had been battered out of me that day, I reckon.

As you can probably imagine, I was pretty stiff, sore and tired for a couple of days after my last great adventure. I didn't even go to church on the Sunday after that fateful last-class day, because my muscles felt as though they'd been nailed into place by a maniacal biologist. I called Mr. Hostetter to tell him I was ill. He said that he was sorry and that they would miss me. Since I was a mere alto unless I was singing a duet with Lucy, I figured he'd get over his sorrow soon.

There was one visit I had to make, however, and I managed to get my sore and scraped body up and ready a little after noon that day. I'd spoken to Johnny and Flossie, and they said that Hilda Schwartz didn't have to work on Sundays and that she lived in premises on the Salvation Army grounds. Evidently they'd set aside some apartments for the women they were trying to help.

Not much was open on a Sunday afternoon in the fair city of Pasadena, but I managed to find a little roadside flower stand on North Marengo near the Chinese Methodist Church. I bought Hilda a pretty bouquet of daisies and roses and set out on my mission of mercy.

Hilda was home. She answered my knock and looked perfectly astounded to see me. "Mrs. Majesty!"

"How do you do, Miss Schwartz?" I thrust the flowers at her. "This is a small thank-you for your invaluable assistance yesterday. If it weren't for you, I'd probably be dead right now."

I guess my words had been a little too blunt, because Hilda staggered back slightly. She grabbed the bouquet first, however. "Dead? Dead? *Ach, nein!*" She straightened herself, looked a little brighter, and said, "Really? I really help?"

"You really helped," I assured. I took a deep breath and then came out with it.

"And I'm hoping to help you in return."

"Oh?" Was that a wary look in her eyes?

Maybe. I'm not good at reading other people's facial expressions. "Yes."

"Please to come in."

She stepped back, and I entered her tiny little place. There wasn't much to it: just a small parlor that I imagine doubled as a bedroom and a kitchen. I presume she and the other residents used the bathroom facilities down the hall. Somewhere. She always looked clean, anyhow.

"Thank you, Miss Schwartz."

She gestured to a sofa, which, I was almost sure, was also her bed. I sat. "I have something to discuss with you."

"Oh?" She didn't seem awfully happy to hear that, but went on, "But first I make tea, yes?"

"Thank you."

So she did, and as we sipped our tea, I told her what I suspected about her — I swear, the woman nearly fainted — and what I aimed to do about it.

When I was finished, she sat still, staring at her lap, for what seemed like several hours. If I'd been in better physical shape, I'd have been twitching by the time she finally spoke. She did so without lifting her head.

"You know . . . I am German?" Her voice was so tiny, I very nearly didn't hear her.

"I guessed," said I gently.

She looked at me then. "And you want to help me?"

"Yes. I want to help you."

"Because I help you?"

"Actually, I wanted to help you achieve legal status before yesterday's incident, although that surely cemented my intentions."

She started crying then, and I swear to goodness, I didn't think she'd ever stop. I finally left my seat on her sofa, which hurt all my damaged muscles and scrapes and bruises, and put an arm around her. The position was awkward for me, since she sat on a chair and I had to lean over her, but I figured she'd saved my life; what was a little discomfort?

After her sobs had quieted to soft hiccups, her story came pouring out of her. I learned that her village in Germany had been bombed to smithereens during the conflict, her family killed, and all of her hopes and dreams had gone up in smoke. Literally. She managed to make her way to Belgium — and I don't ever want to think again about everything that befell her on that awful journey. When she finally got to Brussells, half-starved and frightened almost to death, she learned about the Salvation Army's effort to assist people whose lives had been disrupted by the war. She pretended she was Swiss, and, well, you know the rest of the story.

I finally left her, although she held on to me as if she never wanted me to leave her side. But I was tired, darn it, and I'd done my good deed for the day. When I finally got home, I nearly fell into bed, I was so exhausted. Nevertheless, I felt good about having spoken to Hilda. And about helping her, too, even though she *was* a German.

It was lucky for me that Mrs. Kincaid had already started out on her honeymoon, because I was in no shape or mood to deal with her hysterics. I just wanted to sit at home and sleep and read for a bit. That was okay by Billy, who liked having me around. When he wasn't mad at me for some unaccountable reason. Spike, needless to say, was overjoyed to have another one of his humans in the house more often than usual.

On the second day after my ordeal, I resumed sewing Christmas presents for everyone. Sewing is such a relaxing occupation — for me, anyhow. Evidently some folks consider cooking relaxing; don't ask me why, because I don't know.

At any rate, I was involved in hemming the skirt of a dress I'd made for Ma when Miss Emmaline Castleton telephoned. I think this happened on the Wednesday after the Rossis were captured.

"Oh, Daisy," she said, sounding more elated than anyone had a right to sound. Or maybe I was still sore from my trip with the Minnekes — Rossis, I mean. "Everything's going to work out all right. Father just heard from his congressman, and both Miss Schwartz and Kurt will be allowed to stay in the country. Father's giving Kurt a job at the estate, and Miss Schwartz can remain in Mrs. Bissell's employ. If she decides to leave Mrs. Bissell for any reason — well, other than a serious transgression — I'll find her employment with one of Father's companies."

I stared stupidly at the telephone for a moment, the receiver pressed to my ear. Then I said, "Um . . . I thought you wanted to meet Hilda before you agreed to help her."

"After what she did for you, and after I spoke with Mr. Buckingham and Mr. Rotondo —"

"You talked to *Sam?*" I regret to say I rather screeched the question.

Emmaline hesitated. "Well, yes. I spoke with him on Saturday evening, after we gathered at your home. He was quite receptive to the proposition after hearing Kurt's story. He was already willing to help Miss Schwartz."

He was? He hadn't sounded very darned receptive to me, curse the man. I said, "Oh." Very well, I wasn't feeling very bright and bubbly yet. "I mean, that's wonderful. Thank you very much for helping Miss Schwartz, Emmaline. And thanks for calling with the good news."

"It's my genuine pleasure, Daisy. I'm only sorry you had to go through such a terrible time before the two of them could be assisted by people who count."

"Yes. Me, too. I guess that's just the way life works, though, isn't it? It's not exactly fair."

I heard her sigh through the receiver. "No. It certainly isn't. When I think about your husband and my Stephen, and then think about those terrible criminals . . . well, no. Life isn't fair."

And with that, we said our good-byes. I was very happy for Hilda, and I devoutly hoped Kurt was worth the effort Emmaline had gone to for him.

On the other hand, if it hadn't been for Kurt, Hilda would never have been assisted with her problem, because Emmaline would never have heard about her, and she'd never have forced her father, who forced his congressman, who did who knows what to get both parties to enter and remain in the United States legally. I guess it's true that God works in mysterious ways. Either that, or He makes his minions here on earth go through insane contortions in order that truth and justice should prevail.

But there I go sounding cynical again. I apologize.

The truth was that I'd learned a valuable lesson. It was a lesson Billy'd been trying to teach me for years, but I hadn't been willing to learn it until now. However, I had to agree with him at last. Every nation in the world has its good folks and its bad folks. What the leaders of those nations do often causes the citizens in those same nations to do things they'd never do ordinarily. They — the leaders — get away with it by pretending that their causes are noble and patriotic and by pretending that the guys they hate are universally hateful, rather than merely annoying to them — I'm talking about the leaders again. And we — the citizens — allow them to do it to us time and time again.

Heck, we all fall into the traps our noble leaders set for us. I remember crying when

I heard Enrico Caruso singing "Over There" on a recording machine at Mrs. Kincaid's house during the war. I recall thinking that our men — and my Billy — were fighting for a glorious cause. At any rate, these things always turn out the same way: the ordinary citizens suffer, while the leaders . . . well, I don't know what they do. Sulk, I guess, until the next time they get so peeved they start another war.

I think we human beings give ourselves too much credit for being creatures of a higher order than the base animals of the world. In truth, we *are* only animals, and we behave the way the human animal behaves. We clearly don't learn from our mistakes, or we'd have stopped fighting wars after the very first war ended — and that was thousands of years ago.

But I probably shouldn't wax philosophical any longer. I make a lousy philosopher at the best of times, and these days I'm weary and indignant.

Eventually, I got over my exhaustion. I even gained a modicum of enthusiasm for life once more. With Mrs. Kincaid — I mean Mrs. Pinkerton — out of the picture for a couple of months, I had lots of time to make my Christmas presents.

I was involved in such a pursuit one

afternoon in my sewing room at the back of the house when Billy knocked at the door. I kept it closed and had asked everyone to knock before entering, since I didn't want anyone to know what I was making them for Christmas.

"Hey, Daisy, may I come in?"

"Is Spike with you?"

"Yeah. He's on my lap. Why?"

"Let me put his present away. I don't want him to see it before Christmas."

A long silence ensued, and I realized how stupid my statement had sounded. So I laughed. But I still hid Spike's present, a nice warm jacket for taking walks during our semi-cold Pasadena winter.

"You can come in now," I said after putting a pattern book on top of Spike's gift.

So he did. Then he said, "Johnny's here. Want to take a break and come out and talk for a while?"

"Johnny's here? If he's going to ask me to teach another —"

"I'd never do such a thing to you again, Daisy!" came Johnny's hearty voice from the front of the house.

So I followed Billy and Spike to the living room. Sure enough, Johnny Buckingham, in his Salvation Army captain's uniform, stood before the fireplace, in which a fire burned merrily. We who live in Southern California like to pretend we need fireplaces, even though we probably don't. Still, the weather had been nippy for a few days. It was mid-December, after all.

"It's a good thing," I said, but I smiled fondly at Johnny.

"I wanted you and Billy to be the first to know that Flossie is set to teach the next cooking class, which is going to start shortly after the first of the year."

"Thank God for that!"

Johnny twinkled at me. "Thank God for the class, or thank God for Flossie teaching it?"

"Well. . . ." I eyed Johnny for a moment, but decided he could handle the truth. "Thank God Flossie's teaching it."

Billy and Johnny laughed. Eventually I joined in. Why not? Better to laugh than cry, I reckon.

"But, Daisy," Johnny said after the hilarity died down. "I wanted you to have this as a remembrance of the noble deed you did in teaching that class. I know how much you hated it."

And darned if Johnny didn't hand me *Sixty-Five Delicious Dishes*. "Oh, my," I said. "Did you rescue this or buy a new one for me?" I knew the answer right after I asked the question, because the pamphlet was spotted and creased in spots.

Johnny clarified the matter anyway. "That's yours, Daisy. I figured you might need it again one of these days."

I know it was impolite of me, but I rolled my eyes.

However, Johnny's visit started me thinking about cooking for some reason, and I decided to surprise my family with a creation of my own that evening. After all, during my last class at the Salvation Army, I had created, with my own two hands and the help of that cooking booklet published by the Fleischmann Yeast Company, a lovely egg-and-pea castle. So I set about to surprise my family with an egg-and-pea castle of their very own.

I ought to have known better.

When I carried my creation to the dinner table, flushed and embarrassed, only Pa spoke at first.

"Um . . . what's that, Daisy?"

I heaved an enormous sigh. "It's called eggs and green peas," I said sheepishly. "It's a recipe out of that book Johnny gave me."

"Ah," said Billy. Then he lifted his napkin to his lips. I knew he was trying not to laugh, curse him.

As luck would have it, Sam was dining

with us that evening, too, so my humiliation wasn't limited solely to the family, who were more or less accustomed to my cooking catastrophes.

Vi said, "Um . . . I think you might have fried the croute a little too long, Daisy." She hurried to add, "Not that it doesn't look delicious."

It didn't look delicious. And I'd burned the croute to something only slightly less crumbly than ashes. I stared at the disaster in my hands. "I don't think I cooked the eggs long enough, either." In truth, I *knew* I hadn't cooked the eggs long enough, because the yolks were still runny when I sliced them. I let the drippy parts drain into the sink.

"Well, it's still lovely of you to do this for us, Daisy," said Ma, who was cheerful under most conditions, even this one, bless her.

Sam shrugged. "Might as well give it a try."

So I served him a tiny portion of my eggs and green peas, along with a slightly-less-burned-than-the-rest slice of croute. As I watched him, I saw his mouth pucker. He, too, lifted his napkin to his mouth, but I think it was because he aimed to spit my masterpiece into it.

I must have looked terribly worried,

because Vi hastily took a tiny bite, too. She chewed thoughtfully and swallowed, then reached for her water glass and swigged a large amount therefrom. Then she looked at me.

"Daisy. . . ."

She didn't want to hurt my feelings. I knew that expression well. I sighed. "What else did I do wrong?" I asked with a sense of defeated resignation that bowed my shoulders and brought tears to my eyes.

"Well . . . are you sure you used flour in the cream sauce?"

That brought my head up in a flash. "Yes! Well . . . I think I did, anyway."

Vi smiled kindly. "Daisy, you're a wonderful girl, and we all love you dearly, but I honestly don't think cooking is your strong suit."

Heck, I'd known that for years.

"I do believe you used baking soda rather than flour in your cream sauce, dear."

I stared down at the plate full of burned croute, mushy peas, undercooked eggs and inedible cream sauce. Then I heaved one last sigh and picked the platter up again. "I'll just go and toss this out."

All I can say is that it was a darned good thing we had Aunt Vi to cook for us. If my family had relied upon me for nourishment, we'd all have starved.

ABOUT THE AUTHOR

Award-winning author **Alice Duncan** lives with a herd of wild dachshunds (enriched from time to time with fosterees from New Mexico Dachshund Rescue) in Roswell, New Mexico. She's not a UFO enthusiast; she's in Roswell because her mother's family settled there fifty years before the aliens crashed. Since her two daughters live in California, where Alice was born, she'd like to return there, but can't afford to. Alice would love to hear from you at alice@aliceduncan.net. And be sure to visit her Web site: http://www.aliceduncan.net.

The employees of Thorndike Press hope you have enjoyed this Large Print book. All our Thorndike, Wheeler, and Kennebec Large Print titles are designed for easy reading, and all our books are made to last. Other Thorndike Press Large Print books are available at your library, through selected bookstores, or directly from us.

For information about titles, please call:
(800) 223-1244

or visit our Web site at:
http://gale.cengage.com/thorndike

To share your comments, please write:
Publisher
Thorndike Press
295 Kennedy Memorial Drive
Waterville, ME 04901